DON'T MISS TH...
TIME PASSAGE...
NOW AVAILABLE FROM JOVE!

# Nick Of Time

## Casey Claybourne

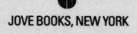

JOVE BOOKS, NEW YORK

# NICK OF TIME

A Jove Book / published by arrangement with
the author

PRINTING HISTORY
Jove edition / December 1997

ISBN: 0-515-12189-4

A JOVE BOOK®
Jove Books are published by The Berkley Publishing Group,
a member of Penguin Putnam Inc.,
200 Madison Avenue, New York, New York 10016.
JOVE and the "J" design are trademarks
belonging to Jove Publications, Inc.

PRINTED IN THE UNITED STATES OF AMERICA

10 9 8 7 6 5 4 3 2 1

*To Judith Reuss*
*for the gift of generous friendship*


*And with thanks*
*to Sue, Shelley, and Candice,*
*the same wonderful crew of women*
*who help make every book happen*

# Nick Of Time

# *Chapter* 1

"NICK DACOSTA HERE."

"Just what the hell are you doing in London? Who do you think you are, for God's sake, the CIA? You're way out of your jurisdiction, daCosta, and I'm telling you right now if you get into any trouble, you stupid son of a . . ."

The gravel-scratchy voice on the other end of the line launched into a long, loud, and unflattering evaluation of Nick's intelligence.

Wincing, Nick shifted the phone away from his ear. Shirley Sokolov might look like a sweet Jewish grandmother, but damn if she didn't have a mouth on her like—well, like the hard-boiled police captain she was, that's what.

"Yeah, yeah," Nick finally broke in. "Okay, maybe I should have run it by you, Shirl, but what did you expect? Did you really think I was going to sit on my hands for six weeks while those bloodsuckers in Internal kept me on ice?"

"You listen to me, you putz," Shirley countered in her distinctive nails-across-chalkboard voice. "We both know this investigation is nothing more than a pile of horse shit, but *I* am the boss. If you think you've got something going in London, you talk to me first, or else your cute little tush is going to be on ice a helluva lot longer than six weeks. We're city cops, Nick. We're not the DEA, goddammit. You don't have any business messing around on foreign turf, and I'm sure as hell not going to cover for you if you screw up."

Nick massaged the bridge of his nose. "I'm not screwing up, Shirl. I'm here unofficially. I got a lead last week that there might be a guy in London who knew something about our drug friends, so I'm here just checking it out."

"Just checking it out, huh? You stubborn S.O.B." Her tone softened, taking some of the sting from her words. "Well, next time you pull a stunt like this, I'll check *you* out, you got it?"

"Yeah, I got it." He sat back on the hotel bed and stretched his jean-clad legs over the length of the lumpy mattress. "So, Sister Sokolov, did you track me halfway around the world just to rap my knuckles?"

Shirley chuckled. Either that or she was swallowing a mouthful of railroad ties. "You Catholic schoolboys. No, I called because I thought you'd want to know about a message that came in for you today. From a Lenny. He says that he's ready to talk."

Nick bolted upright, nearly yanking the telephone from the nightstand.

"I figured this guy might have something to do with—"

"Bring him in, Shirl. Right now. I want you to hold him for me until I can get back to the city. I'll catch a plane tonight."

"Now, daCosta . . ." He heard her hesitation. "You know that until the investigation is cleared, I can't formally let you—"

"I know, I know," he broke in impatiently, raking a hand

through the long hair at the back of his neck. "Don't worry, I'll play by the rules this time, I promise. But Lenny was there, Shirl. He saw the whole friggin' mess play out. He's the one who can blow this case wide open for us." *And clear my name while he's at it,* Nick added to himself.

"And what about your London lead, James Bond?"

Nick suppressed a grimace. "It turned out to be a dud." After he'd maxed out his credit cards hunting it down, too. "I was going to head home in a couple of days anyway."

A hush fell on the other end of the line—the kind of hush that never boded well. "Well, uh, it's a good thing you're coming back sooner rather than later, Nick."

His gut clenched. "Chris?"

"Yeah. The doctors are saying maybe only a few more weeks. Or days."

*Damn.* Nick caught his pained expression in the hotel's mirror before jerking his gaze away.

Though everyone had been expecting this, it still hurt. It hurt bad. Chris had been his partner for the past two years, ever since Nick had come out from Chicago to work for San Francisco vice. In a coma almost a month now, Chris had been shot during a sting operation that had gone sour—the same sting operation that had landed Nick on suspension.

"I'm sorry, Nick."

He ground his back teeth. "All the more reason we've got to make Lenny talk and nail those bastards."

"To the wall," Shirley concurred. "So we'll be seeing you soon?"

"Yeah. Just make sure you hold on to Lenny, okay?"

"I'll take care of him personally." Shirley cleared her throat in a sandpapery sound. "Nick . . . if you want to say good-bye, you'd better hurry."

His stomach twisted again. "I'll hurry."

Nick put down the receiver and stared at it for a moment. A pang shot up the side of his face, and he realized it was from clenching his jaw so tight.

He glanced down at his watch and frowned. He'd never catch that last red-eye if he didn't make some serious tracks.

Snatching up his blue duffel, a twelve-dollar Kmart special, Nick started to stuff his clothes, both dirty and clean, into the bag. His eyelid twitched as he tossed in a pair of tiger-print boxers that Chris had given him as a joke for his last birthday. Nick zipped up the duffel with a jerk of his wrist.

From his back pocket, he pulled out his wallet and quickly peeled off a few bucks for the maid. He was about to close up the bifold when his gaze landed on a worn scrap of paper tucked behind an old movie ticket stub. Slowly he pulled the paper out.

It was a photograph he'd ripped from a travel magazine a few years back, a picture of snowy-white cliffs and the bluest ocean and fields so green they could have come from *The Wizard of Oz*. He'd been sitting in his dentist's waiting room when he'd come across the ad and it had absolutely mesmerized him. It was so peaceful. So perfect. It looked like the kind of place where nothing bad could ever happen—no children ever hit in drive-by shootings, no crack babies ever born to teenage moms.

He'd been carrying the photo around for two or three years now, pulling it out from time to time when the world's ugliness just got to be too much. Too much for even him to take. Chris liked to tease him about it, but Nick swore that some day he would go and find that place. That place of peace and perfection. Just so he could say that once he'd been to paradise.

In fact, he'd been planning to drive out to Dover tomorrow, but Shirley's phone call . . .

He glanced at his watch again. *Shit*. Paradise would have to wait for another day.

Twenty-seven minutes later as Big Ben began to toll midnight, Nick was on his way to Heathrow Airport. A vicious thunderstorm made for relatively light traffic as he drove too fast through the winding London streets.

The night was moonless, dark. Darker than Nick could ever remember seeing. Sheets of rain, driven by the October wind, pummeled the windshield of his rental car. The wind howled. Claps of thunder echoed through his head like a cheap tequila hangover, and Nick wished that he'd thought to pop some aspirin before leaving the hotel.

*Damn this storm.* He had to make that next flight. He had to. He would never be able to forgive himself if he didn't get home in time to say good-bye.

Generally speaking, partners who worked together for any length of time became pretty tight; it was the nature of the business. But with Chris . . . Well, he and Chris had shared something special, an honest-to-God friendship that went far beyond the job. They took in Giants games together, ate at hole-in-the-wall Hunan joints, and freely dissed each other's ex-spouses. Last Christmas the two of them had even gone back to Chicago to celebrate with the daCosta brood, since Chris didn't have any family still living.

*Still living . . .*

Nick's fingers tightened around the gearshift until his knuckles cracked.

Goddammit, Chris couldn't die yet. Not yet, not before he had a chance to explain. It had been a screw-up, an accident. Any kind of sting operation was full of risks and this one had been no exception. Perhaps even riskier than most. They had all known going into it that it was going to be dicey. They had all willingly accepted the danger. In fact, Chris had been the one who had insisted on taking the lead role in the setup. Against Nick's objections.

But knowing all that didn't stop the guilt from keeping him up nights, did it?

He would lie there in bed, replaying the scene in his mind over and over, telling himself that there had to have been some way that he could have prevented it. Maybe he could have covered Chris more closely. Maybe if he hadn't been so intent on hooking those drug-smuggling assholes, he could have kept his partner from being shot. But no, not Nick. Not "Take-no-prisoners" daCosta. Determined to nail those bastards, he hadn't seen the gunman before it was too late. Too late for Chris.

He had to get home.

A mighty gust of wind buffeted the car, sending the back wheels into a fishtail. Nick wrenched the steering wheel hard to the right.

"Cheap imports," he muttered beneath his breath.

Leaning forward, he squinted into the night, trying to get his bearings. The rain all but blinded him. Christ, had he taken a wrong turn?

He looked to the dashboard where the digital clock glowed neon green. Sixteen minutes after twelve. Man, he should have been on the highway by now. Must have been that left turn a few miles back.

A jagged flash of white split the sky, accompanied by a sharp crack of thunder. Nick blinked as an eerie bluish light filled the car, crackling and snapping.

"What the—"

The tires squealed. The ball of light exploded. Nick made a frantic grab for the wheel, but it was too late. The car swerved off the road, hurtling over the sidewalk as if possessed by a demon.

And like in a movie where everything abruptly goes slow motion, a series of images branded themselves into Nick's consciousness.

An iron gate.

A neat row of headstones.

A name carved in silver-gray granite: *Godfrey Woodbaine 1780–1810.*

Then . . . the impact.

Nick's final thought before he was flung through the windshield was one of ironic appreciation. He was going to die in a cemetery.

\*     \*     \*

Pain. Excruciating pain. Agony ripped through his head and arms and chest like the flames of a fire. In fact, Nick thought he could smell the scent of burning flesh. His?

Then mercifully the pain was gone. Nick felt himself floating, easing up and out of his body. All was whiteness and light.

"Nick."

A voice. A familiar one.

"Chris . . . is that you?" Nick knew his lips couldn't be moving—he'd left his body, hadn't he?—and yet the question lingered as if he'd spoken it aloud.

"Yeah, partner. It's me."

"What's happening? What is this?"

"Don't worry about it. We're going to take care of you. Your time wasn't supposed to have come yet, Nick. Your time got all messed up."

*My time?* A weird feeling of apprehension clutched at him.

"Shit, Chris. Are we *dead*?"

"Nah." Through the vast whiteness, Nick thought he heard a low chuckle. "Well . . . at least, not yet."

Panic displaced apprehension. "Jesus, Chris, I can't die yet! I've got to clear my name with Internal, I've got to see you again. God, Chris, I let you down. I am so damned sorry, I should have—"

"Easy, big guy, easy. It's okay."

*Okay?* Nick silently repeated. But he couldn't die like this. Without reclaiming his badge, his honor. Without seeing paradise.

Nick tried to draw closer to his partner's voice, but he couldn't seem to move through the light. "Hey, are you still there?"

Chris's response sounded as if it came from a great distance. "You've got your work cut out for you, buddy, but it'll be all right. They're giving you another chance. No coincidence you landed where you did, I guess. Take care of yourself, Nick."

"Wait!" But Nick somehow sensed that his friend had already left even as the word hovered in his thoughts.

Then, as if guided by some unseen force, Nick felt his spirit drifting, floating back toward the accident. Through the receding whiteness, he could see the rental car crumpled up like an aluminum can, its engine afire as flames shot up into the night. He could see his body, bloodied and burned, lying on the wet ground next to the rubble that had once been a grave marker.

But strangely, he felt distant from the scene. Disengaged. He saw himself lying there on the ground, knowing that was where he belonged, yet he could not move near. He could not seem to take possession of his body. Something was holding him back; he couldn't get into his body because—

*Because someone else was in there.*

Before he could even try to make sense of what was happening, Nick started to spin, to move with a swiftness that defied time or speed.

Suddenly his soul slammed into a body. The torturous pain returned, driving him into unconsciousness.

*At the other end of the white timeless void, a man struggled to locate his mount. Agony gripped him, but he fought it, fought it with ever fiber of his lost, wandering soul. If only he could retrieve the blasted horse, he thought, he could find his way home.*

*But soon he would realize how very lost he was.*

# *Chapter* 2

## THE DOVER COAST, 1810

BENEATH A CRESCENT moon, white-winged gulls dotted the darkness as the lone woman carefully picked her way along the treacherous cliffside path. Below her, waves thundered against the steep ivory bluffs, spraying their mist toward the sky like a salty offering to the gods.

The woman blinked, welcoming the briny sting pricking at her eyes, breathing deeply of the night air. Tonight the scent of the sea blew strong, pushed onto shore by northern gusts from across the Channel.

The woman did not falter along the trail, though her leather walking boots had grown stiff with salt, and the night shone as black as ink. The wind whined, tugging at her cape like a petulant child, demanding and insistent. She merely pulled tighter at the neck of her cloak, indifferent to the plaintive wind, to the biting cold.

Many undoubtedly would have called it madness to wander these cliffs in the frigid October night. But for Anna, these midnight walks helped keep the madness at bay. The sea was her solace, the darkness her friend.

She narrowed her eyes as she gazed out onto the turbulent, white-capped sea. A storm threatened from across the Channel. But its menace was not as great as the other danger from the east: the threat of Napoléon's troops. For months now, the country had been gripped by paranoia, terrified that the French would attack. But Anna did not worry. God help her, but she had much more to fear than a foreign invasion or a thundering tempest.

Nevertheless, as she glanced to the billowing black clouds overhead, she knew that she ought to return home before the rain began to fall. She started to retrace her steps along the path when—

She stilled.

A gull's cry? No, the sound had been too low-pitched. She tilted her head to the side, listening.

Again. She heard it again.

As the mounting wind whipped her hair loose from its braid, Anna peered into the night. The sound might have come from the lichen-covered rocks to the left. Curious, she veered off the path in the direction of the outcropping.

A rumbling groan rent the darkness and Anna froze. There could be no question of it now. A man was moaning. In great pain, it sounded.

Without hesitation Anna lifted her skirts and plunged forward into the high grasses. She did not permit herself to question the wisdom of her actions—the fact that the man might be a wounded smuggler or a highwayman nursing a well-deserved bullet. She only knew that someone needed her help.

Her nose wrinkled as the thick-sweet odor of blood mingled with the ocean's scent. She hurried closer, making out a form, a body. Beside a low boulder stretched the figure of a man. Even in the deep shadows, she could see that he was gravely wounded.

Just then a cloud that had been masking the sliver of

moon slipped aside so that light slanted across the man's face.

Recognition stiffened her limbs. Her mouth went bone dry. Fear coiled inside her, churning her stomach with instant nausea.

The man lay on his stomach, his face turned toward her. His features—features Anna had once believed to be beautiful—were swollen and discolored and it looked as if he might have very well broken his nose. Cinnamon hair, dark and matted with blood, covered a deep, uneven gash above his brow. He was dressed in riding clothes, still clutching a crop in his right hand.

Anna tentatively stepped closer. His breathing came ragged and shallow. He must have been thrown from his mount. But when? Who was to say how long he might have been lying here on the icy ground?

Anna's fists clenched at her side as she dispassionately gazed down at the man's figure. She could not remain dispassionate for long. Like an infected wound once reopened, memories began to ooze forth, bringing with them fury, frustration . . . and loathing.

Especially loathing.

How she hated him. The muscled arms and shoulders that should have portrayed strength, but represented something else entirely. The long tapered fingers both elegant and sinister. The lips, like a cupid's bow, capable of forming the cruelest of phrases.

As her gaze fixed on the hand holding the riding crop, an utterly sinful and wicked thought slithered into Anna's mind. She could walk away. No one would ever know. No one need ever suspect that she had found him. He was far from the road, and sufficiently removed from the cliffside path that 'twould seem reasonable his body would have gone unnoticed. By morning's light he would be dead—if not from his injuries, then from exposure.

Slowly Anna began to back away.

*What of the Reverend Hancock?* Would she be able to

confess this unpardonable sin to the young clergyman? Even knowing all that she had suffered, the priest would still condemn her, as she deserved to be condemned. Always the vicar had counseled her to "turn the other cheek," quoting scripture in his calm, quiet voice until she wanted to shriek and tear at her hair like a Bedlamite. Especially since she knew he spoke the truth.

Anna shook her head. *No.* She would have to make peace with her conscience on her own. After all, this was not the first time she'd considered ending a life—the life of the man who lay before her so vulnerable and weak.

Setting her jaw, Anna willfully turned her back. The wind sighed, lashing the long grass against her legs.

"Chris."

Barely audible, the raspily voiced word stopped her in her tracks. Something in the way he had called out the name—it was so full of need, of yearning. She glanced back, trying to see his expression in the darkness. He appeared to be unconscious.

Anna tried to turn back to the trail. Pulling her cloak closely around her, she swung around in the direction of the sea. But that single word, its heartfelt longing, continued to resonate within her.

*Chris.*

She lifted her face to the heavens, screwing her eyes and mouth tightly shut. This must be some manner of divine trial. The Lord had deliberately placed this opportunity in her path as a test of her strength, of her goodness.

She wasn't good. Anna knew that. But she *was* strong.

With a sharp curse, she tore at the clasp of her cape, marching angrily back to the rocks. A light drizzle had begun to fall, cool and misty. Refusing to look into his face, she spread her woolen cape over his body, biting at the inside of her cheek until she tasted blood.

Blast, she was a fool.

Pivoting about, she hiked up her skirts and began to run back to the house. To summon help. Help for her husband.

\* \* \*

It was at first a distant humming, the gentle rasp of whispers teasing at the edges of his consciousness.

". . . are we to do?"

"Calm . . . cautious . . . Do not fret."

"Angry when he sees . . ."

"I venture to say . . . bedpan."

From a darkness more profound than sleep, Nick labored to focus, to make sense of the garbled, disjointed words. Who was angry? Who needed to be cautious? And what was that about a bedpan?

He struggled to understand, but fragments of phrases floated up and out of his reach before he could grasp their meaning. The low murmurs sounded like nothing more than jumbled nonsense; a burning, throbbing pain clogged his head, making it impossible for him to think clearly.

Where was he? And what the hell had happened? Had someone taken a jackhammer to his skull? In the farthest corner of his mind Nick knew there was a reason he was hurting so much, but he couldn't quite seem to remember it. He did remember taking that bullet in the shoulder last year, which, in retrospect, had been a mere scratch compared to what he was experiencing now.

He pushed himself to concentrate on the voices humming around him. Women's voices. A little urgent, a little frightened. One younger voice. One paper-crackly and reminiscent of his Nona's. Foreign, both lilting in the clipped cadence of—

Memory slammed into him like a sucker punch, catching him unprepared.

*England. The lightning storm. The car accident.*

Nick's head started to swim, the darkness yawning before him again. He fought back, refusing to give in.

*Okay.*

A deep, aching breath steadied him back to consciousness, and he realized that he must have been brought to a London hospital. But it didn't smell like a hospital, at least

none that he'd ever been in. Where was that plasticky sterile aroma? The sharp stench of disinfectant? The room
smelled like . . . the sea. Like salt and fish. And potpourri?

The nurses exchanged more words that Nick couldn't de-
cipher, but he zeroed in on what lay beneath their words:
fear. The two of them sounded not just concerned, but
downright terrified. Terrified for him? Was he that bad off?

He tried to open his eyes.

Nothing. Complete and utter blackness.

*Had he been . . . blinded?*

Adrenaline shot through his veins, bringing the dizzying
darkness looming before him again. Ruthlessly, deliberately, he stamped down the surge of panic.

Although a lapsed Catholic since the age of fifteen—
when, in the same year, his favorite cousin died of leukemia
and St. Ignatius lost the state championship—Nick suddenly
found himself issuing a flurry of Hail Marys.

He was a cop, for the love of God. How could he be a
cop and not see? What would he do?

Then, like a ray of hope, a tiny pale sliver of light
pierced his vision. In numbed relief Nick realized that he
wasn't blind—his eyes were swollen shut. He tried raising
his right arm, thinking that he could physically pry open an
eyelid, but he couldn't. He couldn't lift his arm. It felt
strange and weak and thin.

Was it the drugs? He didn't think so because, although
dazed and confused, he was still hurting too much. Way too
much. How about getting him a decent painkiller, folks? A
Vicodin or a Percodan maybe?

Determined to have a look around, Nick tensed his facial
muscles until they ached. He succeeded in lifting his right
eyelid just enough to open up a narrow view of the room—
like one of those old movies where the top and bottom of
the screen have been sliced off. His vision was fuzzy, but
he was able to make out a . . . dresser. An enormous
wooden antique dresser above which hung a gold-framed
mirror.

*What?* What was this place? London's hospital to the stars?

He tried to search for the nurses, but his stiff neck wouldn't budge and his facial muscles were growing fatigued. He let his swollen eye close. Man, what was his insurance company going to say when they got the tab from *this* place? He'd be paying off his twenty percent of the bill until he hit his grave, for God's sake. Which, judging from the way he felt, might not be so very long from now.

Boy, he sure did hurt. His head may as well have been filled with shaving cream the way his brain was slogging along. Nothing made much sense. The dresser, the mirror. Something was wrong with this picture . . .

*Wait a minute.*

This wasn't a hospital. It had to be someone's home. Damn, had he been rescued by some London do-gooder who hadn't had enough common sense to take him to a hospital? Perfect. He could be lying here, dying from massive internal bleeding or a raging infection, at the mercy of some clueless Florence Nightingale wannabe.

Nick snorted lightly and the faint motion sent a virtual spike through his forehead. Okay, so maybe he wasn't dying. But shouldn't he be?

In his mind's eye he revisited the scene of the accident— the twisted iron gates, the sky-high flames, the car crunched nearly in half. By all rights he probably ought to be six feet deep in a satin-lined box, making cozy with the worms.

But he wasn't. Sure, he felt as if he'd had the crap beaten out of him, but he wasn't dead. Yet.

*Wasn't dead yet*— Why did those words seem to ring a bell?

*Chris.*

Like a flashbulb going off in his head, Nick suddenly recalled floating in that place of endless whiteness, Chris talking to him . . . What else? Nick knew there was more he ought to remember, but his brain refused to make the connection. He only knew that he had to get back to San Francisco. Right now.

He tried to drag himself from the bed. He nearly fainted as he fell back onto the pillows.

". . . stirred. Did you see?"

The whispered question, so near his bed, caught him by surprise. He'd almost forgotten about the nurses. Or whoever they were.

"Laudanum . . . doubt he's able to . . ." a voice said.

Laudanum! Was that what they'd been giving him? No wonder he felt like hell, as weak as a day-old kitten. That stuff was made of opium, wasn't it? Man, Shirley was going to have a shit-fit when his urine test came back next month.

A hand cradled the back of his head. Nick labored to open his eyes to see who it was, but he hadn't the strength. Something metallic pressed at his lips. A spoon. More laudanum.

*No.* He resisted, but he was simply too weak. The spoon inexorably tipped past his teeth and a viscous bittersweet liquid flooded his mouth. A hand massaged his throat, urging his reflexes to swallow the foul medicine, while the other hand held firmly to the back of his head. It was either swallow or choke.

In frustration Nick felt the syrup spill down his throat. Every four-letter word in the book danced across his impotent tongue as he slowly slipped off again into the darkness.

The light shone much brighter when Nick awoke next, his eyes squinting open with greater ease. Although still only swollen slits, they afforded him a much more expansive view of the room.

Delirious or not, his hunch had been right. He hadn't been taken to a hospital. He didn't know how or why, but it looked as if he had been staying in the private home of some wealthy London antique collector. Nick mentally checked off a list of details—the striped green-and-gold curtains surrounding his four-poster bed; the ornately carved fireplace mantel; an armoire almost half the size of his North Beach studio.

Such detailed observation had become second nature to Nick; in his line of work, you had to be able to take in a lot of information in a very small amount of time. Unfortunately, he had only a small amount of time to look around the room before he had to close his eyes again. The sun's glare proved too potent for his poor, pounding head.

After resting a minute or two he tried for another peek. He raised his hand to shield his gaze against the sunshine—

*Whoa.* He stared at his hand. Above the white ruffled cuff of some old-fashioned cotton nightshirt stretched five fingers. *His* fingers.

Amazed, Nick brought them in front of his face for a closer look.

By God, he didn't even recognize his own hand!

It looked like it belonged to one of those San Francisco socialites who spends every Friday afternoon at Neiman's beauty shop. No calluses, no scars; nails pared and cleaned, with not a hangnail in sight. Could it be that he'd been burned during the car fire? A serious burn might explain the paleness of his fingers—the newly grown skin and all— but why were they so slender? Had he been laid up as long as that? A month? Longer?

But, if he had been so very ill, where were his mom and sisters? Theresa daCosta, the self-proclaimed queen of overprotective Italian mothers, would have moved heaven and earth and everything in between to be here tending her baby boy. So where was Mom and her gnocchi and her collection of rosaries? Had no one contacted his family?

Nick closed his weary eyes. The throbbing at his temples mushroomed into a first-class headache. His hand flopped listlessly back onto the bedspread. Okay, so he didn't yet exactly know what was going on here or why he'd been taken in by this antique enthusiast. But he was a cop, and a good one. He'd figure it out.

And soon, too, he told himself, as the tinny grate of door hinges signaled a visitor.

Anna tiptoed into the room, careful to avoid the floor's squeaky patches near the dresser and along the far wall. During the last two days, she'd become rather expert at silently navigating her way around Godfrey's chamber. Of course, she would have much preferred to avoid his room altogether, but someone had to administer his laudanum, and she was scarcely so unfeeling as to ask Mara to perform such a service. Of course, the maid would have obliged—her devotion was heartwarming—but Anna would never ask her to do what she herself dreaded.

The room was awash in the tawny October sunshine, the window curtains pulled back sloppily, the faint scent of lavender water lingering in the air.

*Lavender water?* With a surge of surprise, Anna realized that Aunt Beverly must have pulled back the window hangings, that she must have been in to see Godfrey that morning. But why?

Brow furrowed, Anna crossed to the window and released the curtains from their tiebacks. As the room fell into shadows, the loud rustling of the crisp damask made her wince and cast a hasty glance toward the bed. Godfrey still slept. He'd been sleeping for thirty-six hours now.

At breakfast that morning Aunt Beverly had suggested that Mr. Heyer be called back in for a consultation since Godfrey had not yet awakened. Anna had dodged the question, suggesting they wait another day or so before summoning the doctor. Unlike her aunt, Anna was neither surprised nor troubled by Godfrey's long sleep, for she knew *why* he had yet to stir. For the past day and a half she had been liberally dosing her husband with enormous quantities of laudanum.

Though Anna would have preferred to appease her conscience by telling herself she'd done it to ease Godfrey's pain, she could not deceive herself. She and her Maker both knew that she'd had dishonorable motives for keeping her husband drugged. She needed the time. Time to accept his reappearance, to acknowledge the consequences of having Godfrey back at Cliff House.

After his absence of nearly a year, Anna had fooled herself into believing that he might never return. That she might somehow forget she had ever married such a man as Godfrey Woodbaine. That she might, at last, live her life in peace.

But, no. Godfrey was back. And at her mercy.

Anna's guilty gaze drifted to the laudanum bottle sitting on the cherrywood night table. 'Twould be so easy to administer—accidentally, of course—an excessive dose of the powerful, potentially lethal, medicine. One did hear of it from time to time, the occasional inadvertent overdose. Not that she would do it. She hadn't the courage, as evidenced by the fact that she'd rescued this man, this wretched soulless man, from a certain death.

Why? Why had she not left him there?

She had not slept these past two nights pondering that very question. She had lain in her bed, wondering who Chris might be, asking herself why she had been so affected by the way Godfrey had called out the name. Hour after hour she had sought reassurance, had prayed for a sign that she had done the right thing by saving him. She had, hadn't she? Surely if the Lord had meant it as a test of her righteousness, she had passed. *More or less.*

Yet still, indecision plagued her, made worse by Aunt Beverly's inexplicable and sudden concern for Godfrey's well-being. Why should her aunt fret over whether or not to call in the doctor? A few years past Beverly had chased Godfrey through the house with a loaded weapon, for heaven's sake. Beverly had never cared for him and in fact, up until now, had viewed Godfrey as an unpleasantness to be avoided at all costs. Why, then, was she visiting his bedside?

Granted, the old woman's behavior had become more erratic of late. More than once, Anna had discovered her talking animatedly to an empty room, or dancing to a phantom melody. But then again, her aunt had always been unusual. Some would even have called her eccentric or odd.

Now that Godfrey was back at Cliff House, Anna would have to be mindful of keeping Beverly out of his path. For her aunt's own safety.

A muffled *meow* broke into the quiet. Anna rolled her eyes, clenching her fists into her pinafore.

"Aunt Beverly," she berated beneath her breath. Godfrey despised animals, most particularly the cats that were Beverly's especial delight. Anna shuddered to imagine what Godfrey might do if he discovered a kitten making shreds of his fine silk stockings.

*Meow.*

The soft mewling seemed to originate from the other side of the room. Again avoiding the squeaky floorboards, Anna tiptoed over to the dressing table, one wary eye fixed on Godfrey's swollen face.

Noiselessly she lowered herself to her knees and began her search. Since she could not call out, she was forced to look into every nook and cranny, brushing aside cobwebs and dust balls that had collected over the months. The cleaning of their master's chambers was plainly, if understandably, of minimal importance to the Cliff House staff.

After searching beneath the dressing table, Anna crept over to the wardrobe, hoping against hope that the kitten had not been so foolish as to crawl beneath Godfrey's bed. Fortunately she located Lucky—so named because he'd survived a terrific tumble within days of his birth—hiding in the shadows under the clothes press. He meowed as she grabbed hold of him, but she cuddled the fluffy bundle in her hands, offering him no opportunity to escape. She was attempting to rise when suddenly the curtains snapped open, the sound as sharp as a pistol's report.

She jerked upright. Silhouetted against the morning light, Godfrey stood with his back to her, staring out the window.

She realized that he must not have seen her when he climbed from his bed, for she'd been on hands and knees at the other side of the four-poster. Wildly she wondered if there was any chance of her sidling out the door before he turned around.

Not very likely. So she stood there as still as stone, her heart pounding so thunderously that she feared Godfrey could hear it.

Then the kitten cried. Anna dumped him into her pinafore pocket as Godfrey slowly, very slowly, pivoted toward her. His expression was not what she had anticipated. Though his features were puffy, disfigured by violet and crimson bruises, Anna had already grown accustomed to viewing his injuries. What unsettled her, nay, shocked her, was the confusion so openly revealed in his aspect. Godfrey was not one to reveal weakness. *Not ever.*

But there he stood like a man lost and floundering. Even his palms were turned toward her in unconscious supplication. Anna instinctively drifted back a step.

"Jesus," he said, his voice rough with bewilderment. "Just where the hell am I?"

# Chapter 3

GODFREY MIGHT AS well have spoken to her in ancient Greek or some other esoteric foreign tongue, for Anna was incapable of giving countenance to what she had just heard. She could not even begin to fathom it.

While her husband, a master of sarcasm and mockery, did possess a viciously cruel and biting wit, his language never ran to coarseness or profanities. Never did he employ oaths or avail himself of the cant so popular with the London set. His tongue was as smooth as a snake's, his manner of speech positively poetic. Even on the occasions where Anna had seen him collapse from the effects of excessive drink, he had never abandoned the role of refined gentleman. Not once had she heard even a mild "blast" issue from his lips.

Godfrey took a step in her direction, an impatient frown pulling at the bandage across his forehead. "Where am I?" he repeated, his tone more demanding.

Anna wrapped her arms around her middle, cognizant of the kitten wiggling at her hip. "You are at Cliff House. Don't you remember?"

"No. I don't."

His frown expanded as his gaze traveled the length of her from muddied boot to frumpy cap. She prepared herself for his censure. Throughout their marriage Godfrey had frequently reproached her for inattention to her appearance, calling her slovenly and unfeminine. Never a diamond of the first water, Anna could well imagine how she looked with her pinafore filthy from crawling about on the floor, and her hair slipping from its untidy bun. *But what does it signify to me?* she thought defiantly. If her husband found her lacking in allure, 'twas only to the good.

"Who brought me here?" he asked, surprising her by foregoing the rebuke.

Anna wavered, loath to confess that she'd done him a kindness. "You must have been riding from London when you were thrown from your horse," she answered cautiously.

"Horse? I was on a—" He recoiled, scowling. "Do you hear that?"

Anna placed a protective hand over her pocket. "I don't hear anything."

"No, no." Godfrey waved his hand back and forth, then pointed at his throat. "*That.* I've got a goddamn English accent!"

For the first time Anna wondered if Godfrey might have seriously injured himself in the fall, perhaps done damage to his brain. Of course he spoke with an English accent. Did he think it ought to be French?

She saw him glance down at himself, rubbing the nightshirt between his fingers as if to identify the fabric. Then, to her dismay, he hoisted the gown high, well up above his knees. As he stared at his lower limbs, shock held him motionless until he slowly lifted his gaze to her.

"What's happened to me?" he rasped. "Just how long have I been here?"

Godfrey's strange manner was making Anna exceedingly

uncomfortable. At best, her husband was known to be un-predictable. . . . At worst, he could be dangerous.

She hesitated before responding. "A day and a half."

"And where was I before that?"

She shrugged. "London, I presume?"

A hint of frustration tightened his jaw. "All right then, what day is it? The date?"

"It is the twenty-eighth of October."

"The twenty-eighth . . ."

He stood there, his chest rising and falling very fast.

Anna debated whether or not she should try to return him to his bed or if 'twould be best to merely keep still until she could slip away.

"It can't be the twenty-eighth," he argued. "I was leaving for the airport the night of the twenty-sixth."

*The airport?*

"Unless . . ." He turned away from her to gaze out the window. "Shit. Unless I've been in a coma for an entire *year*."

Anna surreptitiously edged toward the door. It seemed she would have to send someone for Mr. Heyer after all.

All of a sudden Godfrey clutched his head with both hands, heedless of his bandages. "Jesus, this is insane! I feel like I'm living an episode of the *Twilight Zone*." He spun back toward her and she halted her furtive creep to safety.

"What year is it?"

Truly disturbed now, Anna decided to play along.

"It's 1810, Godfrey. October twenty-eighth in the year eighteen hundred and ten."

His face—where it was not bruised—paled to a shade even whiter than the cliffs outside the window. He seemed to sway on his feet. Then, to her complete horror, his limbs went rigid, stiff as pokers. His eyes rolled back in his head as his whole body began to shake violently.

"Dear Lord," Anna whispered.

Godfrey crumpled to the floor.

\*   \*   \*

Blessed darkness. Nick welcomed it, welcomed the respite from the suffocating confusion that had been roiling through his mind. He felt weightless as if he were spinning in a void, a great black void. Spinning endlessly, until finally the blackness began to dim, lightening to charcoal, then to gray. Something was coming into focus—what was it?

Spaghetti? He must be at Mom's house in Chicago. Thank God. Though he'd had some doozies in his day, that journey through Jane-Austen-Land had to be the trippiest, most realistic nightmare of his life. He couldn't remember ever having a dream quite so graphic.

*But hold on. . . .* That wasn't spaghetti in front of him. The shapes sharpened, colors filling and completing the picture. Tubes. Wires. Needles. An IV drip. Man, he had more hardware hooked up to him than the police department's mainframe. Both sides of the bed were flanked by a dizzying assortment of blinking, beeping, clicking machines.

*A hospital.* A bona fide hospital. And he must be pumped up with some bona fide painkillers because his head wasn't pounding as it had in the nightmare. Instead he felt nothing. But it was a strange nothingness, distant and dulled. As if he were lying in the bed, but not really in the bed—only viewing it as though in a movie. But viewing it from the *inside* of the camera.

Uneasy, he reached for the nurse's call button. He couldn't. He tried again, an eerie sensation winding along his spine. He couldn't reach the call button because he could not control his arm. . . .

Because he could not control his fingers. . . .

*Because . . . he was not in his body.*

In a paralyzing flash of memory, Nick relived his journey through the vast white emptiness following the accident. His disembodied conversation with Chris.

*"Your time wasn't supposed to have come yet. . . . Your*

*time got all messed up. . . . They're giving you another chance."*

*Another chance?*

And then Chris had disappeared and Nick's spirit had floated above the fiery wreckage, unable to return to his body. Because it had been occupied. By someone else.

*This can't be,* he thought. *This isn't possible.*

But instinctively Nick sensed the truth. That, against every rule of nature and physics and Papal doctrine, someone else, some other soul, had taken over his body. Nick was nothing but an observer, sharing the same space.

Two spirits in one body.

Then, as if their thoughts had merged, Nick had a name to put on the other being. The same name the woman had called him in his weird nightmare: Godfrey. Godfrey Woodbaine occupied his body. It was Godfrey Woodbaine who had reawakened in Nick's battered physique with a collapsed lung, a broken jaw, burns over a quarter of his flesh, and a vertebrae cracked like a Thanksgiving wishbone. . . . Godfrey was barely clinging to life.

Nick's life.

Suddenly Nick knew a panic so intense, he thought he might melt or explode or shatter. He needed to scream, to bellow, to lash out against the insanity of it all. But here, he had no voice. Trapped in this maelstrom of feeling, Nick felt his spirit reel as his world went black. He freefell through time almost two hundred years.

The next thing he knew, he was flat on his back, roaring at the top of his lungs. But they weren't his lungs. They were Godfrey's.

His ears still rang with his shout when he opened his eyes to find the lady in the white cap standing over him, her blue-gray eyes enormous in her little pinched face.

"Godfrey?" she questioned hesitantly.

Nick didn't answer her. His heart was racing a million miles a minute, yet he was barely breathing. What in the hell had just happened to him? What was that, some kind of seizure? Some kind of time-traveling seizure that had bridged the gap between 1810 and 1997?

Disoriented and dazed, Nick lay there on the floor struggling to recapture reason in an unreasonable situation. *Establish a series of facts*, he told himself, *like any good cop would do*. But unfortunately the only fact he could be certain of was that he had totaled the rental car during the storm. The rest of it was so far outside his boundaries of belief, he didn't know what to think.

What would be a feasible explanation for what he had just experienced?

A hoax? No, he didn't think there could be enough mirrors in the world to pull off a magic trick like that one.

What about a coma-induced hallucination? He gave a mental shake of his head. Not only did the smells and sounds and textures of this world appear completely genuine, but Nick doubted that he had enough knowledge of the time period to produce a delusion with such detailed authenticity.

For example, the woman hovering above him who smelled of rich, loamy earth and sea spray. She seemed authentic, all right. Slender with dark blond hair, she could have stepped right out of that movie *Pride and Prejudice*. The ankle-length dress and the apron and the funny white cap.

So what other explanation was left? Only the most far-out, incredible, totally wacko one of all. That he really had switched souls with this Godfrey guy from 1810.

"Godfrey?" the woman repeated a little louder.

*She most likely thinks me dead*, Nick thought, then wondered if he was. Maybe Father Flynn had been wrong about those Pearly Gates and this was what the afterlife offered, a trip through your Number-One Fantasy. For he had seen his longed-for paradise, hadn't he? Right outside the window? The majestic ivory cliffs of Dover, complete with fields of rolling green and an ocean so blue it couldn't be real. And it probably wasn't real. Probably none of this was.

A gull swooped by the window, its high-pitched cry rattling Nick's nerves like a wake-up call. Gingerly he levered himself onto an elbow. *Damn.* If the pounding in his skull wasn't real, it was as close as he wanted to get. His throat hurt like hell, too, probably from that soul-drifting primal scream he'd let loose. He pushed up into a sitting position, and the woman scuttled back out of his reach.

She sent a distrustful glance his direction, then lifted her skirts and made tracks for the door.

"Wait," he ordered.

She stopped, only half-turning toward him. "I . . . I must fetch Mr. Heyer."

Though Nick didn't know who this Mr. Heyer might be, he figured that she had to be on her way to call 911 to report an escapee from the local loony bin. God knew he felt like one.

"No, wait. Please." He took a deep breath, trying to clear his head. "I want to talk to you."

By her guarded expression, he could tell that she didn't relish the idea of spending even one more second in his company. But she remained where she stood, her stance defensive, her arms wrapped around her middle.

Nick relaxed—a fraction—and mentally searched for a logical next step. His gaze wandered around the extravagantly appointed room, a room that looked like a museum reproduction, before lighting on the gold-framed mirror against the wall. *The mirror.* That was one sure way to determine in what body his soul had landed. He attempted to rise, but his legs buckled beneath him. After that seizure-like ordeal, he was a bit shaky on his feet.

"Could you help me up?" he asked.

He might as well have offered her a spitting cobra the way she eyed his outstretched hand.

"O-o-o-kay." Seemed he'd have to make a go of it on his own. He had just begun to struggle to his feet when her hand wrapped around his elbow. Her touch was dispassionate, yet capable. Like a nurse's.

"Thanks," he murmured.

Her face lifted, her eyes expanding to the size of half dollars. At the back of his mind, he recognized that she was young. In her mid-twenties? As soon as he was standing shakily on his own, she retreated a half-dozen steps. He made for the mirror.

"What are you doing?" She darted in front of him again as if to bar his path.

"I'm going to have a look in the mirror."

Apprehension tightened her features. "Oh, Godfrey, I daresay you should wait a few days."

"Wait for what?"

"You . . . you suffered injuries during the fall. Your face is sadly bruised."

Nick sure as heck didn't need a mirror to tell him that. "I think I can handle it," he wryly assured her.

She bit her pale lips and stepped aside.

Halfway across the room Nick's stride faltered. From ten feet away he could tell that Nicholas Michael daCosta was not reflected in the glass. The man's image was taller and leaner than it should have been. Than Nick was. Slowly—determinedly—he approached the mirror, placing his palms flat on the dresser and leaning forward.

"Holy shit."

His knees wobbled. His stomach turned upside down.

"I tried to warn you," the woman said.

*Warn him?* He almost laughed out loud.

Looking beyond the bruises and abrasions and bandages, Nick saw a stranger. A pretty boy. One of those clean-featured preppy-looking, movie-star-handsome men who usually made him want to puke. Not that he considered himself the dog-faced boy or anything, but Nick—the real Nick—had been more of a cross between Bruce Willis and Al Pacino. Or so he liked to tell himself. The face staring back at him in the mirror belonged on the cover of *Esquire,* for God's sake.

Pale green eyes, a thin straight nose, killer cheekbones

and thick auburn hair—a good-looking guy, all right, if a bit too handsome to suit Nick's taste.

Jeez, so was this what Chris had meant by "another chance"?

In the reflection, Nick's gaze sought the woman's. She was fidgeting as if she wanted to make a run for it.

"How old am I?" he asked hoarsely.

Her response came warily. "Thirty this past June."

Thirty. Godfrey was thirty, but Nick had been thirty-two. What did it mean? Did Godfrey have a job? Did he have family? Kids?

Suddenly Nick wanted to know everything, to pick apart every detail of Godfrey's life until he'd established a connection between them, until he understood the reason for this centuries-spanning swapping of souls. For there had to be a reason, didn't there? . . . Or did there?

Perhaps this kind of thing happened all the time. Maybe instead of dying, people were just zapped through history, be it the past or the future, into another body. Or could it be that some strange time continuum had been disrupted and this was nothing more than a giant cosmic mistake?

Nick squeezed his eyes shut, dropping his chin into his chest. No one could take all this in and not go absolutely psycho. It was too much, too goddamn much. And to make matters worse, that headache he'd been battling all morning was about to do a Mount St. Helens and blow the top of his head off.

"Would you mind getting me a couple of aspir—"

She was gone. The woman was gone.

He pivoted away from the mirror to discover the bedroom empty, the door ajar.

"Hell," he muttered. He'd better go find the Jane Austen look-alike before she had him hauled off to a nice padded cell. Which was probably where he belonged.

# Chapter 4

AGITATED AND BREATHLESS, Anna burst into the parlor, coming within a hair's breadth of crushing a kitten beneath her boot.

"Goodness, my dear," Aunt Beverly chided as Anna hopped aside at the last moment and the tiny ball of fur bounded out of harm's way. "What has you dashing about the house so?"

Seated before the fire with a wool shawl across her shoulders, Beverly bent her head—graying and bare since she scorned caps of any sort—to follow the kitten's retreat into a nearby sewing basket.

Frowning, Anna remembered that Lucky still rested at the bottom of her pinafore pocket. She walked across to the sofa and handed the kitten to her aunt. Her fingers were shaking.

"You are terribly flushed, my dear," Aunt Beverly said as she cuddled the mewling kitten against her wrinkled cheek. "What has overset you?"

Anna curved her fingers over the edge of the marble chimneypiece. Its faint chill steadied her.

"Godfrey has awakened," she said evenly, not wishing to alarm her aunt.

"Oh." From behind her round spectacles, Beverly's hazel eyes sparked with curiosity. "How does he fare?"

"He does poorly. Very poorly indeed. Though I have no desire to disturb Mr. Heyer again, I must send for him straightaway."

She cast a nervous glance to the coffered ceiling, questioning whether even the doctor could treat Godfrey's brand of illness. But then she asked herself . . . what if he could not? Was Godfrey perhaps going mad? Mad enough to be confined? Or was his aberrant behavior due solely to his head injuries?

*How ironic 'twould be if Godfrey were to meet with the same fate with which he had threatened Aunt Beverly all these years. . . .*

Anna bit softly into her lip. *Wicked, uncharitable thoughts.* Naturally, she felt some small measure of concern for Godfrey—however slight. Yet, first and foremost, she must consider her responsibilities to her aunt and to the servants. What if Godfrey were genuinely unbalanced? Might he not do one of them an injury—especially since he had not needed the excuse of madness to behave violently in the past?

"Well, dear," Aunt Beverly said, "if he has finally awakened, I don't know that you need to bother Mr. Heyer again."

Anna's fingers tightened around the chimneypiece. Her aunt would no doubt feel differently if she had witnessed Godfrey writhing about on the floor.

"I don't know, Auntie, I really do think I ought to send for the doctor. Do you know where James might have gone? I could not find him either in the kitchen or in the menagerie."

Beverly's thin silver brows furrowed in puzzlement. "James who, dear?"

"Our manservant James." The same James who had lived at Cliff House these past twelve years.

"Oh. Have we a manservant?" Beverly's expression was curiously blank. "How very nice for us."

Masking her dismay, Anna walked over to stand behind her aunt.

"Yes, it is nice," she softly agreed, stroking her hand across Beverly's salt-and-pepper hair. "Very nice."

She stroked her aunt's hair, quieting the anxiety that churned inside her.

With each passing day Beverly's mind seemed to grow a bit more feeble and unpredictable. Ten minutes from now she might remember James, or it might take two days for her memory of him to return. In either case, up until now, Anna had not worried about her aunt's forgetfulness; she judged that, at seventy-two years of age, and having lived a full and eventful life, Aunt Beverly was more than entitled to the occasional bout of absentmindedness.

But so Anna had felt prior to Godfrey's return. Now she feared she had cause to worry. Good cause.

If only they had somewhere to go, she thought. A place in which to take refuge until Godfrey decided to return to London. A place where Anna could keep her aunt safe.

But without funds their options were sorely limited. Anna had a small nest egg hidden in the attic, but it was not enough for her to spirit everyone away to safety. And she couldn't leave James and Mara at Cliff House; the servants depended on her, if only to shield them from Godfrey's temper. Not to mention that she had her animals to consider; what would happen to them if she fled?

No, there was no hope of escape. At least, not yet. For even discounting all those very sound arguments, Anna knew in her heart that she could not abandon Godfrey while he was so very ill. No matter how great her aversion for her husband—and it *was* great—she simply could not slip away into the night knowing that he was unwell.

"Auntie." Anna smoothed her hands over her aunt's hair,

rearranging the combs in the elaborately braided coiffure. "While James rides for Mr. Heyer, why don't you and I take a turn along the cliffs? The weather has cleared and we could both benefit from the fresh air."

*As well as maintain a safe distance from Godfrey until the doctor arrives.*

"A walk? Yes, I'll fetch my cloak."

"Splendid," Anna said. "I'll find James and send him with a message and then you and I . . ."

Anna's words died in her throat. Aunt Beverly had started to rise from the sofa, but then had stiffened alertly, her gaze swinging to the open parlor door. Anna's followed.

Staring into the room as if undecided as to whether or not he should enter stood Godfrey. A Godfrey Anna had never before seen nor could she ever have imagined.

Disheveled and barefooted, he wore only a pair of breeches and an unbuttoned linen shirt that hung halfway down his thighs, revealing his bare chest. One hand was hooked by a thumb into the waist of his breeches, while the other hand scratched uncertainly at the top of his head. Cinnamon hair shot up like a rooster's comb from the misaligned bandage circling his brow.

"Hi there." He addressed the tentative greeting to Beverly.

*Hi there?* Anna mentally echoed. Where had Godfrey picked up the peculiar Americanism? And why, in heaven's name, had he not dressed himself?

"Good afternoon," Beverly answered in a bright, cheery voice, evidently not the least surprised to find Godfrey standing in the corridor like a half-naked heathen.

Anna set her hands protectively on her aunt's shoulders, willing her to stay seated. Not to draw too close.

"How are you feeling?" Beverly asked. "Anna had said that you were rather indisposed."

"Anna?" Godfrey's gaze traveled past Beverly to her.

"Yes, you know." Beverly tilted her head back in Anna's direction. "Your *wife*."

As she leaned back, Anna saw her aunt send a wink across the room as if she and Godfrey shared in some private jest.

"Godfrey has been very ill," Anna broke in. "I am sure that he wishes to return to his room to rest. Is there something you needed? I was just going to send for Mr. Heyer—"

"Oh, you don't have to do that." He took a step into the room, and Anna's stomach plummeted.

*Not too close.*

"Really, I'm okay . . . Anna." He spoke her name as if he were testing it on his tongue. "I'm feeling fine."

"What . . . what of the fit you suffered?" she persisted, averting her gaze from his bare chest. For some reason, she found Godfrey's state of undress uncommonly disturbing.

"Oh, thanks, but I don't think there's any reason for you to get worked up about the seizure," he said. "Following a blow to the head, an episode like that isn't all that unusual. I'll be all right."

He flashed a wide smile as if to reassure her.

It did not.

"All right?" Anna repeated. How could he claim so when he stood before them in shocking *dishabille?*

"Well, okay." He shrugged, the gesture self-conscious. "I confess I might be a little confused for a few days. You know, forgetting names, stuff like that. But I think it's only to be expected."

*Is it?* Anna's head was spinning, but she kept her sights pinned to her toes, her palms firmly planted on her aunt's shoulders.

There was no question that Godfrey's injury had affected him. He was behaving completely and utterly unlike himself. And though Anna did not understand it, despite the peculiarity of his manner, he seemed to her somehow less . . . threatening.

"If the boy says he doesn't need the doctor, then I suggest you leave well enough alone," Aunt Beverly inter-jected.

*Boy?* Anna nearly swooned. Aunt Beverly's wits must truly have gone wandering for her to dare refer to Godfrey as a "boy."

"I—I . . ." Anna began to sputter an excuse for her aunt when, taking advantage of her shocked reaction, Beverly slipped out from under her grasp.

Anna actually made a grab for her, but her fingers fell short of her aunt's caftan.

"Are you well enough to join us for dinner this evening?" Aunt Beverly asked, as congenial as you please. "We'll be dining in an hour."

*Auntie!* Dear heavens, had she completely forgotten to whom she was speaking?

"Yeah," Godfrey answered with another expansive smile. "I think I will."

Anna swallowed.

"What an extraordinary day," Aunt Beverly mumbled as she brushed past Godfrey. "Positively extraordinary." She sent Godfrey another preposterous wink, then headed down the hall, whispering to herself.

Across the room, Anna's gaze clashed with Godfrey's green stare. She lowered her eyes.

"Shall I send James up to you?" she asked.

"What for?"

"To help you dress?"

Godfrey glanced down at himself. "I guess I do need help, huh?"

*Indeed. And more help than the servant could likely pro-vide.*

Anna stood behind the sofa, waiting—not patiently—for Godfrey to leave the doorway so that she could withdraw. She did not particularly care to find herself alone with him right now.

Not that she ever had.

But Godfrey continued to linger just inside the threshold,

peering around the parlor with studied interest. He ran his finger over one of Aunt Beverly's Egyptian scarabs that was sitting atop the sideboard. He squinted curiously at Uncle John's prized hand-held telescope.

When he leaned over and picked up her Bible from a small card table, Anna had to stop herself from rushing forward to snatch it from his hand. Godfrey was *not* what one would call a man of faith.

He flipped open the Bible to the first page, the page where her name and birthdate were recorded. He appeared especially interested in the information therein, and after a few seconds, he lifted his gaze to find her staring at him. Anna would have sworn his demeanor was almost sheepish.

"Oh." He set the Bible down and rubbed the back of his hand across his jaw. "I guess I should get dressed, huh?"

She gave a small, cautious nod.

Still he hesitated as if he wanted to say something, but didn't know how.

A cramp in Anna's side caused her to realize that she was holding her breath.

Finally, with a courteous dip of his chin, Godfrey turned and walked out, his barefooted tread silent against the parquet floor.

Anna stood there for a long moment, wondering if everyone around her was slowly going insane.

Nick thought he was holding up pretty well.

Nine years as a beat cop on the streets of Chicago, and then another two working vice in San Francisco, had taught him a helluva lot about coping with life's unthinkable realities. Once you'd seen babies starving to death in crack houses, and seven year olds shoot each other over a pair of sneakers, you somehow learned to conceive of the inconceivable.

Not that he found it easy to accept his present circumstances. Not by a long shot. Nothing—not the crisis-management

courses nor the touchy-feely counseling sessions nor the
seminars on post-traumatic shock—ever could have prepared him to deal with *this*.

An I'll-believe-it-when-I-see-it, dyed-in-the-wool skep-
tic, Nick fought it and fought it hard. Time travel and soul
exchanges? Jesus, what kind of nutcase fell for that New-
Age crap? But even while he argued with himself, tried to
convince himself that it was all nothing more than a bad
dream . . . he was living it. He had only to look around him
for proof.

And if the furniture, the clothes, the decor, the absence
of electricity and phones weren't enough to convince him,
there was always Godfrey himself. The memory of Nick
and Godfrey sharing Nick's body in that London hospital
bed was seared into Nick's brain. The experience had
branded him. Scarred him.

Nothing could compare to that brief exchange of
thoughts when their minds had merged, when he had
learned Godfrey's name. No matter what Nick told himself
or how much he tried to discredit it, he knew that what he
had experienced with Godfrey had been real. Frighteningly
real.

So ultimately he had had no other choice but to accept it.
He was in Dover, in the year 1810. And he was in Godfrey's skin.

After surmounting that hurdle—the acknowledgment of
his situation—Nick didn't waste any time on metaphysical
supposition. He set about formulating a plan, and at the top
of his list was figuring out how to return to 1997. First and
foremost, Nick knew he had to get back to his own time.
He had a partner to avenge, bad guys to nail. He had to
clear his name with Internal, and to say good-bye to Chris.

Man, what must Shirley be thinking right about now?
Did she even know about the accident? She was probably
cursing up a blue streak, wondering where the hell he was.
Or . . . was time even progressing in the future while he

was in the past? Jeez, he didn't have a clue. All he knew was that he had to get back.

But how? Obviously, getting tossed into a mental institution wasn't going to help him much. Explanations of lightning storms and near-death experiences and hospitals from the future weren't likely to convince people that he was really Nick daCosta hiding out in Godfrey Woodbaine's body.

No, the only answer was to pretend to be Godfrey. It was the only reasonable solution. He would treat this soul-switching problem like any other case: gather clues, interview witnesses, and most importantly, establish a motive. *Why* had he swapped souls with Godfrey? Why?

Though he didn't like to flatter himself, Nick knew that he was a better-than-average detective because he had really good instincts; and his instincts were telling him that the woman, Anna, was a key player in all of this. Though he didn't have anything solid to pin that theory on, something about her just set Nick's antenna buzzing. Somehow, someway, she was important, he could tell.

When he'd stumbled by the living room and found her stroking the old woman's hair, her expression soft with affection, he'd felt a pang in the middle of his chest. Like he had happened across a private moment that hadn't been intended for his eyes. Nonetheless, he was glad that he'd seen it since it had given him his first clue. Apparently Anna was very close to the woman, protective of her. If only he knew who the old woman was.

The hazy-eyed lady in the wild orange mumu looked too old to have been Anna's mother. Grandmother, maybe? According to Anna's Bible, she was only twenty-two. Young. Younger than his kid sister, Sophia. For a girl just out of her teens, Anna looked unnaturally . . . tired. But, then again, people were supposed to have aged faster in the old days, right?

Though she was hardly what Nick would have described as a knockout, Anna was attractive in a different sort of way. In a small, elegant way. Like a not-so-pretty Audrey Hepburn. She struck him as a little skittish, but not dumb. She was no airhead, he was sure of that. But most important . . . she was his wife. Godfrey's wife. And since he didn't have anything better to work with at the moment, he'd have to use her as the starting point of his investigation. Then hope that she led him in the right direction.

As he clomped down the narrow staircase in Godfrey's knee-high boots, Nick got the impression that Anna wasn't interested in leading him anywhere. He'd just rounded the corner into the front hall when a dark blond head popped back behind a doorway.

Nick smirked to himself. Considering how he'd rolled around on the floor that morning as if satanically possessed, he couldn't really blame her for keeping an eye on him, for maintaining her distance. Yet, at the same time, Nick got the unmistakable feeling that Anna's reserve was due to more than just his lunatic behavior. Something else was afoot.

As he ambled down the corridor to the room into which he'd seen Anna disappear, he idly wondered how long it would take to grow accustomed to the gloom. Lit only by gas lanterns and candles, the shadowy house smelled of oil and beeswax and smoke. And, man, it was cold. Seriously cold. Already Nick was starting to miss the finer points of modern living—like electricity and central heating.

He stepped into the dining room to find both Anna and the misty-eyed old lady seated at the table. Dressed in a hair-raising combo of lime green and purple, the older woman smiled warmly as he entered, fluttering her fingers at him. Anna only gave him a nervous look through her lashes.

Again, Nick found himself blown away by the reality of being in 1810. It was all so unbelievably . . . detailed. In this room, as in the living room—or parlor or whatever it was called—the decor leaned toward an Egyptian theme with pharaoh-like busts decorating the mantel and images of sphinxes plastered in friezes. It was like a movie set, but a thousand times more authentic.

"Uh, sorry I'm late," he said. "James and I had a small communication problem."

Anna's spine went ramrod-stiff. "Wh-what? What happened?"

Nick took the open seat at the head of the table. "It was nothing. He tried to get me into some type of girdle, but I set him straight."

Anna paled to the shade of a marshmallow. "If there is a problem with the servants, Godfrey, you should send for me. I-I can take care of it."

"Oh, there was no problem. I simply made it clear that I wasn't going to be laced into any damned girdle."

Anna gasped lightly.

*What?* What did he say? Was there some secret issue about the girdle?

He glanced across to Anna, who was wearing a plain gray dress that made her appear very sober and Quaker-like. He, on the other hand, looked like a peacock in the gold brocade waistcoat and sky-blue jacket that James had chosen for him. Had the servant known what he was doing, selecting such a getup? Or did Godfrey normally dress like a poster boy for NBC? If so, Nick vowed, Godfrey was about to get himself a major wardrobe overhaul.

"Your bruises are fading quite nicely," the old lady piped in.

"Aunt Beverly," Anna murmured.

Nick looked back and forth between the two women, catching the glimmer of warning in Anna's gaze. She seemed extremely touchy about his injuries—he remembered that earlier she had tried to talk him out of looking into the mirror. Did she care so much? Or was it Godfrey she was concerned about? Nick glanced down at his gold vest again, thinking that maybe *GQ*-handsome Godfrey was the one who was hypersensitive about his appearance.

"Thanks," Nick said. "I'm feeling pretty good, too."

He shrugged, scraping his jaw against the stiffly starched scarf James had swaddled around his neck. A cravat, the man had called it. Nick called it torture.

"You know, about this afternoon, Anna. I'm sorry about all that craziness. I hope I didn't scare you or anything. I think that I was pretty shook up from the fall. In fact, my memory is still a little hazy. . . ."

He let his words trail off, debating how much he should give away. He didn't think it a good idea to go overboard on the amnesia angle. It seemed a bit on the corny side like something from a made-for-television movie: *You see, honey, I've lost all my memory*—

But, realistically, Nick didn't see that he had a whole helluva lot of choice. Since he knew absolutely nothing about Godfrey or Anna or Beverly or anything about 1810 England, he was going to have to fish around for some info. The basics, at least.

"Well," he asked, "how did everything go here while I was in London?"

Anna's blue-gray eyes looked to double in size, giving Nick the distinct impression he'd asked the wrong question.

After an awkward silence Beverly chirped, "Nefertiti had a new litter of kittens last month."

"Great," Nick answered with a touch too much enthusiasm. "That's just great, Bev. How many did she have?"

"Seven." The old woman beamed as if she had given birth to them herself.

"Wow, seven," Nick repeated, then realized how lame he sounded. But he had learned that Godfrey had been away in London for at least a month. And he now knew that Beverly was Anna's aunt. He congratulated himself and put up two mental ticks in the clue column.

Silence stretched out again until Nick was saved by the entrance of a young, dark-haired maid carrying a soup tureen. Nick tried to smile a greeting, but the servant avoided his gaze. She served him first, ladling into his bowl a watery fish stew that smelled like a marine biology experiment gone awry.

"Smells good," Nick lied when she was done serving him. "Thanks very much."

The girl reacted as if he'd goosed her on the fanny. She started so violently that she tipped the tureen onto its side and a small puddle of stew spilled out onto the white tablecloth.

The maid let out a dismayed shriek as Anna jumped from her seat and righted the tureen. Nick scooted his chair back to avoid being splashed, while pulling from his pocket the handkerchief James had given him.

"Hey, easy now," Nick said. He blotted the spill with the handkerchief. "See? It's only a dribble. No damage done."

The overwrought maid looked on the verge of a faint.

"It's okay," he assured her.

Anna had wrapped her arm protectively around the maid's shoulders and was staring at him as if he'd grown a second head. "Godfrey," she breathed. "Your handkerchief. It's ruined."

Nick, somewhat confused by all the fuss, eyed the soggy piece of silk. "Yeah, I guess it is. It's no big deal. . . . Is it?"

"Come, Mara," Anna said. "Let me give you a hand in the kitchen."

Nick watched them leave the room, thinking they'd both been way too whacked out over a harmless splash of soup.

He shook his head and glanced over to Bev. "The maid sure is a nervous little thing, isn't she?"

"Yes, well . . . Mara's father and brother drowned off the coast about five years ago. Mara was to be sent to a foundling hospital, but Anna rescued her. She collects orphans, you know. Both the human and animal varieties."

Nick frowned. Why was Bev telling him this? As Anna's husband, shouldn't he already know all there was to know about her? Or maybe Godfrey and Anna were newlyweds. Nick decided to go for it and take a bit of a risk.

"Gosh, it's good to be back. Don't know how I stayed

away so long." He tipped back in his chair, feigning a pose of reflection. "Time sure flies, doesn't it, Bev? To think that Anna and I've been married, what now—"

"Four years?" Beverly offered.

"Four years. Practically newlyweds. London was fun, but I did hate to be away. Seemed like forever, didn't it?"

She gave him a knowing smile. Almost as if she saw through his ploy. "It seemed like eleven months."

*Eleven months?* Nick concealed his surprise.

No wonder Anna was pissed if her hubby had taken off for a whole year. What had Godfrey been doing? Had he written to her, contacted her? Or had Anna *asked* him to go? After all, she wasn't exactly spinning cartwheels celebrating his return.

Before James had appeared to help him dress for dinner, Nick had made a quick search of his bedroom. He'd found a mountain of Godfrey's clothes, but no evidence that Anna had ever shared that room with her husband. Now he asked himself "why?" Earlier he had concluded that it must be customary in these times for couples to keep separate rooms. But the vibes he was picking up from Anna strongly suggested that there might be another reason for the split sleeping arrangements.

Before he could think of a sly way to pry, Anna came back into the room. Nick admired her poise as she walked behind him and took her seat. For a small woman she carried herself with a natural grace that made her appear taller than she was, almost regal. There was something very appealing about her, he thought. Very appealing.

Anna went ahead and finished dishing out the fish stew, then took her seat. Nick had just raised his spoon to dig in when Anna bowed her head.

"Dear Lord," she murmured.

He quickly laid down his spoon.

"For what we are about to receive, may we be truly grateful. Amen."

"Amen," Nick echoed.

Anna jerked her gaze to his, both censure and astonishment in her expression.

*Now what have I done?*

Nick looked down into his bowl of cooling fish soup and sighed. His first dinner in 1810 England was going to be a long one, he suspected. A very long dinner.

# *Chapter* 5

BEFORE SUNRISE THE next morning Anna crept out of bed and sneaked down the hallway in her night rail and wrapper to the opposite wing of the house. A draft wafted through the halls, flirting with her candle, sending the flame dancing and flickering in the predawn darkness. Anna cupped her hand around the wick to protect it, wishing that she might protect her aunt with the same directness and ease.

Her fears, she knew, bordered on the irrational. Godfrey had never mistreated Aunt Beverly in the past, since, for the most part, he had pretended that she did not exist. He had threatened Anna with the knowledge that he controlled her aunt's fate, but never had he actually harmed Aunt Beverly in any way.

So why was she slinking through the house like a bandit at this hour of the morning?

She cracked open the door to her aunt's chamber. The bed curtains were drawn, yet Beverly's gentle snuffling told Anna that she slept in peaceful repose.

Anna closed the door, her palms damp with nerves. What

had come over her? The answer, of course, was obvious: Godfrey.

He could not dupe her with that act he had put on last night. Something was afoot. He might couch it in kindness, but, beneath all the smiles and pleasantries, there had to be a fiendish reason for this startling shift of conduct.

Dinner last night had proved an interminable ordeal. Though Anna had asked Mara not to bother with re-moves—simply to present all the courses at once to hasten the meal along—Anna had felt as if she aged a lifetime sit-ting at that table with Godfrey. It wasn't that he had been his usual mocking self; it was that he had been completely the antithesis.

Frankly, Anna had thought he'd poured it on a bit thick—in four years he'd never even held a conversation with Beverly, and last night he'd not only complimented her on her hideous green-and-purple ensemble, but then he'd laughed twice at her cat jokes. Honestly, did he think them both fools? Where had been his usual finesse?

*And the curious questions he had asked* . . . At one point he had come close to hinting that he was employed. Surely, Godfrey would not have taken a position while he was in London? Surely not. Above all, Godfrey was a gentleman, a man of breeding. Never would he lower himself to enter a vocation or become involved in trade.

Anna, still fretting, had just finished dressing when there came a quiet scratch at her door.

"Yes?"

Mara peeked her head into the room. "Oh, my lady, I'm sorry to disturb you so early. But you know Jack, the young lad who's apprenticed to the village smithy? Well, he's downstairs, fit to be tied 'cause an iron got dropped on his dog's leg. Looks bad, it does. What shall I tell him?"

"I'll come down with you now, Mara. Is he in the menagerie?"

"He is. I didn't know what else to do with the boy."

Anna followed Mara downstairs to the back of the house

where a light shone in the room they called the menagerie. Formerly a music conservatory, it had been converted into an animal hospital where, over the years, Anna had nursed back to health literally dozens of cats, dogs, rabbits, raccoons, seagulls, geese, a goat or two, and even a wild fox.

Though the majority of the animals, once mended, had been returned to either their natural environment or their rightful owners, a few had made Cliff House their permanent home: a bloodhound named Harry who was so docile he would not give chase to either fox or fly; a pair of bunnies who had been adopted by one of Auntie's numerous cats; and an owl chick who'd made a nest for himself atop the molding.

Anna entered the menagerie and had to bite her lip when she found Jack sitting on the floor, holding his four-legged friend in his arms. The boy couldn't have been more than ten or eleven, his coat threadbare, his hair hacked off at the shoulders as if he'd cut it himself. He lifted his face to her, and she saw how he was struggling to keep the tears at bay.

"Hello, Jack," she said.

"Mornin', your ladyship. I'm sorry to be disturbing you like this, but Rupert here—" The boy's voice cracked and he dropped his chin to his chest.

Anna extended a comforting hand and then let it fall. How she wished she could hold him, hug him until his fears were quieted. But this child knew her only as the lonely lady who lived out on the cliffs and fixed animals. That's all that she was to him. That's all that she was to anyone.

Anna donned the apron hanging on the wall.

"Very well, Jack, let's have a look at Rupert, shall we?"

She helped the boy lay the spaniel-mix mutt on the oversize marble slab she used as an operating table.

"You know what, Jack, my friend? This looks bad because Rupert has a compound fracture, but I'm fairly certain we can save his leg."

The boy's hopeful expression gave Anna her first smile in many days.

As Anna worked, Jack hovering behind her, the advancing dawn filtered through the floor-to-ceiling windows, striping the limestone floor in bands of coral and pink. By the time that Anna tied off the last bandage, the sun had begun to emerge and Rupert was ready to be taken home.

"The splint must be left intact for three weeks," Anna instructed, carefully handing the dog to the boy. "Keep his bandage dry, keep Rupert quiet, and he should mend very nicely indeed."

"Thank you, your ladyship. I-I don't have no blunt—"

Anna waved him off. "I wouldn't hear of it, Jack. It was my pleasure to help both you and Rupert."

The lad's big, brown eyes looked up at her with such gratitude that it was all Anna could manage not to wrap her arms around him and take the payment she truly yearned for. An embrace. The simple warmth of a child's embrace.

"Now, go on," she said. "Before the blacksmith wonders where you've gone off to and finds himself another apprentice."

"Yes, ma'am." Holding Rupert against his chest, Jack left with due speed to make the long journey back to town.

Anna folded her arms across her middle as she watched him go. As if she could hold back the ache inside her. She walked over to the windows, and scooped up Nefertiti along the way, rocking the old mama cat in her arms. It wasn't the same, but it would have to be enough.

She was humming quietly, Nefertiti purring against her neck, when a faint noise turned Anna around. The door closed with a click.

"Mara?" Anna called.

There was no answer.

Shrugging, Anna turned back to the window and watched the sun come up while she sang children's lullabies to a tabby cat.

Nick retreated to the parlor, slightly shaken. The image of Anna standing before the windows had been like—

"Wow," he whispered.

She had looked like a . . . Madonna. A Madonna cradling a fat, mangy cat.

The picture lingered before his eyes. Anna silhouetted in the rosy light of dawn—she had literally taken his breath away. And he didn't exactly understand why.

She wasn't beautiful. She wasn't. But when he had seen her standing there, it was as if the sight of her had struck a chord within him. A chord of familiarity. He felt as if he had recognized her at a deeper level; as if he knew her more fully than a man who had only met her yesterday could possibly know her. Had sharing thoughts with Godfrey planted some memory of Anna inside him? His response to her had been so visceral, automatic . . . intense.

He had woken up that morning filled with determination to get his investigation up and running. Downstairs he'd stumbled across the maid Mara, who hadn't give him the time of day much less any truly useful information. All he'd gotten from her was that Anna was at the back of the house, in the menagerie. He had gone looking for Godfrey's wife with the intention of pumping her like a well for clues.

Then he'd seen Anna in front of the window and he'd done a major double take. His reaction to her had been so strong. Strong enough to make him stop and think. Something Nick daCosta sure as heck didn't do enough of.

Suddenly he had remembered what had gotten him into this mess in the first place. His lack of patience. If he hadn't been driving hellbent to leather in a lightning storm, he might not have crashed and he might not have found himself transported back in time into another man's body. And if he hadn't screwed things up with the sting by being such a goddamn eager beaver, he wouldn't have gone to London in the first place. And Chris wouldn't be dying.

Maybe this time, Nick told himself, he would play it smart. Maybe this time he would learn his lesson. *Look be-*

*fore you leap, daCosta. Think before you open your big mouth.*

So he made himself slow down. Chill. Then once his investigatorial jets were cooled, he found himself able to reflect more clearly on his situation. He wasn't going to be charging ahead like a bull in a china shop this time. *Nuh-uh.* This time, he was going to think. Plan. Play it smart.

Nick was pacing back and forth across the parlor, wondering what step—what smart step—to take next, when he saw Anna walk past the open doorway. She obviously didn't see him.

The front door squeaked open, then slammed shut. Nick hesitated only a heartbeat before deciding to go after her. He ran upstairs and grabbed one of Godfrey's many coats from the armoire. Barreling down the stairs, he reminded himself, *Play it smart.*

The piercing sunshine of early morning made him squint as he located Anna ahead on the path. He studied her unobserved. Like yesterday, her clothing was simple and plain, a small gray hat and matching wool cape. Nick again felt that stirring of déjà vu, as if he'd walked behind her like this before, admiring her gently swaying hips.

He shook his head and turned his gaze onto the sea, his boots crunching over the shell-strewn path. He still couldn't quite believe it. What was it that Chris had said to him?

*"I guess it's no accident that you landed where you did."*

Was this what Chris had meant? That this had been his destiny, this amazingly peaceful place from centuries past? Was that the reason he had been so inexplicably fascinated with that photo of Dover? Because fate had always intended to send him here?

Or, Nick asked himself, had it been the other way around? He had long dreamed of a fantasy world like this, so here he had landed?

As beautiful as it was—and it was breathtakingly beautiful—Nick knew he couldn't stay. He had to find a way home. And the answer to his return trip was marching ahead of him, her skirts swaying in unwitting invitation.

"Anna," Nick called.

By the sudden stiffness of her back, he knew that she'd heard him, but she pretended that she hadn't. She kept walking.

"Anna," he called again. "Wait up."

Even the muted pounding of the surf could not mask his shouted request. Anna stopped and folded her gloved hands before her. Her posture struck him as both meek and defiant; her chin raised, but her shoulders bowed.

"Thanks," Nick said as he closed the final yards between them. She didn't turn but continued staring out onto the horizon, her cape flapping like the wings of a giant gray bird.

Against the brilliant blue background of the sky, her features cut a sharp profile, the stark hollows of her cheeks and the unyielding line of her jaw curiously attractive.

Nick followed her gaze out to the ocean. "It's incredible, isn't it?"

Her brows veed together and Nick realized his error. Just as he took for granted the beauty of San Francisco, so Anna must see the magnificence of Dover as commonplace and familiar.

"What I meant," he said, "is that it's easy to forget how lovely it is here, how lucky we are. You know, when you see it every day . . ."

Nick gave it another try, choosing a subject he knew that she cared about—animals. "By the way, did the horse that threw me ever show up?"

"Anubis trotted into the stables the morning after you were found."

"Oh, good. So he made out better than I did, huh?"

"There was a gash on the left foreleg," she said curtly, "but nothing serious."

Nick nodded. She sure wasn't making this easy on him.

He'd swear that he'd had more animated conversations with his damned toaster.

"I was wondering . . . Where was I found?"

Maybe he could find a clue to the time traveling at the site where Godfrey had been injured.

Anna shifted, pointing to a group of moss-covered rocks to the right. "Over there."

"Ah-hah."

More silence.

Nick cleared his throat. "Anna, do you think maybe we should talk?"

Her wide slate-colored eyes jerked his way for but a fraction of a second before she lowered her gaze. Her lips, already taut, drew into a tight, compressed line.

"Why, Godfrey?" She wrapped her arms about her waist. "Why did you return?"

*Whoa, that's direct.* "You, uh, didn't want me to?"

Her shoulders lifted and fell in what might have been either a sigh or a laugh.

"Anna, look, I'm sorry, but I can't seem to remember much about . . . about . . ."

A lock of her hair flew loose, sliding silkily along her cheek. She brushed it aside, lifting her gaze, intelligent and probing. She measured him from behind a thick fringe of mascara-free lashes while Nick dutifully submitted to her scrutiny.

"Much about *what?*" she finally asked.

"Well." He scratched the side of his neck. "Much about anything, to tell you the truth."

"Are you saying that you have lost your memory?"

Nick nodded. "Yeah."

She appeared to start to say something when her attention was diverted to the fields at their backs. Nick turned around with her.

Walking toward them through the tall green grass came a man. A large, blond man holding determinedly to a high-crowned hat that the wind was trying to sweep from his head.

"So are you telling me," she asked in an obvious test, "that you do not remember this gentleman, for example?"

Nick watched the man's progress. It would be just his luck to find out this guy was supposed to be his brother or his best friend. "Um, he looks familiar. . . ."

Seeing their attention directed at him, the man waved a greeting.

"He is the vicar, Mr. Hancock," she said, returning the salute. "Perhaps you might more readily recall his mother? Lady Robeson?"

A certain note in Anna's voice caught Nick's interest. He tried to define it, but couldn't.

"Lady Robeson," he repeated, pretending to run the name through his memory. "Yes, that name does ring a bell."

Anna's eyes narrowed, but she said nothing, stepping away to pluck a pale pink wildflower from among the grasses. Nick watched her movements, sensing that he had just missed something, missed an important clue.

He would have liked to have pursued it, but the blond stranger approached, hat in hand. Dressed in black from his muddied boots to his unadorned coat, he was carrying a Bible in one hand.

"Lord Woodbaine, how good to see you up and about."

Nick mimicked the vicar's bow, feeling Anna's steady gaze upon him. "Mr. Hancock. How are you?"

"Very well, my lord, very well. And pleased to see that you are recovering so quickly." The clergyman's voice dropped to a respectful whisper. "I learned yesterday of your mishap from Mr. Heyer. Unfortunate. Most unfortunate. But racing on horseback in the face of a winter storm—" He shook his head. "From the physician's description, I had believed your injuries to be even more severe."

With his lemon-yellow hair and his toothy smile and his

demeanor of exaggerated earnestness, Hancock reminded Nick of the children's cartoon character Dudley Do-Right.

Nick dismissed his wounds with a negligent shrug. "Nothing but a few scrapes and scratches and a solid blow to the head. Got off easy, all things considered."

The vicar nodded his agreement. "Indeed. We should all give thanks that the Lord, in His infinite wisdom, saw fit to spare you. Mr. Heyer told me that you would not have survived the night if Lady Woodbaine had not found you."

Anna coughed lightly behind her hand, and the clergyman swerved in her direction. Nick frowned, wondering why Anna had neglected to tell him that it was she who had saved his life.

A blush stole into the vicar's cheeks. "Surely, Lady Woodbaine, the Lord must have guided you to your husband in his hour of need. You must be so . . . grateful to have Lord Woodbaine in residence a-again."

Instantly alert, Nick noticed how Hancock's voice quavered and cracked as he addressed Anna, how his boyish features grew rigid with constrained emotion.

Nick's gaze sharpened, flying from Hancock's red complexion to Anna's bent head.

*For the love of—*

A jolt of completely irrational jealousy caught Nick square between the eyes.

*The goddamn vicar had the hots for his wife.*

# Chapter 6

**W**HILE FEIGNING GREAT interest in the flower she twirled between her fingers, Anna fervently wished herself away. Far, far away.

She hazarded a peek at Godfrey through her lashes. Thankfully his attention had shifted to Mr. Hancock.

"If anyone ought to be grateful, it's me," Godfrey said. "I don't think I would be alive today if not for Anna's tender care."

Anna stilled. Had there not been a trace of sarcasm in those words? Did Godfrey know that her "care" had included inordinately large doses of laudanum?

"Yes, well." Mr. Hancock fiddled uncomfortably with the brim of his beaver.

"And how is your family, Mr. Hancock?" Anna asked, in an effort to diffuse the strained mood.

"Oh, very well, Lady Woodbaine. Thank you for asking. Always very kind, yes. In fact, you remind me of the reason for my visit. I happened to mention to my mother that you had returned to Cliff House, Lord Woodbaine, and she bid me to stop in and issue an invitation to both you and Lady

Woodbaine to dine at Ravenshead next Wednesday. Provided, that is, that your health permits."

Anna's breath caught. An evening in Lord and Lady Robeson's company? *Oh, dear.* She could think of nothing she might less enjoy.

"Ravenshead?" Godfrey echoed. Anna wondered if he had any recollection of the marquess's palatial home.

"Well, what do you say, Anna? Are we free Wednesday night?"

She glanced up in surprise, uncertain as to whether she was actually being given a choice. But before she could respond or devise an excuse to beg off, Godfrey answered for them.

"Tell your mother that dinner sounds great. I'm sure we can shuffle our schedule around, can't we?"

Anna nodded, privately wondering whether the vicar also noticed Godfrey's unusual speech and casual manner.

"Splendid," Mr. Hancock said. "Until next Wednesday then, unless I'm fortunate enough to see you at Sunday's service." He bowed, placing his hat back atop his head. "Lord Woodbaine, Lady Woodbaine."

In relief, Anna watched Mr. Hancock begin his long walk back to the vicarage. The clergyman walked almost everywhere, spurning the ease and comfort of a carriage in order to appear humble and unworldly to his parishioners. Ever since his mother had married into wealth, it had become something of an obsession with the young reverend. Privately Anna thought it a silly practice, but understood that Mr. Hancock took his piety rather seriously.

"Mr. Hancock seems like a nice enough guy," Godfrey commented.

"He is dedicated to his vocation."

"I don't suppose he does any marriage counseling, huh?"

"I'm sure I don't know what you mean."

"I mean that I get the feeling that maybe you and I haven't been getting along very well."

*Oh, for the love of—*

The wind whisked a strand of hair across Anna's jaw, and as she reached up to tuck it behind her ear, she tilted her head up just enough to meet his gaze. His eyes met hers in straightforward appeal.

"This is not a jest?" she asked, though Godfrey had never been the jesting sort.

He shook his head. "Scout's honor," he said, lifting two fingers in an alien gesture. "Honestly, I know it's kinda hard to believe, but I seem to have forgotten everything. I can't remember how we met or what my middle name is or why I ever liked purple-and-gold vests."

"You recall nothing? Nothing of our years together?"

"No. I'm sorry, I don't."

*Oh, how very convenient.*

Without a word, Anna began walking back toward the house, her stride long and determined, her cape flapping furiously around her skirts.

To her annoyance, Godfrey followed after her.

"So I take it we're at war?" he asked.

"Good heavens, have you forgotten even that?" she demanded. "When Napoléon could attack our shores tomorrow?"

Godfrey grimaced. "What I should have said is that I take it you and I are having some problems. Do you want to talk about it? Since I can't remember what they are . . ."

She spun toward him, her eyes flashing.

*The nerve of the man. The very gall.*

"No," she spat. "I do not wish to discuss it."

"All right," he said carefully. "If you don't want to talk about it, we'll just have to start over. With a clean slate. I'm sorry, Anna. I apologize, although I wish I knew what for."

Her hiss of indrawn breath caused him to hurriedly add, "Though I realize that my crime must have been really, really bad for you to be so angry. I can see that. And I'm sorry."

She persisted in her stride, her boots stubbornly crunching along the rocky path.

"Come on, Anna, can't we start over? Put the past behind us?"

She stopped dead in her tracks, amazed. Furious.

Her gloved hand splayed across her abdomen. "If only, Godfrey," she whispered harshly. "If only it were that easy."

As she turned to march away, Nick let her go, held fast by the fervent intensity with which she'd delivered that statement.

*Man, oh, man, was this marriage in the toilet.* A libidinous vicar, a pissed-off wife, a husband who'd disappeared from the scene for nearly a year—

Abruptly Nick put on the mental brakes, his thoughts catching on that last point. Why? Why had Godfrey unexpectedly shown up again in Dover after more than ten months away? Obviously Anna had neither anticipated nor requested that he come home from London and, besides, what was the guy's rush? According to the vicar, Godfrey had been speeding through the night in the face of an oncoming storm.

Why? Had Godfrey experienced a revelation? Had he been dashing home, planning to make amends with Anna?

And suddenly it occurred to Nick that *this* could be the reason he'd been sent back to 1810. To bring Godfrey and Anna together again. It was just like in one of those movies where, in order to win his wings, an angel has to do a good deed and reunite a couple or rescue a child or show someone that his life was worth living. Maybe Nick's mission was to engineer Godfrey and Anna's reconciliation. Maybe once he saved their marriage and set matters straight, he would be returned to his own body and his own time. Could that be it? The answer?

Nick heard Chris's voice floating to him in that vast white place between life and death: *"You've got your work*

*cut out for you, buddy, but it'll be all right. They're giving
you another chance."*

Another chance. This must be it. The Powers That Be
must have set for him the job of mending Godfrey and
Anna's unhappy state of matrimony.

Yeah, that had to be it. The folks upstairs probably figured they were giving him a taste of his own medicine after
he'd wimped out on his own marriage. Sure, the decision to
marry Lisa had been the wrong one, a disaster ranking right
up there with Hurricane Andrew and the Chicago Bears '96
season. But Nick had to own up to his part in it, his share of
the blame. Virtually on his wedding night, he had realized
his mistake, but what had he done about it? Nothing.

But this time he wouldn't be able to sit back and do nothing. Not if he wanted to get back to 1997. Now he'd have
to take care of Godfrey's dirty work and fix whatever was
broken in this marriage. And it looked as if it called for
some serious fixing.

What had it been? Another woman perhaps? Maybe
model-handsome Godfrey had been playing the field, and
Anna had found him out?

Nick sent a skeptical glance heavenward. Above him a
black-topped tern sailed by, leapfrogging past a slower-flying
gull. Nick realized that he was jumping to conclusions as
swiftly and as randomly. If he were going to mend the rift
between Godfrey and Anna, he would need to determine
the exact nature of their dispute.

Bending over, he plucked a blade of grass from the earth
and tucked it between his teeth. The fuzzy-gazed aunt had
seemed rather friendly, he recalled; she might be able to
shed some light on the affair.

Up ahead on the ridge Cliff House stood like an impressive-
looking sentinel standing watch over the Channel. Built of
both wood and stone, the house had been situated to take
advantage of the spectacular views. Though not precisely a
mansion, it was still some pretty fancy digs, Nick thought

to himself. Fancy enough for Lord Woodbaine. *Lord Godfrey Woodbaine.*

Suddenly Nick's legs turned leaden as if they'd been shot up with Novocaine, weakening him almost to the point of collapse. He had to lean over and brace his hands on his knees.

"Godfrey Woodbaine," he rasped. "God."

There it was, etched in his memory as clearly as it had been etched in the gravemarker's weathered stone.

*Godfrey Woodbaine. 1780–1810.*

"Jesus Christ," Nick breathed. Godfrey was destined to die within the next nine weeks.

# *Chapter* 7

THE FOLLOWING AFTERNOON, after convincing Godfrey to lie down for a rest, Anna slipped from the house with a basket of kittens on her arm. In the stables she secured the basket to her mount's pommel, clambered into the saddle, then headed down the lane in the direction of Aylesdown.

The kittens she brought as an alibi, an excuse for her visit to town, should she happen to meet one of her acquaintances—limited though they may be. It might have been silly perhaps, but after all these years Anna still considered herself a stranger among the local townspeople. As a girl she had been painfully bashful, and had rarely ventured into the village. Her uncle's prolonged illness and the remoteness of Cliff House had kept her mainly at home, where she had gathered shells and played on the beach and wandered through the fields, content in her solitude.

Eventually she had outgrown some of her youthful shyness and had felt the need to spread her wings, to venture forth. But before she had that chance, her uncle died. And at eighteen, having seen virtually nothing of what lay outside her own safe, small world, she had wed Godfrey, an impoverished baron and cousin to a friend of her uncle's.

Then, God help her, she had seen too much.

A shiver shook her as she rode into the shade of the woods. The trees grew more densely as one traveled inland, the barren branches of deciduous oak intermingling with the rich, fragrant green of fir and pine. Red, orange, and yellow leaves eddied across the road, welcome patches of color against the wintry-brown landscape.

Anna sighed, wondering, as she often did, if the townspeople knew of her secrets. For one so young, she had many secrets. Too many. Some, she confessed, she was ashamed of; others not. Some festered inside her; others she simply accepted as her due. Though she had regrets, she saw no point in self-pity. She merely did what she must to survive. To care for and protect her aunt.

If Anna had learned anything during these past four years, she had learned the meaning of compromise. Life for her was not to be a cut-and-dried proposition, composed of neat decisions that were either right or wrong, black or white. No, Anna's existence was painted in grays. In almost-wrongs and almost-rights. In half-virtues and half-sins.

If she took risks, if she lied to her priest, if she broke the laws of her people . . . Well, so be it. She wasn't proud of her circumstances. She battled her conscience on a daily basis, keeping her concerns private, confidential. It was not easy for her to share her innermost feelings and fears. In fact, rarely was she able to.

Today, however . . . Today she had to talk to someone or else she was going to explode, to positively burst at the seams. Last night she had roamed the cliffside for hours seeking solace in her customary walks. But to no avail. The salt-tinged darkness and thundering surf, usually so soothing, had failed to ease the tumult rioting within her. She had to talk to someone. And that someone could only be Mr. Hancock.

Though the vicar's sermons on temperance and wifely

duty did not provide much in the way of comfort, Anna trusted the young clergyman. As children, they had, on a few occasions, played together before he had been sent off to school. She remembered Stephen Hancock as her equal in shyness with a boyish tendency to become tongue-tied. When he had returned to the Dover area a little over a year ago, Anna had been surprised by the changes in him, by his unwavering commitment to his calling. Not that she had ever known him well, but he had seemed different to her, more confident in his faith.

At the very least, Anna reasoned, Mr. Hancock was an ear to bend, someone whom she could trust, knowing that her affairs would not end up as fodder for the village gossip mill. With no family other than Aunt Beverly, and no friends, only the confidences shared with the moralizing vicar kept her from teetering over the edge of reason.

The horse's hooves clattered noisily as she rode across the ancient stone bridge that led into the town. A poky little village, Aylesdown comprised no more than a dozen small shops, set up to serve the fundamental needs of the local citizenry. An apothecary, an inn, and a blacksmith's shop provided the basic services, but to purchase anything novel or exotic, one had to travel either to the larger towns of Dover or Folkstone or sometimes all the way into London itself.

Anna slowed the horse to a walk as Mr. Hancock's lodgings came into view at the edge of town. Set slightly apart from the rather famous fourteenth-century church, the vicarage was the best tended home in Aylesdown. The white-and-gray house boasted a fresh coat of paint, a new slate roof, and a thoroughly modern heating stove that had been shipped all the way from Germany. All courtesy of Mr. Hancock's mother.

Though the vicar objected to such luxuries, Lady Robeson believed that her son should live in a fashion suitable for the sole issue of a marchioness. Even if that rather lofty title had been but recently acquired. Two summers past, on the very anniversary of her first husband's death, Ursula Hancock had caused a small scandal by wedding Edward Conning, the Marquess Robeson, a man forty years her senior. Anna did not believe the alliance to be a love match.

As she tied her horse to the hitching post, Anna was glad to find the street relatively empty. Gray skies warning of rain must be keeping the townspeople at home, she thought as she looped her basket of kittens over her arm.

She glanced down the street to the Black Oar's wooden sign, battling a twinge of guilt. "I only do what I must," she reminded herself in a whisper. "Only what I must."

She had just stepped onto the vicarage porch when the front door swung open.

"Lady Woodbaine." The priest's youthful face flushed with surprised pleasure.

Anna's step faltered as she took note of the beaver clutched in his hand. "Oh. Were you on your way out?"

He followed her gaze and drew the hat behind his back. "No, no. That is, I was going to pass by the apothecary shop, but it can wait. I think. Yes, please—" He stepped aside, inviting her into the hall. "Please come in."

Anna bit back a smile. Even as a grown man, eloquence still eluded him.

"Thank you," she said. "I do not wish to detain you. . . . " Her sentence trailed off as she stepped into the vicarage's diminutive yet familiar front hallway. "I brought the kittens you'd promised the Kingsley children."

"Ah, yes. How very thoughtful of you to remember. Allow me." He took the basket from her as she followed him the few feet into the parlor. "I'll ring for tea, shall I?"

"A cup of tea would be most welcome."

A manservant responded to the summons, for the vicar did not think it seemly to keep a female in his employ.

"Tea, please," Mr. Hancock instructed and handed the servant the basket. He turned to Anna with a careful smile. "Kindly have a seat, Lady Woodbaine."

She did, removing her hat and gloves and setting them

beside her on the brocade divan. Lady Robeson's hand was evident in this room as well, in the velvet window hangings and the fashionable Chinese decor. Decorated in shades of blue and gold, the parlor had a calming effect on Anna, the colors reminding her of the ocean view from her window at home.

The vicar took a chair opposite her, threading his fingers together and leaning forward with an earnest expression. "The blacksmith's apprentice told me that he'd come to see you with his dog. He was very grateful for your help."

Anna gave a small shrug. "It was nothing. The dog heals well?"

"Yes, from what I understand."

The tea arrived and Anna poured out.

Mr. Hancock accepted his cup, his gaze lingering on her trembling fingers.

"You are troubled."

Anna smiled ruefully, setting her cup on the table. Her stomach felt too unsettled for food or drink.

"I regret I do not come to call when easy of mind."

"Please, Lady Woodbaine," he said with a smile. "I expect you to seek me out when your spirit is troubled. It is my calling. To cheer the dispirited, calm the distressed— It is my commission from Our Lord."

Anna ran a hand across her brow.

"Does this concern Lord Woodbaine?" the clergyman asked hesitantly.

She nodded, embarrassed.

"Has his return . . . pained you?"

"Oh, yes," she said. "Yes, indeed."

The vicar pursed his lips and lowered his gaze to the Oriental carpet. "Matthew 5:44," he murmured. "'Pray for them that despitefully use you.' Let us pray for Lord Woodbaine—"

"No," Anna interrupted, stretching out her hand in a staying motion. "No, it's not like that this time. It is something else entirely."

The vicar's blue eyes skimmed over her. Not in a bold or presumptuous way, but as if he could locate the source of her distress.

"I am sorry," she said, "but I do not wish to mislead you. It isn't . . . It isn't *that*. Since the accident, Godfrey has been different, changed. Did you not notice it yesterday?"

A thoughtful frown furrowed Mr. Hancock's brow. "Now that you mention it, his lordship's manner did strike me as somewhat informal."

"Yes." Anna's eyes widened. "His manner, his speech. Everything about him is different."

"How so?"

"For example"—Anna took a quavering breath—"James our manservant has always served as Godfrey's valet when Godfrey is in residence. Today James told me that Godfrey has refused his services, insisting that he can dress himself. And you should see him, Mr. Hancock. He attires himself like a . . . like a gentleman farmer. He spurns his elegant waistcoats and has set aside his rings. He goes without a coat and refuses even to wear a cravat."

Mr. Hancock appeared nonplussed. "No cravat, you say?"

Anna nodded. "And he leaves—" She could not meet the vicar's eyes. "He leaves his collar unbuttoned."

"I see."

"And it's not merely his attire that is changed, but his conduct, too. He has been—" Anna threw up her hands, feeling foolish, but knowing no other way to describe it. "Well, he has been *kind*. At dinner he pulls out Aunt Beverly's chair for her, then asks about her cats. And last night not only did he help himself to three servings of turnips— Godfrey detests turnips—but then he complimented our cook on their preparation.

"I swear to you, since his return to Cliff House, he has been all that is pleasant and genial and gentlemanly. It frightens me, Mr. Hancock. I fear that he hides some underlying purpose in this change of character."

The vicar ran a finger along the side of his collar. "You say 'pleasant' and 'gentlemanly,'" he repeated. "Yet Lord Woodbaine has always possessed a certain polished urbanity—"

Anna vehemently shook her head. "But that is precisely my point," she argued. "I do *mean* pleasant. Where before Godfrey used flattery to mask slyness, politeness to mask deception, he is now completely the opposite. He is candid, direct. At times, almost tactless."

Mr. Hancock's nose twitched as he mulled over her words.

"Well, I have heard of cases where, following a brush with death such as Lord Woodbaine has experienced, a man may undergo an epiphany of sorts, a divine illumination of his role in God's plan. Perhaps the accident has caused your husband to reexamine himself."

"I believe it is more than that. More than an examination of his soul."

"And what makes you say so?"

Anna toyed with the gold tassels adorning the cushion. "Godfrey claims that the accident has caused him to lose his memory."

The vicar sat back in his chair. "Really."

"Yes. He says that he remembers nothing."

"Nothing of . . . your marriage?"

"Nothing," Anna flatly confirmed. "And, since he remembers nothing about our relationship, he says that we must begin again. Begin our marriage anew." She huffed a bitter laugh. "Convenient, is it not?"

"You do not believe him, then?"

Anna frowned, recalling her conversation with Godfrey yesterday. He had *seemed* sincere. . . .

"I-I do not know what to believe," Anna said, hearing her voice quiver. "Never have I been so confused. I vow I do not know what to do, how to go on."

"Oh, my dearest Lady Woodbaine—" Mr. Hancock started to reach out to her, then stopped himself, visibly struggling. Naked emotion shone in his face, a frustrated longing that forced Anna to swiftly glance aside.

Embarrassed color rushed into her cheeks, her breath caught. She blinked twice slowly, listening to the steady ticking of the clock. Good heavens, how had she failed to see it before?

Surely, she assured herself, the vicar's admiration must be a chaste one. *Surely.* Never would the conscientious Mr. Hancock allow his feelings to trespass into the realm of the physical or the lustful. It was not possible. He was her clergyman, her confessor. He was not truly a man; he was a priest.

Mr. Hancock's hand fell to his side. In numbed relief Anna realized that her judgment had not been wrong. His affection for her was pure, virtuous. Safe.

He cleared his throat as a blush turned the tips of his ears a vivid pink. Fixing his attention to a spot over her shoulder, he took a few moments to compose himself, to reclaim his ecclesiastical decorum. The clock ticked on, its steady meter underscoring the awkward silence.

"Ahem," he said, at last. "I, uh, I would remind you, Lady Woodbaine, of Christ's teachings wherein he urged us to set aside our doubts and fears, to have faith. Faith in our fellow man. Perhaps Lord Woodbaine has turned over a new leaf."

*A new leaf?* Anna's embarrassment faded as resentment surged up inside her. How could Mr. Hancock speak to her of faith when he knew perfectly well what Godfrey was capable of? When he had seen with his own two eyes evidence of her husband's duplicitous nature?

An insane idea, born of desperation, began to form in her thoughts.

"Mr. Hancock, I had hoped that you might be willing to help me."

"But, of course, my lady. Of course, I wish to help you. My mission is to serve."

"Yes, to serve." She licked at her parched lips. Was it

wrong to use the vicar's feelings? To manipulate his affection for her?

"Would you know of a place, somewhere—*anywhere*—where my aunt and I might go to be safe?" Her words came faster, rushing together in a self-conscious, yet hopeful, torrent. "A place far from here? London? Dover? To the north? I don't know precisely what I could do other than to act as a companion or a lady's—"

Mr. Hancock's expression silenced her. Silenced her hopes.

"A wife is to cleave to her husband," the vicar said, his eyes sad with understanding. "Though I empathize with your suffering, Lady Woodbaine—I honestly do—we cannot work against God's word."

Anna's shoulders sagged. Dear Lord, what had she been thinking? Had she honestly believed the young clergyman would spirit her away, save her from herself?

Though her spirit still raged, she forced herself to calm. Outwardly, at least.

*If only I possessed Mr. Hancock's depth of conviction.*

Yet, she did not. In spite of hours at her prayers and her desperate willingness to believe, Anna had yet to find all her answers in faith.

Resigned, she shook her head and let go the last of her resentment. After all, she had come to the vicar for guidance. She should do her best to try to heed his well-intentioned counsel.

Mr. Hancock stood and retrieved his prayer book from a round occasional table.

"Shall we pray?" he invited.

# *Chapter* 8

FROM THE UPSTAIRS window, Nick watched Anna leave the house, a mysterious basket swinging from her arm. With every dozen steps or so, she darted a look behind her, her face a pale ivory oval against the steel-gray canvas of the sky.

Even from a distance Nick could read the wariness in her expression, in her hunched shoulders and industrious stride. He didn't need years of police surveillance to recognize that Anna was sneaking away from the house.

For a moment he toyed with the idea of trying to follow her, but then decided against it. It was always tricky trailing someone in unfamiliar terrain, and if, by chance, Anna were to discover him, it would be a serious setback. A setback in his goal of establishing a climate of trust between them.

From what Nick had seen so far, trust was an element that had been sorely lacking in Godfrey and Anna's previous relationship. Last night, for example. A simple request to Anna to please pass the turnips, and she had reacted as if he'd asked for her to donate a kidney. The look she had given him would have been laughable if Nick hadn't recognized that her suspicion was real. She had acted as if he was after more than just turnips. So what did she think? That he was concocting some fiendish plan to take over the world . . . involving tubers?

No, he sure as hell couldn't afford to make any mistakes with Anna. He didn't have time. Not when this body he was occupying could be dead as early as tomorrow. Or tonight. Or an hour from now.

Frustrated, Nick swung away from the window, catching a glimpse of himself in Anna's bedroom mirror.

"Jesus," he muttered, still unaccustomed to wearing Godfrey's movie-star face.

Of course, Godfrey's face wasn't quite as handsome as it had been earlier that morning. Though the bruises had faded significantly, Nick had done a number on himself trying to shave with that straight-edge razor. At least a half-dozen wounds speckled his jaw and cheeks, and he decided that maybe tomorrow he'd let James have a go of it again.

Nick grimaced at his reflection.

"Good looks aren't going to help much once your number is called," he muttered at the mirror. Not once old Woodbaine found himself shuffling off to the Great Beyond.

*When would it happen? And how?*

Nick turned his face to the ceiling.

Damn, the fates probably thought this some terrific entertainment: *Okay, daCosta, you've got to fix this marriage and you have less than nine weeks to do it.* The clock starts and . . . go! He felt like a contestant in some kind of paranormal game show where the prize was life or death, marital bliss or misery. The big question, though, was who was really going to die when Godfrey's body bit the dust? Nick daCosta or Godfrey Woodbaine? Or both? Nick half expected Alex Trebek to appear out of thin air with the answer—or maybe Saint Peter clutching a sealed envelope.

Of course, he still didn't know *why* he'd been sent to reconcile a marriage that was doomed to end in a few weeks anyway. But, hey. Who was he to challenge the Almighty Gods of Time Travel?

Nick rubbed his hand across his eyes, laughing softly, if humorlessly, to himself. No, he didn't have any answers and no game-show host or angel was likely to suddenly materialize with them in hand. All he had to go on was instinct. He was going to have to rely on his gut intuition and trust that Godfrey was not destined to die before Nick's mission was fulfilled.

Yesterday afternoon he'd gone out to the rocks where Anna said she had found Godfrey that fateful night. After scouring every inch of the area, Nick had nothing more to show for it than skinned knuckles and broken fingernails. The most interesting discovery he'd made had been a slug the size of a small Buick. If there was a secret time tunnel hidden among those rocks, he sure couldn't find it. No, he'd just have to keep looking for clues a little closer to home.

Raking a hand through his hair, Nick glanced around Anna's bedroom, wondering where to start. A narrow curtained bed, a plain oak wardrobe, a small yet orderly writing desk; the room's furniture presented a spare simplicity that reminded Nick very much of its owner. Only the thick patterned rug underfoot hinted at even the slightest luxury, and one of its corners was tattered and worn as if chewed away by a dog.

"Well, I might as well see what we've got here."

He walked across the room and flung open the doors to the armoire. Neatly folded stacks of clothing in shades of brown, gray, and black filled but half the shelves. Nick frowned, knowing that down the hall Godfrey's wardrobe was practically overflowing with a rainbow of vests and coats and pants and God only knew what else.

He clicked his tongue against his teeth. The contrast between the Woodbaines' style of living was pretty obvious. But was it by choice? Did Anna prefer this Quaker-like existence or was it forced on her by her husband? Godfrey didn't seem to mind spending a few pennies on his own comfort, but was he as generous with his wife?

Swiftly Nick rifled through the clothing, looking for what, he did not know. After stumbling upon a hideous assortment of corsets and balloonlike knickers, Nick found himself wishing for a Victoria's Secret catalog. He could just picture Anna in a silky midnight blue—

*Hold up, daCosta.*

Okay, so something about Anna got his juices flowing. He couldn't help that. It was simply good old-fashioned, red-blooded American boy lust. But getting himself all worked up in knots wasn't going to help him focus on the job at hand. He needed to rein in his hormones and stick to his primary purpose: figuring out how he was going to return to the future.

Banishing visions of satin-trimmed teddies, he closed the armoire and moved over to the desk. A journal, a diary . . . He had just begun to flip through a stack of letters he'd found when a slight breeze wafted across the back of his neck. He spun around to find Anna's Aunt Beverly standing in the doorway, a kitten nuzzled against her electric-blue polka-dot dress. She sure had her own sense of style, he'd give her that.

"Good afternoon," she said.

With as much nonchalance as he could muster, Nick slid the drawer closed. "And good afternoon to you, Bev."

There was no point in inventing an excuse for his snooping, since every cop knew that when burned like this, the best course of action was to keep your mouth shut. And divert attention from yourself.

"It seems that neither of us took that nap Anna was pushing on us," he said with a smile. "You weren't sleepy either, huh?"

"Oh, no. Anna thinks I need to nap every afternoon like I'm an invalid or a child. I appease her by going upstairs, but"—she leaned forward and said in a confidential stage whisper—"I don't nap, you know."

Nick was waiting for her to fill him in on what she *was* doing instead of napping, when her inquisitive gaze shifted from him to the desk.

"Come," she said and waved him forward. "I want to show you something." Then she headed out the door, as if assuming he would follow. He did.

She led him down the hall to a door that, when opened, revealed a narrow, dusty wooden staircase.

"What's up there?" he asked.

"The attic."

"Yeah, I can see that. But what's in the attic? What do you want to show me?"

Nick suspected he was being paranoid, but he was suddenly remembering having read *Jane Eyre* in his junior year of high school. Wouldn't it be just his luck to find some knife-wielding maniac locked in the garret?

Beverly turned to him, the top of her gray-brown head barely reaching his shoulder. She raised on her tiptoes and said quietly, "Answers."

He tensed. How the hell did she know he was looking for answers? Or was dear Aunt Bev simply rambling again?

Lifting her skirts, she started up the stairs as spryly as a high-school cheerleader. Nick grinned in admiration. He had to admit that he kind of liked the old girl, quacky or not. She had spunk—like his Nona Carolina. And unlike his "wife," Beverly seemed comfortable with him. She didn't treat him as if he were a saliva-dripping leper the way that Anna did.

Nick trailed Bev up the stairs, remembering to bend low under the rafters since, in Godfrey's body, he stood about four inches taller than his usual five-feet-eleven. With a lump the size of a golf ball still adorning his temple, the last thing he wanted was to crack his skull open again.

Long and narrow, the attic was actually fairly tidy despite being cramped and overrun with dust bunnies. Two dormer windows let in just enough light so that you didn't need a candle, and Nick felt grateful for small favors. Already he'd burned his hand three or four times with hot wax, by forgetting to keep the candle stand level.

Aunt Beverly was sitting beside an open trunk, humming to herself as she rummaged through the contents. The kitten scrambled along the floor, chasing after a dust ball.

"Oh, look." She sighed, and held up a piece of paper, a sketch of some sort.

Nick scootched closer and dropped to a squat. "What is it?"

"This is a drawing I copied from an Egyptian tomb painting, oh . . . thirty years ago, I would say. The Egyptians were such a fascinating people. Did you know that they revered the cat? Just look at this. Is it not magnificent?"

With a gnarled finger, she pointed proudly to the paper, indicating a group of elongated figures standing atop rows of hieroglyphics. "It depicts the four deities: Osiris, Isis, Nephythys, and Duamutef."

*Duamutef?*

"So that Egyptian stuff in the parlor is really from Egypt?"

"Oh, yes, John and I loved to bring back mementoes from our excursions. Before Anna came to live with us, we traveled extensively—North Africa, India, the Continent."

"You don't say?"

Nick was impressed. Aunt Bev might not be as sharp as she once was, perhaps a bit past her prime, but at least she'd *had* a prime. From the sounds of it, this old lady had lived.

"John and I often reminisce about our journeys, the people we met, the amazing sights we enjoyed. Only yesterday we were discussing our encounter with a rare albino rhinoceros. . . . " Her voice trailed off, dreamy and hushed, her spectacled gaze unfocused.

Nick scratched lightly behind his ear. Why did he get the feeling that something wasn't right here?

"John?"

"John Radcliffe, my husband. He passed on in 1806."

*Oh, boy.* "Hmm-mm. And you and John were talking about the rhino . . . yesterday?"

Her hazel eyes cleared. She looked to be returning to the planet Earth.

"Why, yes. You see, ever since John died, I have been able to converse with the spirits. It really is shockingly easy. Once I had made contact with John, then—" She lifted her frail shoulders.

"So you've been what? Holding seances up here?"

Beverly smiled and bent toward him. "Is it not amazing," she whispered, "how much more there is to our existence than we ever could have realized?"

Nick sat back on his heels. Why was she asking *him*?

But Beverly didn't appear to be expecting an answer, for she dug into the trunk again, sorting through a variety of knickknacks and whatnots and doohickies that all probably belonged in a museum somewhere. Or probably were in a museum in 1997.

"Ah, here it is." She pulled from the trunk some sort of gold locket. "This watch belonged to my nephew, Anna's father. He was the last of the Allenbrooks, you know. My father had so hoped I might be a boy to carry on the family name, but alas—" She shrugged. "He gave me a boy's name anyway."

"What about the watch?" Nick asked.

"Oh, yes." Beverly refocused her attention to the time-piece in her hand. "As I said, it belonged to Anna's father, Benjamin. He had her likeness painted on the horn outer case the summer that she turned six. Sadly, that same summer, he and Georgia, Anna's mother, were both taken by a fever epidemic."

Nick accepted the watch from Beverly and studied the portrait. Wide-set eyes, a dot of a nose, a trusting yet bashful smile. It was a face of pure innocence.

"This is Anna?"

"Yes."

An unexpected smile tugged at Nick's lips, and he felt as if he'd snagged a clue, snuck a peek into Anna's childhood. It really wasn't much, only a portrait, but for some reason it pleased him.

"So, Anna has lived with you since she was six?"

"Yes, here at Cliff House."

"Was she what you'd call a happy kid?"

Beverly poked at the bridge of her glasses. "She was quiet, but happy. Anna laughed much more in those days," she added wistfully.

Nick dipped his head and examined the portrait again.

"Why won't she talk to me, Bev?"

"She doesn't know you."

*What was that supposed to mean?*

Before he could ask, Beverly reached over and triggered the watch's gold clasp. "Here, have a look."

Large Roman numerals gave the hour as sixteen minutes after twelve.

"Nice," he said. "Very nice."

He handed the watch back to Beverly, but she wagged her head.

"No. I think you should keep it."

She shut the trunk, scooped up the kitten, and rose to her feet. Show-and-tell was obviously over.

Nick weighed the heavy gold watch in the palm of his hand. "Hey, wait a minute, Bev."

She turned to him, her eyes glassy and distant again. "Yes?"

"Why are you giving this to me?"

She looked through him as if she didn't actually see him, as if she were looking past him into her own private world.

"Time is important to you, is it not?"

"Auntie?"

Anna hung her damp cape on the hook in the hallway, then untied her bonnet with cold-stiff fingers. Her ride home from Aylesdown had not been a pleasant one. Dense fog had drifted in from the Channel, blanketing the land in a bone-chilling mist. She shivered as she walked down the hall, rubbing her palms together. The lamps had not yet been lit in the parlor. The house lay dark and quiet. Could Godfrey and Beverly still be resting?

She was headed upstairs to look for her aunt when she spotted a light flickering at the rear of the house. In the menagerie.

A rush of warm air welcomed her as she pushed open the menagerie door. Her gaze wandered from the fire in the screened hearth to—

Her fists clenched defensively.

Dressed in the casual manner he had adopted of late—no cravat, no waistcoats, no jewelry—Godfrey stood to the back of the room, cuddling a midnight-black kitten against his shirtfront. Beside him, Aunt Beverly played with George, a massive, overfed orange-and-white cat she had disrespectfully named in honor of their royal prince.

Both glanced up as she entered. Anna recognized the far-away look in Beverly's gaze—an indication that Auntie was not in one of her more lucid periods.

"Hi there," Godfrey greeted in his strange Americanized speech.

Anna tried to answer, but she could not push a single sound past the knot of disquiet in her throat. Godfrey never came into the menagerie. Never. Except for his horses, he abhorred animals; he thought them dirty and smelly and ugly. Many was the time he had threatened to throw all of Anna's pets over the cliff. Of course, she did not believe that he would. Not because she doubted him capable of such cruelty—Lord, she understood all too well precisely what her husband was capable of. But to carry out such a threat, Godfrey would first be obliged to touch the animals, and this he would never do. At least . . . he would never have done. Before today.

"Aunt Beverly," Anna said, struggling to keep the alarm

from her voice. "Would you care to freshen up before dinner? It is fast approaching six o'clock."

"Dinner?" Behind her glasses, Beverly's eyes squinted as if searching for the word's meaning. "Oh, yes, dinner. Very well, dear." She returned George to his basket, then shuffled across the room, her vividly blue skirts rasping over the limestone floor.

Anna attempted to read her expression, to see if Godfrey had overset her in any way, but it was impossible to tell. Aunt Beverly was too far gone, lost in her own world.

"John will be pleased to hear we are to dine," Beverly mumbled as she walked past Anna. "He said earlier he was peckish this evening."

As the door closed behind Aunt Beverly, Anna prayed that Godfrey had not overheard her aunt's comment. More ammunition her husband did not need. Years ago he would have committed Aunt Beverly to a mental asylum if not for Anna's vehement protestations. And, after all this time, the only weapon Godfrey still wielded over her with any success was Aunt Beverly's fate.

"Where have you been?" Godfrey asked as he walked over to her, snuggling the kitten against his chest.

By force of will, Anna kept herself from stepping back.

"I had business to see to in Aylesdown," she said, choosing her words with care. "Do you remember the village, Godfrey?"

"No. My memory isn't returning very quickly. Only a little bit here, a little bit there."

His lopsided smile and relaxed manner did not put Anna at ease. Not at all. Though Mr. Hancock had urged her to trust Godfrey—to trust in this sudden change of character—she thought it far more easily said than accomplished. How could she trust this man after everything she had suffered at his hand?

In her heart Anna knew that there must be some explanation. There had to be a reason for this newfound affability on his part. Not for a moment did she actually believe that this change was due to head injuries suffered during Godfrey's fall. If it had been merely a case of memory loss, she might have believed it. After all, she had heard of such rare occurrences. But a complete reversal of personality . . . It was too much. Too much for her to accept.

"Youch," Godfrey growled softly, and peered down at his front. The kitten's claws appeared to be caught up in the fine linen of his shirt.

Anna tensed. On impulse, she reached out to take the kitten from him at the same time that he tried to pry loose the tangled claws. Their hands met atop the silky, black fur. Instantly Anna tried to pull free, but Godfrey secured his fingers over hers, wrapping both their hands around the mewling kitten.

Shocked, Anna jerked her gaze to his. Surely that could only be terror quickening her pulse. . . .

"Soft, huh?"

"Wh-what?"

He directed her fingers in a back-and-forth motion over the downy fur. "Soft little fella, isn't he?"

Anna's heart pounded loudly, so loudly that she could not hear herself think.

"It's a girl," she countered inanely. "Amy."

His green eyes sparkled. *With amusement?* Logic urged her to run, to tear her grip from his and run. But something else, some other part of her was not afraid. Some other part of her was almost . . . enjoying his touch.

*But how could that be?* an inner voice cried. He was a scoundrel, a man totally without morals or conscience. Good God, she despised him. She had always despised him. And he despised her.

Then why—why was he looking at her like that? With feeling, with warmth. Was this how he had won over Aunt Beverly, how he had coerced her into forgetting what manner of man he truly was?

But she was not Aunt Beverly, dash it. Her wits were still acute, her memory sharp. It would take more—much,

much more—than two days of this gentlemanly performance to wipe clean *her* memories.

No, Anna Woodbaine would not forget.

And neither would she forgive.

With a swift jerk, she tugged her fingers free. Godfrey had to clutch at the kitten with both hands to keep it from falling.

"Hey, easy now," he said. "Let's not scare the little critter."

Anna's mouth compressed into a thin line, a line that shook with emotion. "I daresay your loss of memory prevents you from recalling how little you care for animals."

Godfrey frowned at the kitten who was busily gnawing at his thumb. "Me? I didn't like animals?"

"You loathe them."

"No kidding." He shook his head, smiling slightly. "I suppose next you'll tell me I didn't like children, either."

The blood drained from her face. *How dare he mock her?*

But before she recovered sufficiently enough to answer him, Godfrey pulled from his pocket a watch which he tilted toward her. On its face was painted the likeness of a young girl.

"Speaking of children," he said. "That's you, isn't it?"

Anna's teeth clenched. "Where did you get that?"

"Bev gave it to me when we were rummaging through the attic. She said that it belonged to your father."

*Oh, Aunt Beverly.*

Anna had hidden in the attic the sum of her savings: twenty-three pounds, four shillings. Though far from a fortune, it was all they had, all that Godfrey had left them. Did Auntie not realize that they would be destitute if he discovered their hidden cache? It might not be so very much, but without it they would have nothing. Godfrey would take it all, as he had always done.

When she remained silent, Godfrey bent forward, as if

trying to catch a glimpse of her face. "Do you mind? That she gave it to me?"

"Does it matter whether I mind or not?" she answered despairingly.

"Well, sure it does. I mean, the watch did belong to your father. If you'd rather I didn't keep it—"

He held out the watch to her, but she ignored it, meeting his gaze as calmly as she could.

"Since when, Godfrey, did my wishes become of the least concern to you?"

"I—" Indecision twisted his features. "I don't know, Anna. . . . A lot has changed since the accident."

"So you claim."

"You don't believe me?"

By God, did he honestly sound wounded by her distrust?

Looping her arms around her waist, she shivered and glanced away. "I swear to you, Godfrey, I do not know what to believe anymore."

# Chapter 9

NICK'S EYES NARROWED. A minute ago he had thought that Anna was actually responding to him, that she was at last letting her guard down a bit. He'd felt how her pulse had sped up when their hands had joined. He'd seen a feminine awareness flare at the back of her eyes. But then, in the space of a few seconds, her walls of distrust were solidly back in place. She'd closed herself off from him again, wrapping her arms around herself in that familiar stance.

He noticed that Anna did that a lot when she was feeling threatened or emotional. She would fold her arms around her waist or lay a protective hand across her stomach. Reading body language was one of the more useful skills he'd picked up over the years, and right now Anna's was saying to him, "Back off, buddy."

So he did.

Even though he really didn't want to. He was feeling antsy, on edge. Part of it he recognized as plain old sexual frustration. Anna might not know it, but she sure had his number. There was an indefinable quality to her, a gracefulness, a delicate sexuality that he responded to at gut level.

Yet just look at how Anna responded to *him*. She flinched whenever he got too close. Too close to her . . . and to the truth.

Nick wanted to push her for answers, to push past her walls. But all his instincts were telling him to give her some space.

*Be smart, daCosta.*

He turned around and walked across the room to return the kitten to its mother. When he glanced back at Anna, she had her hand on the door latch.

*Goddammit.*

"That really pisses me off when you do that," he blurted out. But what he meant to say and how it came out just didn't sound right. Somehow "pissed off" just wasn't the same when voiced in that uptight-English-prissy-Lord-Woodbaine drawl.

Anna stilled. "I beg your pardon?"

Despite his good intentions, Nick's temper was on the rise. "What I'm saying is that I don't much like the way you just take off, disappear, whenever the discussion starts to get too hot for you to handle."

She looked at him as if he were a sideshow freak.

"Is that how it's always been?" he demanded. "We have a disagreement and you go slinking off?"

*Man, no wonder this marriage was the pits.* It was a text-book case of that age-old male-female-miscommunication syndrome. Okay, so back in 1997, Nick daCosta might not have been the most enlightened guy to ever walk the streets, but, as the product of a Portuguese father and an Italian mother, he had been raised not to hold anything back. If you were mad, you said so. If you were really mad, you did something about it. But this British stiff-upper-lip routine was as foreign to him as . . . *Well, it was just plain foreign.*

He and Lisa didn't have a marriage made in heaven, but

they'd at least aired their differences. Aired them loud and clear so that the whole neighborhood got an earful. Why couldn't Anna just let loose with whatever it was that had her so angry? What was it that Godfrey had done, what crime had he committed, that had put her panties into such a twist?

"Slinking off?" she repeated. Her expression was an interesting blend of belligerence and caution. Nick thought she could give lessons in passive-aggressive behavior.

"Yeah, slinking off. Like today when you snuck away from the house. Why the secrecy, Anna? What were you doing in town anyway?"

Anna flushed . . . guiltily?

"I-I called at the vicarage."

"The vicarage."

Nick stiffened, seeing again in his mind's eye the clergyman's blatant infatuation as he'd practically drooled all over Anna the other day. Damn it, maybe something *was* going on between Anna and Hancock.

*Enough pussyfooting around*, Nick decided. He was going to find out once and for all.

Ignoring the warning bells blaring in his head, he marched across the room. He took hold of Anna's shoulders, drew her close, and covered her mouth with his.

Her lips were passionless, unresponsive, and cold. Gently Nick increased the pressure, slanting his mouth across hers, urging her to participate. The softness of her small, round breasts rubbed against his chest as he tentatively slid the tip of his tongue along the seam of her mouth. The touch of his tongue made Anna freeze up on him like a block of ice.

He pulled back and stared into her ashen face. Her blue-gray eyes were huge, her nostrils quivering with barely controlled breaths. She looked at once defiant, yet resigned. Detached, yet terrified.

And he, God help him, felt like a first-class jerk.

Dropping his hands, he released Anna from his grasp, yet

she continued to stand there like a martyr bound for the stake.

*Brilliant*, Nick berated himself. *Friggin' brilliant.*

He'd only intended the kiss as an experiment, as a way of testing the waters. He'd thought a trial smooch would give some indication as to whether or not Anna had any real feelings for her husband.

Apparently not.

Apparently this marriage stood in some seriously deep doo-doo.

So, was she involved with the reverend? Hell, he didn't know. All he knew was that he felt damned awkward right now. Like a pimply-faced kid with chronic halitosis.

He scrutinized Anna's averted face. Should he apologize? Or would that be too weird, a husband apologizing to his wife for stealing a kiss?

Nick shoved his hands into the back waistband of his pants.

"Anna, I—"

God, what could he say?

She held herself so still, she didn't even look as if she were breathing. Nick wanted to kick himself.

"I-I'm sorry, Anna," he mumbled. Then he walked out the door, realizing that this time he was the one doing the slinking.

Anna waited until she heard Godfrey's bedroom door close before she peeked out into the hallway. She had retired more than an hour earlier, leaving Godfrey and Aunt Beverly to finish their card game. Her aunt had come upstairs a good twenty minutes ago, yet Godfrey had lingered below. Anna wondered what he'd been doing.

Unconsciously her fingers rose to her lips, stroking their fullness. Her mouth still burned. Her pulse still beat too fast.

With silent steps she left her room and walked down the hall, shooting an anxious glance at Godfrey's chamber. A light glowed beneath his door. She quickened her pace, hurrying along to her aunt's room, where she rapped, almost soundlessly, at the door.

"Come in."

Anna slipped inside to find Aunt Beverly reading in bed, the first volume of Denon's *Description de l'Egypte* laid open in her lap. Indian and Egyptian artifacts cluttered the desk, the dressing table, every conceivable surface. Uncle John's old desk still sat along the far wall, squeezed up against the bed. This room had been his study in the days when Anna's aunt and uncle had occupied the grander apartment which Godfrey had later claimed.

"Auntie, I hope it's not too late—"

"It's never too late, my child. Come, sit." She patted the counterpane invitingly.

Anna went and perched herself at the side of the bed.

"Have you hurt yourself, dear?" her aunt asked.

"What—" Then Anna realized that her fingers were once again pressing against her mouth, and she jerked her hand from her face.

"No, no. I only wanted to talk to you about Godfrey."

Anna hadn't discussed with her aunt Godfrey's supposed memory loss, chiefly because she had yet to fully countenance his claim.

"What do you make of him?" Anna asked.

"Make of him?"

"Yes. What do you think of him since his return?"

"I think that he seems"—Beverly smiled, her eyes crinkling at the corners—"rather nice."

"Yes, but *why* do you think, Auntie? Have not the changes to his appearance and temperment quite astonished you?"

"Oh, not really," her aunt said with breezy indifference, waving a wrinkled hand. Lavender water drifted on the air.

"But how can that be? How can you not be taken aback by his strange new ways?"

"Oh, Anna, I am an old woman, love, who has seen a

great deal during her lifetime. Very little surprises me anymore."

Anna felt vexed by her aunt's nonchalant attitude. "Well, you do seem to have lost the strong aversion you held for him."

"Mm-hmm," Beverly agreed in a cheery sing-song. "And what of you, Anna dear?"

"I—" She clenched her fingers. "I do not know. I have no explanation for Godfrey."

"Do you still fear him?" Her aunt peered at her over the top of her spectacles.

"I fear the man he used to be."

Beverly flipped a page over in her book, making no comment.

"I did worry for *you* at first," Anna said. "I was very much concerned over the fact that you seemed to have no fear of him at all."

"*I* am not worried. So why should you be?" Her aunt's gentle smile took the sting from the words. "For me, that is."

Anna smoothed her fingers over the counterpane. "I am concerned to hear that you were showing Godfrey around the attic. You do understand that my . . . income is sporadic at best. If Godfrey were to find our small savings, we might find ourselves in very dire straits, Auntie."

"How you fret, my dear. He won't take our money, I assure you."

"You trust him so thoroughly?"

Her aunt flipped another page. "I do."

Anna masked a frown. Were her aunt's weakening wits to blame, or did Beverly see Godfrey with a truer eye than Anna could?

"But—" Her aunt shrugged. "You must come to your own conclusions, Anna child. You must decide for yourself whether you are capable of trusting the man."

*Never*, Anna's heart cried. But her fingers strayed again to her mouth and she asked herself why she had not been more repulsed by his embrace. She had never before taken the slightest pleasure from her husband's touch. Had she this evening?

She met her aunt's curious stare. What had come over them all? Had Godfrey cast a spell upon them—had he employed some evil black magic to draw forth their sympathies?

Perhaps his goal was to drive her mad. Perhaps he was succeeding.

Prior to the accident, she had at least known what to expect of him. She had known how to protect herself, how to remain on her guard. But since his return, everything in her world had tilted upside down. Everything.

A part of her refused to accept the changes in him. It infuriated her, it did. When Godfrey held out her cloak for her, she did not feel like thanking him—she wanted to rip it from his grasp. When he served her at the table, she longed for nothing more than to slap the spoon from his hand and upend the dish into his lap.

She wanted to reject him. To reject his kindnesses.

But it was becoming increasingly difficult for her to do so.

Aunt Beverly closed her book and set it aside.

Anna gave a quiet sigh. "It is late. I should let you get to sleep."

Yet she did not rise from the bed.

"Did you wish to sleep in here tonight?" her aunt asked.

Gracious, was it so obvious? Obvious that she feared Godfrey might come to her tonight?

"No. Thank you, Auntie, I'm a grown woman now. No more nightmares." She reached over and brushed her lips against her aunt's weathered cheek. "Sleep well, darling."

Her aunt clasped her hand. "You, too, my dear."

But as Anna left the room, she knew she would not rest easy. Not as long as her husband slept but a few yards from her bedroom door.

# *Chapter* 10

NICK WAS IN a bad mood. The kind of bad mood that, had he been at home, would have called for a night alone with a "Dirty Harry" movie and a six-pack.

*Oh, man, a beer.*

The mere thought of it made his mouth start to water. He hated to think what lengths he would go to get his hands on just one ice-cold draft and an order of potstickers. *Potstickers. Or a mushroom pizza. Or a heaping plate of linguini con pesto . . .*

His stomach growled as if warning him to keep his memories under wraps. Especially since, based on what he'd sampled of nineteenth-century food, it wasn't too likely he would be served any of those delicacies tonight. Compared to the cuisine of 1810 England, school cafeteria lunches would qualify as gourmet fare. And they were probably a lot healthier, too. Had he even seen a green vegetable in the last week? If he had, he sure as heck couldn't remember it.

Yeah, the food was bad. But it wasn't meal after meal of watery fish stew that had brought on Nick's current state of grouchiness. It was this "thing" between him and Anna.

The cold shoulder treatment had eased off a bit—Anna had finally begun to treat him civilly. But she treated him like . . . like he was nothing.

She avoided him every chance she got, didn't speak to him unless it was absolutely necessary. She wasn't rude or hostile. She just totally and completely ignored him.

Though no stranger to stress, Nick felt the constant tension starting to wear on his nerves. It made him feel antsy, made his skin crawl. *And the worst part about it was that it wasn't even his own damned skin.*

Godfrey had gotten into this mess, not him. If Nick had to atone for the other man's sins, he'd at least like to know what the Baron Woodbaine was guilty of; why, for all Nick's efforts at playing "nicey-nice," Anna continued to treat him as if he had the plague.

Nick tugged at his neckcloth and sent an exasperated look across the carriage. Her eyes downcast, Anna sat quietly—silently—with her hands folded in her lap. Tonight she wore what must have been her best outfit, a simple golden-brown silk dress with a lace scarf tucked around the neckline. It wasn't exactly a Cinderella-going-to-the-ball kind of dress, but it looked nice on her. The color matched her hair, put a golden flush into her cheeks.

He had complimented her when she had come downstairs earlier that evening, but rather than answer him, she'd acknowledged him with a glacial tilt of her head. She hadn't warmed up any during the carriage ride, either, sparing him not a glance nor a word since they'd left Cliff House nearly twenty minutes ago.

Nick thrummed his fingers on his thigh, uncomfortable with the silence. He'd been raised in a big noisy family and wasn't accustomed to long bouts of quiet. At home he usually kept the television tuned to *American Movie Classics* or opened his window to the clamor of the San Francisco streets.

"You don't want to go to this dinner, do you?"

His abrupt statement caused Anna to flinch before she

looked up at him, one slender brow arched. "I do not often go about in company."

"Oh." He gave an apologetic shrug. "I guess I didn't know that when I accepted the invitation."

Nick might have offered to bag the dinner and return to Cliff House, if only to please Anna. But tonight presented too promising an opportunity to pass up. Neighbors were notoriously the best source of information, and Nick was determined to get to the bottom of this rift between Lord and Lady Woodbaine.

"About tonight . . ." Nick began. "Could you tell me something about the people we'll be meeting? So that I don't make a fool of myself right from the get-go?"

Though it would have been far easier to simply claim amnesia on Godfrey's behalf, Nick felt that it put him at too great a disadvantage. The amnesia bit left him in a defenseless position, giving away too much. It was tough enough going into this situation blind; he didn't want the rest of the world to recognize it.

Anna's lips compressed. "What would you like to know?"

"Well, have we known the Robesons long?"

"I made the family's acquaintance when I moved to Cliff House as a child. At that time Lady Robeson was Ursula Hancock, married to Jeremiah Hancock, the vicar's father."

"A second marriage?"

Anna nodded.

"And when did I meet the family?"

"After we . . . wed."

"How did we meet?"

She returned to the careful contemplation of her gloves. "It was arranged."

"Arranged?" Like *Fiddler on the Roof*? "Arranged by who?"

"By Uncle John."

"Beverly's husband?"

"Yes."

Nick frowned. Of course, he knew of the custom—his family was from the Old Country, after all. But arranged marriages were of the past, a tradition that had gone the way of the dinosaurs.

But this *was* the past, he reminded himself.

"Did you not want to marry me, Anna?"

She fidgeted with a button on her glove. "At the time I did not oppose it."

*At the time. Today would be another story, wouldn't it?*

"Were we ever happy? In the beginning?"

The carriage wheels rumbled. The lanterns squeaked, swinging from their iron hooks.

"No."

A simple "no" that said so much more. He wanted to ask her if she'd ever loved him. If Godfrey had ever loved her. But he could tell that he had already probed as far as she would allow.

Nick tugged aside the window curtain. The moon shone nearly full tonight, brushing the landscape with an unearthly ivory glow. In the distance spun the blades of a windmill, twirling and dipping in their slow circular dance.

Nick had just begun to question how much longer they'd have to rattle along in this bouncing box when the carriage crested the hill. A house loomed ahead, exactly the kind of house Nick had pictured an English marquess might live in. It was enormous and important-looking and the only comparison Nick could make was that it looked like a smaller version of Buckingham Palace with its rows of windows and long, rectangular shape.

"Nice digs," he commented as he let the curtain fall. "Lord Robeson must do okay for himself, hmm?"

Anna peered out her window. "I don't know, but I have heard it rumored that the marquess has twelve thousand a year."

By the tone of her voice, Nick assumed that twelve thousand a year was a respectable amount of dough. He wondered how much old Godfrey brought in.

James pulled up to the front of the house, and a servant rushed forward to help them from the carriage. As Nick followed Anna toward the front door, he casually laid his hand on the small of her back. It was a spontaneous gesture, one he didn't give any thought. But the instant his fingers grazed her, Anna jerked around, her gaze distrustful and wary. Nick dropped his hand. Anna sidled away.

Entering Ravenshead's front hall, Nick forgot all about Anna's brush-off as he caught an amazed whistle between his teeth. Nick had never seen anything like it. Never.

The foyer, glistening with gold everywhere he looked, had to be half the size of a regulation football field. It was like a cavern with columns of white marble as wide as the oldest redwoods flanking both sides. The ceiling stretched twenty feet high—maybe higher—and was painted with half-naked gods and goddesses prancing about. Compared to Ravenshead, Cliff House was but a quaint seaside cottage. And Nick had thought Cliff House pretty swanky.

They were led to another room which Nick figured had to be the equivalent of Anna's parlor. But it was much larger and much grander. He didn't waste time appreciating the furniture or art, but did a quick count of the guests. He and Anna made for a total of thirteen.

Beside him, Nick felt Anna tense up as a woman separated from the main group and glided toward them. *Not too rough on the eyes,* Nick thought appreciatively, his gaze latching on to the deep cleavage framed by the woman's wisp of a dress. Light blond hair curled around her face, and as she drew closer, Nick recognized that she was older than he'd first thought. In her forties, but well preserved. Logically speaking, she would be their hostess Lady Robeson, but Nick was having a hard time picturing this seductive, well-endowed woman as the mother of the staid, sturdy vicar.

Anna curtsied. "Lady Robeson," she greeted quietly.

Lady Robeson extended her hand and Nick bowed over it, nearly choking on the heavy fumes of her cologne. When he straightened again, he noticed the gleam of interest in the woman's hooded gaze.

"Lord and Lady Woodbaine, how delightful that you could join us tonight," she murmured, though she never once glanced at Anna. "I cannot tell you, Lord Woodbaine, how distraught Lord Robeson and I were to learn of your accident. So very distraught." She gave his fingers a light squeeze before he released her hand.

"When Stephen informed us that you would be able to join our party tonight, the marquess and I were ever so pleased. It has been far too long since you have graced us with your company. Oh, but I see that—"

Before Nick realized what she was doing, she reached up and boldly traced the pink, puckered flesh still healing at his temple.

"—you carry a scar," she whispered huskily.

The blatant come-on forced Nick to pull back, and Lady Robeson's hand fell away. Nick shot a look at Anna, who was deliberately averting her eyes.

"Yeah," Nick agreed. Embarrassed, he fingered the scar and joked, "But Anna assures me it doesn't detract from my devilishly good looks."

*That* got Anna's attention. She turned to him, her expression plainly saying she'd never told him any such thing. Lady Robeson's dismissive gaze flicked over Anna before she looped her arm through Nick's.

"Come. Let us join the party," she said. "After your long absence, we are eager to hear all the latest news from London." She led him toward the center of the room, where the guests milled together. Anna followed behind them.

Nick knew a moment of panic, surrounded by a sea of faces that he felt certain Godfrey should recognize. But his "Good to see you again" seemed to satisfy most everyone, except for one short, silver-haired guy whose reception Nick decided was definitely on the chilly side. Unfortunately he didn't catch the man's name.

After the brief round of welcomes, and before Nick

could be drawn into the general conversation, Lady Robeson dragged him over to a throne-type chair, where sat a very heavy, very old man wearing the sorriest excuse for a wig Nick had ever seen.

"Darling," Lady Robeson said, releasing Nick to drape an arm across the old man's shoulders. "Look, who has returned to us from the gay haunts of London. Our dear friend, Lord Woodbaine."

Nick tilted forward at the waist, schooling his features into pleasant passivity. On the inside, though, he was reeling with surprise. This old guy was the Marquess Robeson? No wonder then that Lady Robeson had been coming on to him so strong; her husband was old enough to be her grandfather.

Nick turned, searching for Anna. She stood just behind him, head bowed, like a servant or a faithful dog. With a vague sense of annoyance, Nick drew her forward by the wrist, feeling the muscles in her forearm go rigid.

"Anna and I want to thank you for your kind invitation, Lord Robeson," Nick said as he overpowered Anna's faint resistance and pulled her to his side.

She curtsied and covertly yet firmly swept his fingers from her arm. Above Anna's bent head, Lady Robeson awarded him a hint of a smile, her pale brows lifted in question.

"So you've returned, eh, Woodbaine?" Lord Robeson barked. His dark eyes glittered with an intelligence Nick did not fail to appreciate. "Glad to see you've brought your little bride along tonight. She's a clever little piece, she is. For all her mousy manners, she's no shatter-brained chit. Are you, girl?"

Anna pinkened beneath the man's beady-eyed scrutiny and Nick detected some understanding, some awareness, pass between her and the marquess. Something that kept the color high in Anna's cheeks even after they'd been supplanted before Lord Robeson's throne by another guest.

A servant pressed a glass of champagne into Nick's

hand, and he gratefully took a swig. Until now he had not taken notice of the fact that alcohol wasn't served at Cliff House. At least it hadn't been since he'd shown up. Only tea and cider and bitter hot chocolate.

"I say, Robeson," a portly, middle-aged man called out loudly, hoisting his glass high so that champagne sloshed onto his sleeve. "Damn fine wine you're serving here tonight. You wouldn't know where I could get my hands on some, would you now?"

A spatter of chuckles met the man's question while the marquess smiled smugly from his chair.

"I might be able to arrange something for you, Cafferty," Lord Robeson drawled. "But it will cost you . . . *mon ami.*"

More sly laughter followed, and Nick got the feeling that he stood on the outside of an inside joke. He glanced over to Anna to see if she had grasped its meaning. To his surprise, her pink cheeks had assumed an even brighter shade of red.

"And what about tobacco, Robeson?" another man put in. "Do you think the tide will wash in tobacco any time soon?" He winked at the room in general, and several gentlemen burst out in raucous guffaws.

Under the cover of laughter, a sultry whisper suddenly came from behind Nick's back, accompanied by the whiff of expensive perfume. "It is too good to have you home, darling."

Nick didn't have to turn around to identify the speaker. "Thanks," he said.

He began to get a clearer idea of just how close a "friendship" Godfrey had shared with Lady Robeson when her breasts pushed up against his coat, her taut nipples drilling into his back. Before Nick could decide what he ought to do or say, she stepped away to attend her husband's summons.

Nick glanced around the room guiltily, hopeful that no one had seen Lady Robeson rubbing herself against him like a love-starved cat. His gaze clashed with that of the

man who'd been so conspicuously reserved with him earlier. The short man with the thick silver hair who reminded
Nick of a college professor.

The man's lip barely curled, but enough for Nick to
know what he must be thinking. Nick shrugged, as if to say
he hadn't a clue why the marchioness had been massaging
his back with her boobs.

But the silver-haired man wasn't buying it. He dismissed
Nick with a scornful narrowing of his eyes, then turned to
speak to a woman standing at his right.

*Great. Just great,* Nick thought to himself. Apparently
Godfrey had been doing the horizontal mambo with Lady
Robeson while Anna could very well have been boinking
the vicar's brains out— Was it a question of tit for tat?
Who had strayed first, Anna or Godfrey? If Anna honestly
was involved with the vicar, had she only done it out of
spite? To get back at Godfrey? Or had it been the other way
around?

*Anna.* Anna and Hancock. Nick's jaw clenched. For
whatever reason, damn it, he didn't want to believe it. He
just didn't.

Seemingly summoned by Nick's thoughts, the vicar suddenly entered the room looking windblown and cold, wearing the same austere black attire.

"Stephen." Lady Robeson welcomed her son with a kiss
that Nick didn't find all that maternal.

Instinctively, possessively, Nick drifted closer to Anna,
who stood apart from the core of guests. She was cradling a
champagne goblet in her palms, lost in its pale gold depths.

"Having a good time?"

"Oh, yes," she answered blandly.

Nick shot her a calculating look. Though she rarely revealed it, Anna possessed an edge of sarcasm that Nick
didn't think fit her. Or her circumstances. It was almost a
kind of world-weariness that reminded him of women he'd
known from his time. Women who'd been forced to grow

up too fast—runaways living on the streets, youngsters raising siblings because their mothers were addicts.

The hard edge didn't suit Anna. It didn't seem to fit. And Nick wondered where it came from.

Out of the corner of his eye he caught the professorial-looking guy staring at him again.

"Who is that man?" Nick asked. "The one over there, talking to the woman with all the purple feathers in her hair?"

"Do you mean Mr. Heyer?"

"Heyer? The doctor?"

"Yes, he attended you after the accident. You don't remember?"

Again Nick heard it in Anna's voice. The doubts, the questions. As if she never really believed that Godfrey had lost his memory. Nick wanted to ask her what the doctor had against him, why he'd been glaring at him since they arrived. But since Anna would not even explain the nature of the grudge *she* carried . . .

Hancock made the rounds on his mother's arm, and Nick watched the vicar closely as he smiled and bowed and frowned in that earnest little way of his. Truth be told, Nick kind of liked the young clergyman. Except when it came to his regard for Anna.

Lady Robeson swept her son up to them and the greetings exchanged between Hancock and Anna struck Nick as somewhat terse. As if they were both embarrassed.

Or feeling guilty.

Nick surreptitiously listened to the vicar greeting the rest of the guests. By the time they went in to dinner, Nick was able to put a name to every face. He figured that if worse came to worst and he got backed into a corner, he'd have no choice but to fall back on the memory loss excuse.

At the table Nick was not overly surprised to find himself placed next to Lady Robeson, even though he had learned from Anna that seating arrangements were normally determined by rank. By all rights, Godfrey, a baron, should have been placed lower at the table beneath the Viscount Hayton. Lady Robeson glossed over the matter by making some reference to the "informality" of the gathering. Anna sat across from him, but down a seat.

The first course was a soup. *Not* a fish stew, thank God. Though hardly a devoted follower of Miss Manners, Nick managed to remember enough of his mother's lectures so that he didn't humiliate himself. At least, not immediately. He was sipping at his soup, listening to Lady Hayton blabber on about hats, when Lady Robeson cupped him. As cool as you please, she wrapped her fingers around his crotch and squeezed.

Nick's spoon wobbled a bit, but he never let his smile falter. Nor did he turn to Lady Robeson. He just sat there, feigning sympathy with Lady Hayton over the high cost of lace caps.

While his hostess gave him a hand-job through his pants.

As the soup bowls were cleared, Nick seized the opportunity to reach beneath the table and wrench her fingers from him. And not a moment too soon. Though he'd been trying not to respond to her caresses, a man could only withstand so much. Nature had taken its inevitable course. And quickly.

Nick's heart pounded, his groin ached and his breathing was slightly labored. Lady Robeson laughed low and husky, knowing damned well what she had done. Nick did not so much as glance at her. And certainly not at Anna. He concentrated instead on bringing his traitorous body—actually Godfrey's traitorous body—back under control. Before he lost it.

He squirmed to the side of his chair, attempting to relieve the pressure between his legs. *Shit*. Wasn't this just downright amazing? He had to travel nearly two hundred years into the past, to a time of elegance and refinement, in order to play some wealthy woman's boy toy. Jesus, he felt like Richard Gere in *American Gigolo* or something.

For the remainder of the dinner, Nick was on the run and

Lady Robeson was on him like an NFL cornerback. Hands everywhere, toes sliding up his leg, whispers, touches. He had to give her credit, the woman was slick. She seemed to know just how to couch a caress behind an innocent gesture so that no one saw her tongue slip into his ear, her fingernail score up his inner thigh.

And the worst of it was Nick couldn't even *enjoy* it. He felt guilty, ashamed. Like he was cheating on Anna. Which technically he was. Or Godfrey was.

Not until the ladies retired and the men were left with their port was Nick able to refocus on his mission. To gather information about Godfrey and Anna. Among the gentlemen, there was more talk about "French silk" and "Guinea boats," similar to the jokes that had gone on before dinner. Nick wasn't quite sure what it was about, but laughed with everyone else. He did offer up one or two references to Anna before it became evident that the fellas weren't interested in discussing their wives. It was horses, hunting, and gambling.

And peeing into bowls hidden in the sideboard. Nick opted to wait.

As the servant kept circling with the decanter, Nick was dismayed to discover that Godfrey was a lightweight. Whereas Nick, in his own body, could have put away the same amount of wine and port and not blinked an eye, he noticed that his speech began to slur, his wits to grow cloudy. He was laughing too loudly like every other man in the room. As soon as he realized what was happening, how Godfrey's body was getting plastered on him, Nick cut back. Not so the rest of the crew. The wine kept flowing, cigars were puffed one after the other, and the sideboard urinals were put to heavy use.

After about forty minutes, Lord Robeson announced it time to rejoin the ladies. Half the men had trouble keeping to their feet as they stumbled back toward the parlor. It wasn't pretty.

Steering clear of Lady Robeson, Nick was making a beeline for Anna when he was yanked aside by Sir Avery. Sir Avery, pickled like a Vlasic, demanded to know in no uncertain terms if Hoby was worth the blunt, damn it. Nick rashly assured him it was. *Whatever the hell Hoby is.*

When he finally shook off Avery, Nick saw that Anna was in conversation with the doctor.

*Bingo.* This was just the opportunity Nick had been waiting for. All evening he had been watching Heyer. The doctor appeared to be an okay guy. Easygoing, friendly. Except with him. Except with Godfrey.

Nick walked up and clapped the man on the back. "Dr. Heyer, I'm glad to have a chance to talk to you. I wanted to thank you for piecing me back together after my accident last week."

Heyer gave him a brusque nod. "Thanks are due Lady Woodbaine, not me. Had she left you there in the cold, you would have died before dawn."

*Left me there?* The way he'd phrased it, the doctor made it sound like that had been an option.

Nick forced a light smile. "The vicar had mentioned something along those same lines. That Anna had saved my life. For some reason, though, she hadn't told me of her good deed."

Anna smoothed her skirts, pretending no interest in the discussion.

"She did save your life, I assure you," the doctor asserted. "Though I cannot maintain that I am of such a charitable character. I rather doubt that I would have done the same in her place."

Even Nick, with all his years undercover, couldn't keep the surprise from his expression. "Really?"

"Indeed. And let me tell you what's more, Lord Woodbaine," Mr. Heyer whispered savagely. "I took a most unholy pleasure in being called to Cliff House to tend *your* wounds for a change!"

# *Chapter* 11

NICK STOOD TO the side of his bedroom window, a finger crooked around the edge of the rich damask curtain. Through the narrow gap he peered down into the night, his gaze following Anna as she left the house through the kitchen door.

*Where the hell is she going at two o'clock in the morning?*

White as the moon, her face shone like a beacon in the inky darkness. With her gray cape billowing about her and a ghostly fog encircling her feet, she reminded Nick of a character from a gothic novel.

And he felt like the mysterious and brooding hero, lurking in the tower.

The night had grown bitterly cold, so cold that patches of icy frost clung to the outside of the window panes. Nick's warm breath clouded the glass, and he rubbed it clear with the sleeve of his night robe.

For the space of a second, he wondered if Anna was meeting with the vicar. But almost as soon as the thought entered his head, he quashed it and quashed it good. This jealousy he felt on Godfrey's behalf was not productive. It muddled matters. Nick didn't exactly understand why he should be feeling so possessive about Anna. So, he was sexually attracted to her. But he was only borrowing Godfrey's body—not the man's emotions. . . . *Right?*

Nick craned forward, but Anna had moved out of his line of vision. He saw no point in following her. On the open bluffs, he'd have a hard time concealing himself and, frankly, he wasn't all that excited about tramping along the fog-shrouded trail in the dead of night. He didn't know the path the way that Anna did. She seemed to know every turn, every rock like the back of her hand.

Besides, he suspected that like him, Anna was just having trouble sleeping and had gone out for a stroll. Beverly had mentioned something about Anna taking midnight walks along the cliffs. Which was what she probably had been doing the night she had discovered Godfrey's body.

A draft from the window sent a shiver up Nick's spine. He dropped the curtain and walked across to the fireplace, where he heaped two more scoops of coal onto the grate. He then dragged a chair close to the hearth and sat down, tucking his robe around his legs.

He wasn't all that surprised that both he and Anna were having trouble sleeping tonight. They both had plenty to think about following their evening. At least, he sure did.

They had returned from the dinner party well over an hour ago, Anna feigning sleep during the carriage ride home. Nick had had too much on his mind to care whether she was really snoozing or not. He'd been too busy reviewing all that he'd learned, trying to piece together the clues he'd picked up during the evening.

The dinner party had been his first opportunity to see Anna in a social situation. Though she'd said practically nothing the entire night, the evening had brought home to Nick the realization that Anna was different. Special different. He'd always felt it but, not until he'd seen her among a crowd, juxtaposed against people of her own time, had he recognized just how unusual she was. She had stood in the background, apart from the other guests, not as a wallflower, but as a quiet observer. She hadn't seemed uncomfortable or judgmental. She hadn't acted as if she set herself above the other guests in any way. It had just seemed to Nick that she didn't belong in that milieu. His Nona Carolina would have said that Anna had an old soul.

Yet, in spite of that, there was a vulnerability to Anna, also. A quality that made Nick want to gather her up in his arms and protect her from life's every sadness. She was such an odd mix; she was an innocent wearing a hard shell of worldliness. Nick hated to think that Anna could ever have experienced anything that would have left her worldly or embittered.

But . . . she had.

And, thanks to the doctor, Nick now had a suspicion of what that experience might have been. An ugly, wholly repugnant suspicion that he could not shake off.

*"Tend* your *wounds for a change,"* the doctor had said.

Mr. Heyer's hostility, Anna's skittishness . . . Could it be possible?

*God, not Anna.* She was so small, so fragile. But there was some of the look about her. The hunted look that Nick had seen hundreds and hundreds of times during his years on the force. He knew the signals, too. And many of them were there, had been there from the beginning. He simply hadn't thought to look for them. Not in paradise.

He dropped his head into his hands, pressing the heels of his palms into his temples. Jesus, it was inconceivable. Nonetheless, he had to pursue it. To know for certain.

Pushing himself up from the chair, Nick walked over to the dresser where he'd put the gold watch Beverly had given him. He picked it up and studied Anna's portrait, aware of a sudden tightening in his chest. Though a pretty child, she had been far from beautiful, his Anna. There was something too ordinary about her features, too expected. She looked pretty much the same today as she did as a child. She had the same pointy chin and round eyes. The same nose a fraction too wide.

Nick's gaze caught in the mirror.

And then, of course, there was Boy Gorgeous Godfrey. Godfrey, who surrounded himself with beauty, from his flashy clothes to his luxurious bedroom furnishings. Why, Nick wondered, had the superficial, materialistic baron chosen the very average-looking Anna for a wife?

Anna had said that it was an arranged marriage. Okay, so what had she offered him that he had wanted? Had he loved her despite her plainness? Or had Godfrey even known her when they wed? Had she known him?

Nick wrapped his fingers tightly around the watch and carried it back to his chair.

Jesus, if his suspicions proved accurate, he was going to make damned sure Godfrey got what was coming to him. Nick didn't know how, but he swore he would find a way. A way for Godfrey to get some seriously overdue payback.

Nick sat there and stared into the fire, wondering how he was going to set everything aright. Wondering what it was going to take for him to return to 1997. He had been living in the past eight days now. Was it already November in his time? Had Halloween come and gone without him? Was Chris still alive?

Nick sat there in the chair staring and wondering. Staring and wondering until dawn slipped into the room, the beginning of another day.

Nick awoke later than usual. Right about the time that the sun had started to come up, he had nodded off in the chair. Now he had a crick in his neck that extended down into his back. He stood and stretched, groaning as his muscles pulled taut.

Rather than ring for James, he decided to try shaving himself again. The second go-around went much more smoothly than the first, as he only cut himself twice, despite the fact that he rushed through the process.

He threw on his clothes, slicked back his hair and walked down the hall to Anna's room. The question that had kept him up all night was eating away at him, driving him nuts. He needed an answer. Right this minute.

He tapped at Anna's door. No response. She, too, might be sleeping late this morning, he thought. He knocked again more loudly and, this time, the door swung open beneath the pressure of his knuckles.

The bed was made, the fire banked. Anna had already gone out. Nick turned to head downstairs when a white bundle on Anna's dressing table snagged his attention. Tied up in a rich silk pink ribbon, it caught his eye since Anna never wore anything as fancy as that ribbon. Curious, he walked over and picked it up.

*Handkerchiefs?*

He untied the bow, his brows hitching together when he lifted a snowy-white infant's gown from the top of the parcel. Though the miniature frock didn't look large enough to fit a doll, Nick knew—thanks to his amazingly fertile sisters—that babies actually did start out that small.

He held up the gown, noticing how the embroidered yellow curlicue design at the hem stretched only halfway around the dress. Almost as if the person doing the embroidery had grown tired, or had given up on the project. Nick checked the rest of the pile and discovered that they were all baby's gowns. Six tiny pristine dresses, and not a single spit-up stain between them. Brand, spanking new.

Nick refolded the clothes and tied them up again in the ribbon. As he placed them on the dressing table, he asked himself if Anna could possibly be pregnant. But if Godfrey had been away almost a year—

*No.* Nick categorically refused to believe she could be expecting the vicar's child. He didn't, wouldn't, couldn't believe it.

The gowns most likely had been part of her trousseau. She had brought them out to— To what? To dream someday of being a mother? Or to mourn the loss of that dream?

Nick had seen how she liked to rock that big tabby-cat in her arms. He was pretty sure she had the maternal instinct.

But she had said something the other day about Godfrey not liking animals or kids. Was that the problem? Or did it have to do with Mr. Heyer's insinuations? Maybe Anna didn't want to bring a child into a violent home.

Nick shot a glance to the bed.

Maybe *that* was his purpose in being here. To get Anna with child. Maybe Godfrey was infertile and—

Nick mentally slapped down his libido. As much as the idea appealed to him, he didn't honestly believe he had been sent into the past to serve as a sperm donor.

"Nice try, daCosta."

He tugged at the ribbon one last time, making sure that he left it exactly as he found it. With one more lingering and hopeful glance at Anna's bed, he left, closing the door behind him.

He felt a bit hung-over from lack of sleep as he entered the breakfast room. Mara came in from the kitchen to inquire if he wanted chocolate or tea. It had taken a few days but she had finally warmed up to him and was no longer spilling their dinner every night.

"Mara, do you know where Lady Woodbaine is?"

"Her ladyship goes into town like clockwork, every Sunday for church services and, then again, every Thursday morning."

"Church on Thursday?"

"Oh, no, m'lord. I believe her ladyship takes care of other business on Thursdays."

Nick sat down at the table, wondering what Anna's other business might be.

"Oh, a note came for you just a few minutes ago, m'lord. I set it beside your plate."

"Thanks," Nick said, and glanced curiously at the ivory square tucked next to his cup.

He settled himself before his lukewarm tea and toast—

he'd still not managed to face the gray, lumpy porridge that was served every morning—and picked up the note addressed to "Lord Woodbaine at Cliff House."

A thoughtful pucker pursed his lips as he opened the letter, which was nothing more than a piece of paper folded and sealed with a blob of wax. The message was direct and to the point.

*I must see you. It has been too long.*

It was signed simply with a flowery, curvaceous *U*. As in Ursula. The 1810 English version of *The Graduate*'s sex-starved Mrs. Robinson. Nick smiled slightly.

*Robeson. Robinson.* Could it merely be coincidence?

Nick ripped the message into shreds and set the pieces at the edge of his saucer. He didn't imagine that he would be answering Lady Robeson's note. Mainly because he didn't know how. Without understanding the sordid particulars of the relationship, he was reluctant to break off whatever liaison Godfrey and the marchioness had going. Nor did he really want to see the lovely Ursula again even if it was to end the affair. Last night she'd practically mauled him and he had the evidence to prove it. This morning he had found fingernail marks in his thigh.

The easiest response, Nick figured, was to simply ignore the message. . . . Or should he? Might Lady Robeson be a source of information that he was mistakenly planning to overlook?

While Nick second-guessed himself about how to handle Godfrey's girlfriend, Aunt Beverly waltzed into the breakfast room. As usual, she was dressed outrageously, wearing a short purple jacket over a bright orange plaid dress. The hideous ensemble brought a reluctant grin to Nick's face.

He rose and pulled out a chair for her. "Morning, Bev. Do you want me to call Mara for you?"

"No, thank you," she said brightly. "I ate earlier with Anna."

In her arms Bev carried a pair of matching gray kittens.

She presented him one as if she were handing him the morning paper.

"Uh, thanks," Nick said, rejecting the feline offer with a wave of his hand. "Maybe after breakfast." He took a sip of his tea. "So I understand that Anna drove into the village? Into Aylesdown?"

"Yes, every Thursday morning."

"Is it far?"

"Not very far," she said. In her lap the kittens hissed and tumbled over one another. "Twenty to thirty minutes in the whiskey. About half the distance to Folkstone or Dover."

Nick watched Beverly over the rim of the china cup. A bit fuzzy the past day or so, she appeared to be clearer-headed this morning.

"Bev."

"Yes?"

"I was wondering if I could talk to you about Anna."

"Certainly." An adventurous kitten started to scramble up her sleeve. She paid it no mind.

"Last night at the dinner at Ravenshead"—Nick scratched at his chin—"some things were said that got me to thinking. Thinking about my past relationship with Anna, that is. Did Anna happen to mention to you that, since the riding accident, I seem to have lost my memory?"

"Gracious, Anna didn't need to tell me. It was plain to see."

Nick set down his cup. "It was?"

"To me it was."

"Huh. Really." Jeez, he had thought he'd done a fairly good job of masquerading. But apparently old Bev saw more than he gave her credit for.

"Anyhow," Nick pushed on. "Last night some comments were made, by the doctor in particular, that worried me. I was thinking that maybe, before the accident, I might have been somewhat of . . . a jerk."

Beverly smiled placidly.

Nick tried again. "You see, since I can't remember anything, I don't know what kind of husband I was to Anna. Before the accident. I'm worried that maybe I didn't always treat her with the proper respect."

Bev still smiled.

Nick recognized that he'd have to be more direct. "What I'm asking is, in the past, do you know if I ever was violent with Anna? Did I ever . . . hit her?"

The smile faded. Beverly laid a gnarled finger against the tip of her nose and sat that way for a very long time. Nick concentrated on the piquant fragrance of his cooling tea. A metallic *clang* sounded from the kitchen.

"Yes," she finally said in a soft, emotionless voice. "Godfrey did strike Anna."

Nick blanched. His stomach felt as if it turned inside out, and he had to work to keep his tea down.

*The bastard. The goddamn bastard.*

He hadn't wanted to believe it. Even after Mr. Heyer had virtually spelled it out for him, Nick had resisted it, had resisted the truth. It was too horrible, too personal. Too close to the world he'd come from.

He clenched his fists beneath the table, struggling to hold on to his temper. God, he wanted to smash his fist into a wall, do anything to release this rage corroding his insides.

*Anna, sweet Anna . . .*

"Godfrey, you see, has a frightful temper," Beverly said in that faraway, dreamy voice that told Nick her mind was wandering. He noticed also the strange way she referred to Godfrey in the third person, but he let her go on talking without interruption. He wanted to get as much out of her as he could.

"My husband John was on the hotheaded side, you know, and sometimes his temper got the better of him. But he never gave rein to violence. Never. He was the dearest, kindest, most gentle of men.

"Godfrey, however . . ." Beverly shook her head. The manner in which she stroked the kittens' soft fur reminded

Nick of how a child takes comfort from a beloved stuffed animal.

"Godfrey is not like John," she said. "His temper is a cold, calculated fury. An anger that, I think, is all the more terrifying for its deliberation.

"In the beginning Anna hid it from me. As you probably have noticed, she is very protective. I think she wished to hide from me the knowledge of what John had done. Poor John. If only he had known the true character of the man. But he honestly believed it would be a good match for Anna. He wanted to see her taken care of, and Godfrey's title impressed him."

She sighed. "But, of course, Anna could not keep the truth hidden forever. When I realized what was happening, I dragged out John's old dueling pistol and went in search of Godfrey."

Nick sat back in his chair. "You what?"

"Unfortunately, I never was much of a marksman. I missed." Beverly let out another sigh, this one of disappointment. "Although Godfrey did begin to spend more time in London after that."

*No kidding.* Nick was just sorry Bev hadn't nailed the scumbag.

"So . . ." Nick started to say "I" but couldn't bring himself to claim Godfrey's name. "So Anna was often hurt seriously enough that the doctor had to be called in?"

"Every few months or so."

Nick squeezed his eyes shut, unable to bear it. Unable to bear the thought of Anna, strong in her stoic silence, at the mercy of such a man. No wonder she hated him. Nick hated him. Hated Godfrey with a profound intensity that coiled around him, its grip suffocating. He felt almost dizzy with the depth of his emotion—

Not almost. He *was* dizzy. His head started to spin, his stomach to churn. He was losing consciousness. *Oh, God, it was happening again.*

*Another seizure.*

* * *

Godfrey felt it. He felt Nick's loathing wash over him in dark smothering waves, pounding into him like the storm-driven surf crashes against the cliffs of home.

Unmoved by the power of the man's enmity, Godfrey merely chuckled. Chuckled softly in his head, unable to put voice to his derision because his jaw—Nick's jaw—had been wired shut by the white-coated barbarians from Nick's future. The same barbarians who kept him a prisoner in this place, bound with ropes and pulleys. Who continuously probed his aching flesh with endless needles and tubes.

Not a day passed that Godfrey did not hunger to return to his own body and to leave this inhumane torture to its rightful owner. But, no matter how he tried, he could not will himself back. Nor could he seem to control these episodes where their spirits joined, coming together, mingling and fusing so that one man's thoughts became the other man's.

These episodes where neither man fully mastered either body.

*Are you offended, Mr. daCosta? Repulsed to learn that my character is not as lily-white as your own?*

Oh, he was so like the vicar, this righteous officer of the law, wedded to his notions of moral rectitude and respectability. He was weak, this man from the future. Yet not weak enough that Godfrey could overpower him.

Even now, Godfrey fought to repossess his body. He felt their two souls at battle, locked in the no-man's-land that lay between 1810 and 1997.

*Curse you, daCosta.*

*You bastard, Woodbaine.*

Godfrey fought, but victory would not be his. At least, not this time. He felt himself slipping. Slipping back into the world where he either slept or suffered, trapped in a body that was not his own.

# Chapter 12

ANNA WALKED INTO the room, and it was like walking onto a stage when she knew not what part she was supposed to be playing.

At the breakfast table sat Aunt Beverly, calm as you please, cuddling her kittens, completely ignoring the man unconscious at her feet. On the floor beside her lay Godfrey, his limbs rigid, his body trembling, his face contorted into a grimacing mask.

"Dear heavens!"

Anna rushed forward and dropped to her knees at his side. "How long has he been like this?"

Aunt Beverly glanced down at Godfrey as if noticing him for the first time. "Ten minutes?" she guessed, tapping her fingers on the tabletop.

"Ten minutes?" Anna repeated. His previous seizure had lasted but a minute or two.

She met her aunt's eyes, and suddenly she was filled with misgivings. Though at first she had assumed that Godfrey was suffering another one of his fits, she now began to question if Aunt Beverly might have—

"Auntie, you did not give Godfrey anything, did you? None of those odd potions you'd brought back from Northern Africa?"

"I gave him nothing, Anna dear. He was drinking his tea when"—she shrugged lightly—"he collapsed."

Anna laid her hand on Godfrey's chest. His heart rate, though rapid, beat steady. Beneath his closed lids, his eyes moved swiftly back and forth. As if he were experiencing a nightmare.

"And you . . . you didn't put anything in his tea?" she persisted. She didn't think her aunt would intentionally poison Godfrey, but Beverly did play around with her Eastern medicinals.

"I shouldn't fret so, dear. When he awakens, I daresay he will be in perfect health."

Aunt Beverly gathered up her kittens and rose from the chair, literally yanking her skirts out from under Godfrey's arm.

"I am going to lie down in my room, dear. I have a touch of the megrims. Call if you have need of me."

Anna glanced up, her eyes wide. Lately her aunt had seemed rather fond of Godfrey. How could she now be so indifferent to his suffering? "S-so you don't think I should send for the doctor?"

"Not necessary, dear. It looks as if he is starting to come around." And with that, Beverly left. Just like that. Left Anna alone with her husband, her husband who was either deranged or dying.

Anna bit into her lower lip. Aunt Beverly was quite right; surely Godfrey would be fine. After his last seizure, he had appeared to recover almost immediately.

Moreover, she did not know why she should care one way or the other. She didn't care, did she? Or did she? He had been so different this past week and a half. So different that she had come close to forgetting all the many, many weeks that had gone before.

She knelt there in an agony of indecision, wondering

what, if anything, she ought to do. She stroked her hand across his hair, hating this feeling of helplessness. Hating the fact that it mattered to her whether or not he was in pain. He was so changed of late that he had begun to seem to her a stranger. A kinder, more considerate stranger.

Last night at Ravenshead he had not humiliated her as he had done in the past. He had not mocked her or shamed her by flaunting his affair with Lady Robeson. He had been considerate, even attentive to her needs.

And evidently shocked by Mr. Heyer's cryptic remark.

"Anna."

She exhaled a sharp breath. He called for her. He called for her in the same voice that he had called for "Chris" the night she had discovered him. A voice of desperation, of infinite yearning. And as before, the mere sound of it pierced Anna to the core.

Then, without warning, Godfrey went limp, his body abruptly released from its attack. His eyelids fluttered once or twice.

Anna hurriedly stepped away, shocked by the profound relief she felt in that moment. Was it only because she had saved his life? Was it only her instinctive need to heal that made her care? In truth, it should not matter to her at all what happened to this man. Not at all.

Yet . . . it had begun to.

On the floor Godfrey moaned and his eyelids trembled, then slowly began to open.

"Oh, thank the Lord," she whispered before she realized what she was saying.

She pressed the back of her hand against her mouth, wishing she could call back the words.

*I shouldn't care,* she told herself. *I shouldn't care.*

But she did.

Shamed to feel the prick of relieved tears burning behind her eyes, Anna lifted her skirts and dashed from the room.

She grabbed her cloak from the hall hook and ran out the

front door. The cool, fresh air helped her recover her equilibrium. She took a deep breath.

Perhaps James had not yet had enough time to unhitch the gig. Though she'd only just returned from the village, Anna thought that she might make a call on the Wilson family. Last month she had treated their cow for stoppage of the stomach; she could pretend that she had stopped by in order to follow up on its recovery.

*Any excuse to keep away from Godfrey,* she told herself. Any excuse whatsoever.

As she marched across the frosty-crisp grass, she asked herself how this could have happened. How she had begun to think of him as someone entirely separate from the Godfrey she had known, the husband she had lived with these past four years.

Inarguably, he was a changed man.

Evidence of it was everywhere. Like what she had witnessed two days ago, for instance.

She had been outside, digging up worms to feed the owl chick. She had glanced up and through the menagerie window had spied Godfrey and Aunt Beverly. She had started to scramble to her feet to call her aunt away, when the sound of their laughter had frozen her in place. Squinting to the other side of the glass, she had seen Godfrey delicately extricating a kitten from the snarled mass of hair at the back of Aunt Beverly's head. Evidently one of the inquisitive kittens had become entangled in her aunt's thick bun and both Aunt Beverly and Godfrey were laughing at the difficulty of removing the unhappy cat.

Anna had stood there on the other side of the window spellbound. For her, it was like waking up one morning to find the ocean orange instead of blue. It was incredible. Utterly unbelievable.

This man that laughed and teased and smiled—this was her husband?

As she pushed open the stable doors, Anna allowed the

tiniest hope to creep into her thoughts. Maybe it was time. Maybe it was time to let herself hope.

Nick awoke from the seizure cold and alone. And sick to his stomach.

The reality of seeing into Godfrey's mind had left him nauseated, sickened with the knowledge that such a heartless, soulless little shithead like Godfrey had shared a life with Anna. Everything that Nick had learned during the seizure, during the sharing of their thoughts, confirmed what Beverly had already told him. Godfrey Woodbaine was the lowest form of life on the planet.

Nick pulled himself up into a chair, still weak from the attack. If only he knew what triggered these damn episodes. If he knew, then he might know how to bridge the gap between the two time periods.

He had made a few useful discoveries, one of which had been the depth of Godfrey's frustration. That had come through loud and clear, no question about it. Godfrey was literally trapped in Nick's body. Nick's majorly messed-up body. From what Nick had seen, during the past ten days Godfrey had been floating in and out of a coma, struggling to stay alive.

*Ten days.*

That had been another insight gained through Godfrey's mind. Time was progressing in the future. Nick couldn't be positive that it was progressing at the same rate in 1997 as it was for him here in 1810, but he had gotten the feeling that time was elapsing. Far too slowly for Godfrey, that was for sure.

Also Nick had sensed that Godfrey was closer this time than he'd been during the previous attack. It had felt as if the commingling of their spirits had blurred the lines, so to speak, between their bodies. Although not all their thoughts had been available to each other, their minds had crossed more fully, more beliefs and emotions had been shared. For a second there, Nick had even felt that Godfrey had been close to reclaiming his body. But Nick's presence had somehow prevented it.

*Damn.*

Nick slammed his palms onto the table, abruptly conscious of the predicament this placed him in.

*Damn, damn, damn.*

Now what was he going to do? He had to get back to his own time. He had to. But once he was able to return to his body, what would that mean? . . . Would it mean that he'd be leaving Anna to Godfrey again?

Anna returned to Cliff House in the late afternoon as the winter sun began its plunge into the distant hills. The skies shone clear, glowing in dusky shades of lilac and rose. Anna took a deep breath and looked to the east, where the waves were rolling calmly, in harmony with the tranquil sky.

Tonight, she thought, would be a good night for Lord Robeson's men.

She entered the front hall on tiptoe. She had seen Godfrey's mount in the stables so she knew that he must be at home. In the past he had never spent so much time at Cliff House as he had done this past week and a half. Normally, when in residence, he was off hunting with friends or out searching for a gaming party. Or dancing attendance at Lady Robeson's side.

The house was very quiet. Anna wondered if Godfrey was resting, if he felt unwell in the wake of his seizure. Her lips flattened with concern as she recalled how he had looked when last she'd seen him. *Pale, weak—*

She slipped along the corridor to the back of the house. In the menagerie she smiled to find the bloodhound Harry curled up with the kittens in their basket. The mother cat, though an extraordinary mouser, had not proved to be the most attentive of parents, and Harry had gladly stepped in to take her place.

Still smiling at the sight of the bloodhound as nursemaid,

Anna retrieved the lamp from the mantel. She lit the lantern, using the fire's banked coals, then walked across to the row of east-facing windows. Outside the sky had darkened to a deep violet, the evening's first star twinkling high above.

She centered the lamp in the middle window, then squinted her eyes as she gazed out to sea—

"What are you doing?"

Anna gasped and spun around, her heart skipping a beat.

Godfrey stood just inside the doorway, his eyes slightly narrowed.

"I . . . I'm checking on the animals," she said, twining her fingers together behind her back.

"What are you doing with that light?" He bobbed his chin in the direction of the window.

"I—um . . ." Anna pivoted and stared at the lamp as if hoping it would miraculously produce an answer for her. It didn't.

"Looks to me," Godfrey said as he listed to one side, trying to look around her to the lantern, "as if you're signaling to someone."

Anna closed her eyes. Her thoughts scattered every which way. Oh, why couldn't she think?

Godfrey walked into the room, coming to within a few feet of her. "Is that what you're doing, Anna? Are you signaling to someone? To Hancock?"

Anna jerked her gaze to his. "Wh-why would I signal the reverend?" she asked in genuine confusion.

Godfrey's eyes twitched at the corners. "Who *are* you signaling then?"

Anna hugged herself. There was no hope for it now. She did not see any avenue of escape.

"Lord Robeson's men."

Godfrey's scowl deepened and he marched right up to the window, glancing first to the lamp, then to the graying sky. "I don't understand. Explain it to me."

*Explain it to him? What was there to explain?*

"Well . . . as you know, Lord Robeson employs a troupe of men to bring in goods from France—"

"Bring in goods? Do you mean *smuggle*?"

"Y-yes—"

"Smuggling?" Godfrey snapped. He suddenly looked very fierce. And very frightening. "What are they smuggling? Drugs?"

Anna recoiled, but, backed up against the window as she was, there was nowhere to go. "Spirits, primarily. Tubs of brandy and wine. Tobacco, laces."

"And your job is to signal them with this light?"

Anna gave a hesitant nod. "On Thursdays I am to go into Aylesdown. If the Black Oar's innkeeper has reversed his sign from back to front, I know that the blockade men have come down from Dover. If the sign hangs in its normal position, I am to leave a lantern in the window so that Lord Robeson's men know that the coast is clear. . . ." Her voice faded. Godfrey was literally shaking.

"Correct me if I'm wrong," he said in a slow, deliberate drawl that did not come close to masking his anger. "But in 1810 this smuggling you describe is illegal, isn't it?"

"Well . . . yes."

"So you are aware of the fact that you are breaking the law?"

"It isn't as if anyone is hurt by it—"

Godfrey's fingers curled. "And how do you know that? Have you gone out with them, Anna? Have you seen what happens when a job goes bad?"

She shook her head in the smallest of movements, her gaze darting to Godfrey's fists balled at his sides.

"I suppose these men don't carry weapons, huh? No guns, no knives?" he continued relentlessly. "I suppose it's all very civilized and proper the way you damned English do everything, isn't it?"

Anna licked at her lips. Godfrey had apparently lost all memory of how, in the past, he had shared in Lord Robeson's spoils.

"It isn't a large enterprise," she tried to explain. "It's only for the marquess's benefit."

"And because it's only a *small* smuggling operation, that makes it all right?"

"N-no."

"No," he repeated. "It's not all right. It's against the law, Anna. Do you understand that? Jesus, don't they put people in jail for this kind of thing?"

Before she could answer, Godfrey slapped his forehead so hard Anna was amazed he was still standing.

"God," he muttered, "a smuggling operation. This is just too damned much. Too goddamn much." Then, before she realized what he was doing, he grabbed her hard by the shoulders, his green eyes boring into hers. "Listen to me, Anna—"

She flinched. She could not bear it. She couldn't. Only a few hours earlier, she'd given herself permission to hope, to believe. To believe that he might truly have changed. To believe that she and her aunt might enjoy a life free of God-frey's threats.

*Now—*

Anna lifted her chin, glaring at him, daring him with her eyes. By heavens, she would not run, but neither would she stand here and meekly submit to him. Never again.

Godfrey had stopped midsentence, staring at her in wonder. His grip on her slackened, then fell away.

"Are you quite done?" she asked, pitching her voice low to conceal its quavering.

"Anna . . . you don't understand. It's only because I'm concerned for you—"

She turned and marched for the door. She did not look back.

# *Chapter* 13

NICK BLASTED HIMSELF first in English, then in his limited Italian.

*Idiot. Moron. Jerk.* For good measure, he tossed in some graphic descriptions—the four-letter variety that would have sent his mom racing for a big bar of soap.

Nick tilted his head back and shook it from side to side. How could he possibly have done anything so stupid? Talk about a misstep. That one had been huge, enormous, right off the scale.

*Shit, daCosta, and you call yourself a veteran cop.* In the last week he'd made more mistakes than a rookie, bungling matters with Anna practically every chance he'd got. The kiss, the assumption of infidelity . . . now this. The only justification he could offer for his ongoing screw-ups was the fact that his circumstances *were* somewhat unusual. What with time traveling and soul switching—

Nonetheless Nick wasn't happy with himself. Not one bit.

He had heard Anna come into the house, and he'd gone looking for her with the best of intentions, planning to talk to her about the "situation." He had recognized from the outset that it was going to be a delicate matter, one he'd have to handle with kid gloves and an extra-large helping of male sensitivity. Though he had dealt with women in abusive relationships before, he had never had to confront the problem from the perspective of the abuser. He knew he'd have to be more than careful; he'd have to be the personification of tact.

And then—*wham*. He'd blown it. Big time. Yet once again, he'd charged ahead without thinking, allowing his emotions to take over. Bull-in-a-china-shop Nick.

Disgusted, he shot a scathing look at the lamp in the window.

It had been the smuggling. The smuggling issue had struck a nerve—a 1997 nerve. Granted, gin and silk hankies weren't quite the same thing as heroin, but the smuggling issue had totally sidetracked him, pushing buttons that were personal. The buttons that reminded him all over again of the sting, the department's investigation . . . and Chris.

Hell, *that's* why he'd lost it. If he'd been thinking clearly, he never would have touched Anna, knowing what he did about her past. Never. But he'd been trying to get her attention—he was scared for her, damn it—and she, quite naturally, had recognized his anger and assumed the worst. The worst of Godfrey, curse the man's black soul.

Nick swung around and stared at the door. Should he go after her? *No. Bad idea, detective.* Right now, Anna was probably terrified out of her wits, too frightened to listen to reason. If ever there were a time for a tactical retreat, this was it.

Nick kicked irritably at a fuzzy red ball of yarn lying on the floor.

Most likely the smartest course of action was just to give Anna some space. To show her that he knew when to back off, knew how to keep his anger in check. Then, after they both had the evening to cool off, tomorrow morning he could try to set up a "nonconfrontational" confrontation. A meeting where Anna could take the power position, where she would feel safe and in control. And where Nick could finally address the ugly truth of Anna and Godfrey's relationship.

Sighing, Nick leaned against the window frame, resting his forehead in the crook of his arm. Outside the night fell swiftly in a curtain of murky, bleak shadows. *Murky and bleak.* Those two words summed up just about everything in Nick's world at the moment. He thought he had begun to unravel the mystery of his traveling through time, right?

Wrong.

Reuniting Godfrey and Anna obviously was not in the celestial cards. The man was evil, a classic example of sociopathic behavior in action. During those long, hideous minutes of shared "mind-time," Nick had sensed not even the slightest remorse on Godfrey's part. No regrets, no repenting for the years of abuse he had put Anna through. The only regret Nick had perceived was Godfrey's frustration at being caught in Nick's body. A body that was in seriously critical condition. Traction, skin grafts. Broken jaw, fractured spine. At least, Nick realized with no small sense of satisfaction, Godfrey wouldn't be going anywhere anytime soon. From the looks of things, he'd be stuck in that hospital bed for quite a while yet.

But . . . how long?

Today was the second day of November. Less than two months before the year was out. Less than two months before Godfrey was destined to croak.

So what was Nick's role? What was he supposed to accomplish before Godfrey's death? Instinctively Nick knew he'd been brought to this time and place for a reason. But why? For Anna?

Out of recently acquired habit, his fingers drifted to the painted gold watch he'd taken to carrying with him.

"Anna."

*She* was the reason he was here. Perhaps his mission was nothing more complicated than taking care of her. Of healing her, mending her wounds before Godfrey died. Then when Godfrey died . . . did Nick get returned to his own body?

His eyes narrowed as he shoved away from the window.

Hell, the next time he was zapped two hundred years through history, he was going to make damned sure he was sent with an operating manual.

The following morning Anna lingered in her room much later than usual, in an attempt to avoid meeting her husband at the breakfast table. Whereas the "old" Godfrey had rarely arisen before ten or eleven o'clock, the "new" Godfrey seemed to awaken with the sun. This meant that, more often than not, their paths would cross at the morning meal—scarcely the preferred beginning to Anna's day.

She had briefly entertained the idea of ringing for breakfast in her room. But with only James and Mara to see to the bulk of the chores, she felt it would be too selfish of her to interrupt their work. So she spent the early hours darning stockings in her bedroom before heading downstairs midmorning to steal a biscuit from the kitchen.

She'd just rounded the stairs into the hallway when Godfrey's "good morning" gave her a start.

"G-good morning," she answered, and edged back a step. He must have been lying in wait for her.

Dressed with more formality today, he wore a plain blue waistcoat and a cravat tied loosely at the neck. He'd been holding his hand behind his back and suddenly he thrust it forward, presenting her with a disorderly nosegay of autumn wildflowers.

"Sorry about last night, Anna." His apologetic smile reached to the back of his eyes. "I lost my temper and I shouldn't have."

Anna wavered. This was wholly unprecedented.

He continued to hold out the straggly bouquet, his expression hopeful. She relented, accepting the peace offering.

He smiled in obvious relief. "Up late this morning, aren't you?"

"I was sewing."

"Oh, do you like to sew?"

"Not particularly," Anna answered, eyeing the narrow gap between Godfrey and the other corridor wall.

"You do a lot of work around here. Taking care of your aunt, sewing, tending the animals. What is it that I usually do to help?"

"You?" Anna glanced again to the space between Godfrey and the wall. "You, uh, generally aren't at home for long periods of time. You stay in London or visit friends at country house parties . . ."

"So you run Cliff House by yourself?"

"Yes." She gathered her skirts. "And I should be about my duties, so if you'll excuse me—"

He pushed away from the wall, turning his shoulders just enough so that she could not pass by without brushing against him. She held back.

"I don't suppose I could talk you into playing hookey for a few hours, hmm?"

*Hookey?* What was that—a card game?

"I was thinking that we really should talk, Anna. I thought maybe we could go for a drive, and you could show me the countryside. And we could set matters straight between us."

"I—"

"I've already asked James to hitch up the cart. The sun's shining. It's a nice day."

Anna bit at the inside of her cheek. In the wake of last night's squabble, she was still feeling very wary. And very confused. Never before had she seen Godfrey in a similar temper. His anger had been . . . peculiar. Not at all what she was accustomed to. Even when he had taken hold of her, his touch had felt different to her. Foreign.

In retrospect, she could appreciate that she'd been more angry with herself for letting down her guard than actually alarmed by his anger. True, Godfrey had been upset. But she hadn't honestly been frightened; she hadn't honestly feared that he would strike her.

She'd been taken aback, also, by the fact that he had not pursued her. In the past, Godfrey would never tolerate even the slightest show of defiance from her. Never had she been able to simply walk away.

"Aunt Beverly—"

"Bev is happily knitting away in the parlor," he said. "I already told her we'd be going out. Come on, Anna, what do you say?"

She could say "no." If nothing else, Anna recognized that this new Godfrey had given her that much, the courage to contradict him, to stand up for herself. She feathered her fingers across the limp blossoms of blue lupine, curiosity taking hold of her. She needed to know who this man was. To really know.

"All right," she decided. She turned around and plucked her cape from the foyer's hook.

"Great." Godfrey grabbed his own coat. "I asked Mara to pack us a snack. I thought a picnic might be kinda fun."

Anna shook her head. Every day Godfrey's speech grew more casual. Stranger yet, as the days passed, he did not seem at all concerned by the fact that his memory was not improving. She would have expected him to search the four corners of England seeking help for his condition, but he did not appear to care whether he recovered his memory or not.

She sidled him a glance as they settled side by side on the whiskey's narrow seat.

Without the benefits of his custom-blended pomade, Godfrey's auburn hair, once his supreme vanity, hung across his brow in thick waves. Though Anna had long ago ceased to find Godfrey handsome, she had to admit that she preferred the boyish untidiness over the fashionably arranged curls he had previously favored.

He picked up the reins, balancing them carefully in his

gloved hands. A gentle slap of the leathers and the single horse gig bounced into motion.

"Hey," he said, grinning with pleasure. "This isn't too tough."

She shot him an astonished look. "You've forgotten how to drive?"

His smile broadened. "Well, not according to the DMV. It's just that I've never tried my hand at a horse before."

The cryptic statement brought a frown to Anna's eyes as she shifted her gaze to the road ahead. They both fell silent while Godfrey attempted to familiarize himself with the feel of the ribbons. He maintained a cautious pace, taking the turn toward the open countryside in the opposite direction of Aylesdown.

For November the weather was unseasonably warm, the sky a sharp, clear blue. Across the fields a gray rabbit zigzagged through the grasses, stalked from above by a hungry white-tailed hawk.

"Anna . . ."

She folded her hands in her lap, mentally preparing herself for she knew not what. Godfrey's behavior had become so erratic, she could not begin to guess as to the topic he wished to discuss.

"First off," he said, his voice gravelly, "I'd like to say again that I'm sorry about last night. I didn't mean to scare you, but I was upset. I'm sorry."

*Another apology?* Good gracious, he'd begged her pardon more often this past week than he had during the entire four years they'd been married.

"After the Robesons' dinner party the other night, I was thinking about some comments the doctor had made and . . ."

*Oh, dear.* Anna squeezed her fingers together. She knew that Mr. Heyer was well-intentioned, but his goading of Godfrey had been bound to result in unpleasant consequences for her. She was only surprised that it had taken this long for Godfrey to address them.

"Well, some of the stuff the doctor said made me start thinking and—" Godfrey coughed behind his hand. "And I asked Beverly a few questions about us and about our relationship. Anyhow, Anna, she told me something. Something I don't want to believe, but I'm afraid it might be true."

Anna's every nerve leaped to attention, her heart abruptly hammering beneath her ribs.

"She said that in the past I . . . I have hit you."

Anna closed her eyes as heat suffused her face. She felt suddenly dizzy and had to steady herself with both hands to the side of the cart.

"So, it's true," he said softly.

She could not answer him; she could not look at him. Amazement and frustration and shame roiled through her in a maddening chaos of feelings. *My God, to hear him talk of it so freely, so openly—*

"Anna, I know this is hard for you to believe—it's hard enough for me to believe—but, since the accident, I have become a . . . a different man. I know it probably doesn't make much sense to you, but the Godfrey you knew before is not the same man sitting next to you now. Do you— haven't you noticed?"

"I have noticed certain changes," she conceded in a whisper, still refusing to meet his gaze.

"Good." He gave a decisive nod. "Good, because I am changed, Anna. I really am."

He pulled the cart over to the side of the road. They were now about halfway between Aylesdown and the even tinier village of Postcliffe, very much alone on this rarely traveled route.

He turned to her, his hands cradling the reins. "Anna, will you look at me? Please?"

She forced herself to comply. Her breathing sounded to her ears unnatural. Shallow and quick.

"Anna, the man I am today is disgusted, sickened even,

to think that anyone—*me*—ever struck you, ever laid a finger on you in anger."

He spoke slowly, injecting each word with an earnestness that Anna actually found credible.

"I can't explain to you how I could have hurt you in the past, because I don't remember that man. I don't know him. But at the same time, I won't make excuses for him—for me—because there are no excuses. There just aren't."

He took a ragged breath and swept his hand over the top of his head. "I can't ask you to forgive me. At least, not without proving to you first that I can be trusted, that you can trust me not to hurt you again. I realize that it might take some time, Anna, and that's okay by me. After what you've been through, I don't figure I have a goddamn right to ask anything of you. I just want a chance to make amends, to show you that I am . . . changed."

Anna was quaking from the inside out, shock pulsing through her in stomach-churning waves. To hear the secret she had been living with so long trotted out in the light of day as if—

She shook her head. *No.* No one had ever spoken of it. Not ever. The doctor had mended her, the vicar had counseled her, her aunt had been incensed for her . . . But no one had ever talked about it in this way. Not ever. The matter had been couched in euphemisms and sympathetic glances, in half-truths and fatalistic shrugs. And always the crux of it had come down to the undeniable truth that Godfrey was her husband. According to both man's law and God's law, he could do with her what he willed.

She stared at him. At his expression so solemn, his gaze so sincere.

A pair of thrushes chirped noisily from the trees overhead. Anna turned toward their song, feeling something inside her stir. And in that moment she realized that she hardly knew herself. Twenty-two years old, and she still did not know who or what Anna Woodbaine was. For beneath her shock and anger, she was amazed to discover that she *wanted* to believe him. She wanted to believe him more than anything she had ever wanted before in her life.

She would not have thought it possible, but under the layers of scar and bruises and hurt, there lay buried within her that hope. She felt it now, trying to fight its way up through her, trying to claim a piece of her again.

Over the years, had not she prayed a hundred times for an opportunity to start anew? Hadn't she wished above all else for the chance to be eighteen once more so as not to repeat the mistake that had forever destroyed her life?

Well, she could not turn back the clock. She had not the power to alter history. But this . . . this might be her chance.

Beside her Godfrey sat patiently waiting, allowing her the time to confront her feelings, her thoughts. Strangely enough, as she watched his fingers idly fidget with the reins, she knew that she believed him. Godfrey *was* different. One had only to look at him to see that it was so.

"I thought that maybe," Godfrey said haltingly, "it would help us both if I went by another name. I know that it sounds kinda crazy but, since I think of myself as a new person now, I'd prefer to go by a new name."

Anna frowned. "What name?"

It might have been the morning light reflecting off the crimson-leaved trees, but Godfrey actually appeared to blush. "How do you feel about Nicholas? Or Nick?"

She turned to stare into the trees, confused and unsettled. "You are asking that we should all call you Nicholas from this day forward?"

"Well, maybe not everyone. But I'd like it if you could call me Nick."

It *did* sound crazy, Anna thought, changing one's name as one changed one's hat.

"Why . . . Nick?" she asked.

His lopsided grin tipped to the left. "It just seemed to fit the new me."

She nodded slowly. It did seem to fit.

"So, can we begin with the name?" he asked. "And go

from there? I'm no saint, Anna, but I promise you *this* man"—he pressed a fist against his chest—"this Nick will never lay a hand on you, I swear it."

Again hope flared in her, a tiny, flickering flame of hope that she could not douse. How should she answer him without leaving him with hope? Hope that she could ever forgive him for what he had done?

The pounding rhythm of approaching hoofbeats drove the question from her mind. Godfrey took firmer hold of the reins as a horseman careened around the bend ahead, riding like the very wind. A brown cloud of dust eddied around the man and beast.

"Mr. Kingsley," Anna murmured in recognition as she rose to her feet.

Spying her, Mr. Kingsley pulled up, his horse rearing up on its two back legs. Miraculously the man held his seat.

"Lady Woodbaine, thank the good Lord I run into ye," the man panted. "I'm ridin' to Aylesdown for the doctor."

"Mrs. Kingsley?" Anna asked in alarm. The Kingsleys' fourth child had been expected two weeks past.

"Yes, m'lady. And somethin's not right. She begun her pains last night and the babe still ain't comin'."

"Oh, God." Inexplicably Anna glanced down at Godfrey. "Mr. Heyer is in London, do you remember? At the Robesons' party, he mentioned that he'd be away for at least a fortnight."

"What's that?" Mr. Kingsley's eyes bulged with panic. "Mr. Heyer ain't in town?"

"No, Mr. Kingsley. He had—"

"Can't we just get another doctor?" Godfrey interrupted.

Anna sat back down on the seat. "There isn't anyone else."

Mr. Kingsley swept his cap from his head and used it to mop his brow. "Ye're good with animals, Lady Woodbaine. Can't ye come see if there's anythin' ye can do?"

Anna paled. "Mr. Kingsley, people and cats aren't at all

the same. I doubt I could be of much assistance to you."
Yet, she knew she must at least try.

Godfrey suddenly leaned forward, determinedly wrapping the reins around his fists. "Lead the way, Mr. Kingsley," he said.

He didn't look at her as he added out of the side of his mouth, "And for God's sake, Anna, hold on."

# *Chapter* 14

FORTUNATELY THEY DID not have far to travel. After only a ten-minute drive—at breakneck speed—they pulled up in front of the Kingsleys' farmhouse. Anna had visited there once before, to tend an ailing goat. Then, as now, she had been charmed by the tidy, two-story farmhouse with its gabled roof and stone exterior. While not the most affluent of families, the Kingsleys were respectable, hardworking people, who traveled the fifty minutes into Aylesdown every week for Sunday services. The vicar spoke well of them.

The dust from Mr. Kingsley's passage was yet settling onto the hard-packed earth when Godfrey reined in the gig. The anxious farmer had already leaped from his horse and gone into the house by the time Godfrey jumped down and helped Anna from the seat.

In the yard to the side of the house a young girl of perhaps nine or ten was holding a toddler in one arm while plucking beans from wooden stakes. Anna waved to her— *Joan, was it?*—as her gaze lingered for a moment longer on the infant. The November sun gilded the fine downy curls

on his head until they shone like spun gold, and his cheeks
were as pink as heather in spring. An ache settled in Anna's
middle, and she turned away, cradling her waist with her
arms, yet still feeling the emptiness.

As they approached the shallow porch, a keening, high-
pitched wail arose from within the house. It echoed mourn-
fully through the desolate garden, causing Anna's step to
falter. Godfrey scarcely seemed to take notice.

The door opened directly as Mr. Kingsley, disheveled
and dusty, ushered them inside. "She's in a bad way," he
whispered.

In the front kitchen Anna recognized Kate, the Kingsley's oldest daughter. The girl stood over a steaming tub of
wash, her pinafore smeared with what might have been
dried blood. She had a look of her father about her in her
round face and sturdy arms. Her tentative smile of welcome, though, could not mask her evident weariness.

The house was as neat as a pin, comfortable in its country simplicity. A wood-burning chimneystack at the center
of the house filled the room with the aroma of oak. Freshly-
baked bread added a hint of yeast to the air. A small parlor
adjoined the kitchen, boasting both a grandfather clock and
an aged pianoforte.

Anna snuck a peek at Godfrey. In an instant his gaze
took it all in, revealing interest but not the condescension
she would have expected from the Godfrey of old.

"The missus is back here," Mr. Kingsley said, leading
them through the kitchen toward the rear of the farmhouse.
He entered a bedroom while Anna waited a few paces back.
To her surprise, Godfrey started to walk past her toward the
open doorway.

"Wh-what are you doing?" she asked.

He paused and smiled down at his arm where she had
unthinkingly laid her fingers in a staying gesture. Anna
snatched her hand back.

Godfrey nodded toward the bedroom. "We're going to
help this woman deliver a baby."

Surely she had misheard him. "We?"

He shrugged as if to say "why not?"

"But . . . but what do you know of it?"

He leaned forward so that their faces were separated by no more than the length of a nose.

"A lot more than you might think," he said quietly.

In spite of herself, Anna felt a spark of awareness shiver through her, an awareness that was not altogether unpleasant.

From the bedroom Mr. Kingsley called, "Lady Woodbaine?"

Godfrey raised his brow in question. "Are you ready?"

No, she was not ready. She was terrified. Terrified to her very core. She had never assisted at a birthing, at least not a human one. And after her own experience—

She balled her hands tightly. Beyond that door a woman lay in need of help. Of her help.

"Yes, of course," she murmured.

Godfrey winked at her, his eyes warm with reassurance, then preceded her into the room. Anna stiffened her spine and followed.

Mrs. Kingsley lay on the plain box bed, her sweat-soaked hair clinging to the pillow, her fists clamped around a length of rope overhead. Anna remembered Mrs. Kingsley as a pretty woman, but with her eyes sunken from lack of sleep, she appeared haggard and old.

Godfrey wasted no time, but set to business, stripping off his jacket and tossing it onto a chair. "We're going to need lots of hot water and soap," he said. "And clean sheets and towels."

Standing at the side of the bed, Mr. Kingsley swung around and sent a bug-eyed look toward Anna. Quite understandably, he looked astonished that the local lord was planning to attend his wife's laying in. Anna offered him a hesitant nod, and the gentleman farmer did not need any further convincing. He rushed out to fetch the requested supplies while Anna removed her cape, her own perplexed gaze riveted to Godfrey's back.

*Who was this man?* Was this her husband, rolling up his sleeves with purposeful confidence as he spoke soothingly to the woman in the bed?

Almost immediately Mr. Kingsley hurried back in, lugging a black iron pot. Kate, his daughter, followed with a stack of clean linens.

"All right," Godfrey said. "Let's get started by washing our hands."

Mr. Kingsley gently nudged his daughter toward the door. "Ye go on and watch after yer brother and sister now, Katie girl."

Young Kate seemed all too anxious to heed her father's directive, patently relieved that her presence was not required. Anna could not help but feel a twinge of envy as she watched the girl go. What would it have been like to have had a daughter of her own?

Another hair-raising cry from the bed sent goose flesh rippling along Anna's arms. Of a sudden she began to ask herself what in the name of God she was doing here. She splinted broken wings and mended mangled paws. *This was beyond her, this was—*

But she had no opportunity to further question herself, for Godfrey set them to washing up. It took some time as he insisted that fresh water be poured into the basin after each person washed. Anna was the last in line. As she scrubbed at her nails, in the manner Godfrey had shown them, Anna could hear Godfrey comforting Mrs. Kingsley, his voice calm and sure.

She listened to him, her brow furrowing, as she rinsed her hands with hot water from the ewer. It *was* Godfrey's voice. It was. Yet . . . she did not recognize it. She did not recognize the tenderness in his tone, the confidence he conveyed with his every word.

She turned halfway around to look at him, and her gaze fell on the blood-soaked bed.

*Oh, God.*

She turned back to the washstand, her hands shaking. With careful movements she replaced the towel, trying to drive the image from her mind.

*A woman lying in a bed. Blood. So much blood.*

Anna refolded the towel and smoothed it with her fingers. She took a deep breath and slowly walked toward Godfrey, her steps deliberate and light. She felt like a figurine tottering on a shelf—any quick movement would send her over the edge.

"Anna," Godfrey said, kneeling on the edge of the mattress. "We're going to have to put clean sheets under Mrs. Kingsley. Can you find some in that pile and bring them over? We're going to have to slide them underneath her, I guess."

Anna's stomach seized up. Her head grew hot and heavy. Memories long locked away flooded through her, frightening and so real.

*The blood, the cries—*

Anna's ears began to tingle and burn. Her head felt on fire as if she were possessed with fever. She could not take her eyes from the woman on the bed.

*White sheets. White legs. Red, red blood.*

"Anna, did you hear me? We need clean shee—" Godfrey's voice rose in pitch. "Jesus, Anna, are you all right?"

She wasn't all right. Hadn't the doctor said that she might die?

From a distance she heard Godfrey say, "Mr. Kingsley, I don't think my wife is feeling too well. Could you help her from the room please?"

A hand touched her elbow. She was cold. Bitterly cold.

Was she dying?


*Shit.*

Something was wrong. Something was very wrong with Anna.

Nick gritted his teeth, resisting the urge to run after her, knowing he first had to determine Mrs. Kingsley's condition and make sure the baby was hanging in there.

"Just relax, now," Nick said softly. "You're doing great. Just great."

Though only twice during his years as a cop had he been required to assist in a delivery, he'd had enough emergency medical training to deduce that Mrs. Kingsley wasn't so very bad off. Or, at least, that's what he was hoping. The blood made it look worse than it was, but then again Nick didn't think the woman had lost much more than was normal.

"Huh," he said on a half-laugh. "I think I've figured out the reason for the holdup. You've got yourself a pair here."

The woman's tired brown eyes widened, the crucifix at her throat glinting in the muted light. "A pair?"

Nick quirked a grin. "Yeah. *Due.* Twins."

Mrs. Kingsley's head fell back on the pillow and she closed her eyes. "Oh, dear heavens." But at least she was smiling, Nick noticed.

He pulled the sheet back up over her and grabbed a clean towel to wipe his hands. "It's okay, Mrs. Kingsley. I think it's going to be A-OK."

From what he could tell, the babies were only a bit tangled up and just needed some help straightening themselves out. She seemed close to zero-hour.

"Mrs. Kingsley, I'm going to check on my wife for one quick minute and then I'll be right back. We're going to get these babies out into the world before you know it. Sound like a plan?"

She opened her eyes and gave him a look so full of trust that Nick had to swallow around a knot in his throat. He hadn't seen that kind of trust in anyone's face since . . . well, since Chris.

After another pat to her hand, Nick raced down the hall. In the parlor, Mr. Kingsley was just lowering a dazed Anna into a chair. She was pale, shaking. A sheen of sweat glistened on her forehead.

*Shock*, Nick realized. Anna was suffering from a mild case of shock.

"Hold on," he said. "Not the chair. Lay her down on the sofa and put a cushion under her feet. Kate, can you fetch a blanket or a shawl? I think she's going to be fine, but we need to keep her warm."

Nick hovered over Mr. Kingsley as the farmer carefully settled Anna onto the sofa. Kate reappeared with a blanket and covered her from head to toe.

Holding his hands high and away to keep them relatively sterile, Nick dropped to his knees beside the divan. "Anna. Anna, can you hear me?"

She blinked and looked straight through him.

"Unbutton her coat and blouse," Nick instructed.

Mr. Kingsley flushed, but did as he was ordered.

"She feels like she's warmin' up some," the man said.

"Yeah, it looks like she is," Nick agreed. Anna's color was coming back even as her eyes began to flutter shut.

Nick glanced over his shoulder. "Kate, would you mind staying with her, please? And make sure that she keeps warm, keep her covered?"

"Y-yes, m'lord," the girl stuttered.

Nick made a face as he dropped his chin to his chest. For a moment he'd almost forgotten the role that he was playing. For a moment he had just been Nick the cop.

Once Anna was settled, Nick headed back to the bedroom, Mr. Kingsley dogging his heels. They entered the room as Mrs. Kingsley was starting to launch into another contraction. Her features twisted, her face colored a bright red. The cords of her wrist stood out as she pulled hard at either end of the rope.

"Oh, boy. We're off and running," Nick muttered. *No panicking now, daCosta. Let's just shift into crisis control mode.*

"Mr. Kingsley, I want you to wash up again. And fast. I'm going to need some help here."

Twenty very long minutes later a sweating, beaming

Nick was thanking God for small miracles. The small, pink kind with healthy, powerful lungs. The first baby had presented breech, but it had taken only an instant of maneuvering to straighten the tiny legs, then out she had popped. After that, it had been smooth sailing. A boy had joined his sister, and, though the two of them were a bit on the runty side, Nick thought that they looked pretty damned good. Based on his vast experience delivering babies.

Once he recovered his breath, however, the effects of adrenaline started to wane and Nick started to worry. In a big way. Infection, hemorrhage, blood clots. Had he tied off the cords correctly?

While he'd been caught up in the moment, he hadn't allowed himself any room for apprehension or doubts. He had simply focused on getting the job done. But, he tried to assure himself, the babies appeared healthy and the afterbirth delivered without complications and Mrs. Kingsley's blood loss was easing off. . . .

"Looks like we came through all right," he said.

"Ye can say that again," Mr. Kingsley agreed, laughing in that tremulous way people did when they got emotional. "Two of 'em, praise God. Two of 'em. I-I dunno what to say, m'lord. The missus and I can never thank ye enough for what ye done."

Nick grinned and cast a proud glance to the babies swaddled on either side of their mother.

God, it felt good. *This* was why he'd become a cop. To help people. Okay, so maybe delivering babies wasn't part of the standard job description, but this warm, do-good feeling was the reason he'd joined the force in the first place. To do the right thing.

Lately, he seemed to have forgotten that. During this past year or so, he seemed to have forgotten the reasons he loved being a cop. In the face of all the ugliness he'd witnessed, the depravity, the corruption, he'd lost touch with the bright side. And there was a bright side to the world. He just needed the occasional reminder.

"Look, I'd like to stick around and make sure everything is copacetic, but I think I need to get my wife home."

"Is Lady Woodbaine unwell?" Mrs. Kingsley asked.

"Oh, I'm sure she's going to be fine. She's lying on the sofa, having a rest. Some people just get a tad woozy at the sight of blood, you know?"

Yet even as the words left his lips, Nick sensed that they did not ring true. Only a few days ago he'd watched Anna sew up the insides of a rabbit that had tangled with a hungry predator—a sight that had made even Nick's breakfast spin uneasily in his stomach. Somehow he didn't think that it had been the blood itself that had upset Anna so very much.

He thought back to the pile of baby clothes he'd found in Anna's room. Did she yearn for a child? Had Mrs. Kingsley's delivery been too difficult for her to witness while that stack of baby gowns sat gathering dust?

"Will you not join us for a meal?" Mr. Kingsley offered. "Our oldest girl is a first-rate cook."

Nick was starving and a meal sounded awful tempting right about then. But Anna—

"Thanks, but we'll have to take a rain check." Nick picked up his jacket and slung it over his shoulder. "But let us know if you need anything. We're not that far down the road."

Mrs. Kingsley smiled wearily. "Thank ye, m'lord, but don't ye worry none 'bout us. We know how to get on from here, don't we, David?"

The round-faced farmer squeezed his wife's hand, and Nick felt his heart squeeze inside his chest. The look that passed between husband and wife . . . For the first time in a long time, Nick wondered if he would ever have that. If he would ever share that kind of love with a woman.

Shaking his head, he thrust the question aside. No time for that, he told himself.

Anna needed him.

# *Chapter* 15

COMPREHENSION CREPT UP on her slowly, like the lazy awakening following a long dream. She felt warm and cozy. And a little disoriented.

A trace of spiciness tickled at her nose, familiar and yet not. Fabric, smoother than the texture of her cotton pillowcase, rubbed silkily against her jaw. Why did she feel so weak?

Anna tried to lift her head and it bumped against ... a chin. Arms. A chest. Hands—

*Dear heavens.*

She struggled to rise and Godfrey's voice whispered across the top of her hair, "Easy now. Easy does it, sweetheart."

She went absolutely still, attempting to make sense of her circumstances. Godfrey was cradling her in his arms on the divan in Cliff House's parlor ... and he was calling her sweetheart.

In a flash Anna was wide awake, every inch of her skin sizzling where it rested against Godfrey's chest and arms and lap. Then, before she knew what she was about, he tilted her back until her eyes encountered his. Pale green eyes that crinkled with concern.

Her breath caught. What on earth could have happened to bring her here?

*Godfrey had wanted to take a drive, Mr. Kingsley . . .*

"Oh," she gasped.

The corners of Godfrey's mouth lifted. "So it's coming back to you now, is it?"

Anna's lungs could not draw air. She was suffocating, her chest heavy, her heart pitter-pattering at an extraordinary rate.

"Just calm down," Godfrey said in a hushed, crooning voice. "You've had a doozy of a reaction. Are you cold?"

She jiggled her head from side to side.

"That's good. What about your stomach? You're not going to toss your cookies or anything, are you?"

Despite the question's peculiar phrasing, Anna was able to gather his meaning.

"N-no."

He smiled a soft smile, one not edged with malice or cunning.

Anna relaxed the very tiniest bit, silently questioning why she was not scrambling to rise. She ought to be. She ought to be battling to pull herself from Godfrey's embrace, petrified by his nearness. In truth, she was experiencing a sort of paralysis. But it did not originate from fear, did it?

"Feeling better?"

"Yes," she choked. Would he now let her up?

"Bev told me that you haven't been eating a lot lately. It probably wasn't such a hot idea for me to ask you to skip your breakfast."

Anna recalled that she'd not eaten last night, either, for she'd been too upset after their confrontation.

"Do you feel like some tea?" Godfrey asked.

"Oh, yes, please. I'll ring—" She began to sit, but his left arm came across her like an iron bar, trapping her against his chest.

"No need. Got some right here." He reached across her to the sofa table, where he poured the fragrant brew into a waiting cup.

"Sugar, right?"

"Yes. Th-thank you." She blushed to hear herself stutter. But how could she hope to speak normally when her face was tucked into the crook of his neck, his warm breath fanning across her temple?

He leaned back again, balancing the saucer in his left hand, his right hand still cupping her shoulder.

"Here we are."

She accepted the cup and stared up at him in bewilderment. Did he quite expect her to drink her tea sitting upon his lap?

Evidently he did.

Anna's lids flickered and she glanced down into her cup, unsettled by the feelings pulling at her from so many directions. Why was she not responding more negatively to him? Was it a reaction to what she'd experienced at the Kingsleys' farmhouse?

She licked at her lips, memory stealing over her again. *The blood . . . The fear . . .* An involuntary shudder sent tea sloshing over into her saucer.

"What is it, Anna?" Godfrey asked. "What happened back there?"

"No." Her answer was terse, immediate.

She didn't want to speak of it. Never. Not ever.

"Anna, please. You were practically catatonic on the ride home. Something obviously got to you. What was it? Was it the blood?"

She hesitated, then bobbed her chin in the barest affirmation, giving him what he wanted. A half-truth.

"Oh, well." He sounded relieved to have the lie. "Plenty of people react that way, you know. It's nothing to be ashamed of, though I am surprised that you're okay with animals and not with people."

She took a sip of her tea and glanced up at him through

lowered lashes. His lips were curved in a gently teasing smile.

*Blood, pain, the memories* . . . By God, she could have died. There were times when she wished that she had.

Fury began to well up within her, a smoldering anger that she had kept secreted in the deepest, darkest corners of her being. She tried to subdue it, send it back to its home, but her fury would not be denied. Shock had unleashed the rage, long-suppressed, and Anna was too vulnerable to its power.

She had to fight it.

Impulsively, frantically, she shoved herself from Godfrey's grip, not caring that hot tea spilled onto her hands and skirt.

"Hey—"

Her knees were trembling with such frenzy that all she could manage was to scoot along the sofa away from him.

"Anna."

She set down her cup, breathing hard. She had to regain control of herself. To regain control of the tumultuous emotions that were churning her insides to acid.

"You're angry, aren't you?" Godfrey abruptly asked.

She folded her hands together. She couldn't lose control. She couldn't.

*The Lord is my shepherd, I shall not want—*

"Hey, don't do that." Godfrey shifted over until he sat by her side. "If you're pissed, let's talk about it, huh? I told you, I am not going to hurt you. You can say whatever you need to say and I'll listen."

Anna scrunched her shoulders up around her ears as if she could keep his voice out. *He maketh me to lie down in green pastures—*

"Look." Godfrey raised his hands at his sides. "I'm not going to touch you, all right? Just admit that you're angry. It's okay."

Anna wrapped her arms so tightly around her waist that

her fingers almost touched at her back. *He leadeth me beside the still waters—*

"Anna, it's all right to be mad. It's downright healthy, in fact, considering what you've been through. Just start by confessing that you've got this anger inside you? From there, we can work on taking care of it, of healing it."

She couldn't do this. She couldn't.

"Come on, let it out. I can see it in you, you know. You're like a transparent bomb ready to blow."

*He restoreth my soul; He leadeth me in the paths of righteousness for His name's sake—*

"Anna."

*Yea, though I walk through the valley of the shadow of—*

"For God's sake, just say it, won't you? Say 'Nick, I'm feeling kinda—' "

"Nick!"

She exploded. She whirled on him, her fingers curling. "Nick," she repeated. "As if a *name* makes a difference!"

He had the audacity to smile. "Are you miffed, Anna? Peeved? A bit put out?"

She leaped to her feet, caution abandoning her in the hour she needed it most.

"What is it that you want? Do you need so very much to hear how greatly I despise you? How I despise myself for carrying your name, for the fact that I was once young and foolish and naive? Is that what you want to hear? The depth of my scorn for the both of us?"

She splayed her fingers over her face, trembling uncontrollably, sensing that it was all starting to crumble. Restraint. Forbearance. Discretion. They were forsaking her.

Out of nowhere, a defeated laugh caught her unaware, bubbling out of her like steam from a cauldron. Her hands fell to her sides, as she turned her back, unable to look at him.

"Yes, I feel anger, Godfrey," she whispered. "A rage so powerful it frightens me. A sinful, murderous rage that works on me like a curse."

Across the room her oft-read Bible called to her, drawing her gaze.

"Not a day goes by that I do not fight it," she said, her voice now quiet and flat. "Fight this ungodly enmity I feel for you—have felt for you for years. Each night in my prayers I ask forgiveness, knowing it is wrong. Wrong to feel such hatred for one's own husband. But I also know that there is nothing to be done for it. It is the cross I bear."

And then . . . there was silence.

Behind her, she heard the sofa creak. But like Lot's wife, another who had sorely wanted for prudence, Anna was incapable of moving. She did not so much as stir when Godfrey's body heat warmed her back.

Her eyes squeezed shut, her shoulders squared with defiance.

A puff of breath blew past her ear, then came the whispered words: "Good for you, Anna. Good for you."

Her eyes flew open. Hot tears abruptly flooded her vision. And without understanding it, Anna turned around and clung to him, sobbing until all her tears were finally spent.

Anna did not like to think of that encounter as a turning point, but from that day forward she could not help but view Godfrey through different eyes.

It was as if he alone, the source, the creator of her fury, had held the key to unlocking her bitterness and anger. Strangely, after her heated declaration of rage, she *had* known a certain sense of relief, an easing of the tension within her.

She had also come to realize that her animosity—once brought into the light—felt old and stale, directed to the man Godfrey used to be. She could not summon that same degree of anger for her husband today, since there was no fresh fuel with which to stoke the fires of her enmity.

The morning following that tearful confrontation, Anna took on the Herculean chore of cleaning the menagerie. She shooed the kittens and the bunnies and Harry out the kitchen door, thinking that the work would prove calming, as well as allow her to hide away from Godfrey for a few hours. She was proved wrong on both accounts.

Dressed in her oldest frock—the one with patches at both elbows—Anna first set to work scrubbing down the menagerie walls. There was something unaccountably relaxing about rolling up your sleeves and donning an apron and sloshing around in buckets of warm, soapy water. The world narrowed to the job at hand, the simple, mindless act of guiding your brush up and down, round and round.

Anna knew the moment that Godfrey entered the room even though her back was to him. He had a presence about him. He was vibrant, alive. She sensed him like she sensed an oncoming storm; he exuded the same sort of charged intensity.

"There you are," he said. "I must have come down to breakfast too late. I missed you."

"I did not eat," Anna answered, intent on her work.

"Didn't— For Christ's sake, Anna, you've got to eat. I can practically see right through you as it is."

A stubborn stain beneath the windowsill required an extra-strong rubbing. "I regret that you find me overly thin."

"I don't think that you're *too* thin. I just think you should eat."

"I wasn't hungry."

Footsteps advanced behind her.

"What can I do?" he asked.

Anna smothered a sigh. She still felt raw from yesterday; she wanted this time to collect herself.

"Why do you not take a walk?" she suggested.

His rumbling laugh turned her around. He appeared very at ease with himself this morning, one thumb looped into his waistband, his shirt open at the collar.

"In case you haven't noticed, it's raining cats and dogs out there." He gestured to the window, where outside Harry was cavorting about in the mud like the happiest of pigs. "Or maybe you had noticed?"

Anna frowned. Rain gushed from the sky, pouring from the clouds in sheets of gray.

"Besides," Godfrey said. "I meant what can I do to help *you*? Here?"

A lock of hair dangled in front of her eyes. She brushed it back with her forearm since her hands were wet, then sat back on her heels. "Godfrey—"

"Nuh-uh." He smiled broadly. "Nick, remember?"

She chose to use no name at all. "This is not precisely gratifying work," she explained. "Every inch of this room must be spotless. Cleanliness is of the upmost importance when sewing up gashes or washing out wounds."

Godfrey nodded and started rolling up the left sleeve of his shirt. "All the more reason you could use a hand, right?"

*A few hours of peace and quiet. Had it been too much to hope for?*

"As you like." Anna did not hide her want of enthusiasm. "If you wish to sweep up cat hair and wash up dog drool, who am I to argue with you? Though I daresay the labor will soon lose its appeal."

"Are you kidding? I can't think of anything I'd rather be doing."

Anna pursed her lips. She would *not* respond to that boyish grin. She wouldn't.

"On the table, there are additional rags and brushes. Help yourself," she invited, then turned her back on him to convey her lack of interest.

Behind her, she heard him whistling as he selected his supplies. Anna set to scrubbing with a vengeance, alternating between the soapy water and a precious cleaning solution of lemon juice that, though extremely expensive, worked wonders on stains.

"You're going to rip the wallpaper if you keep on like that," Godfrey commented at her shoulder.

"It isn't paper," she countered. "It is silk. Old and faded, but nonetheless silk."

"No kidding. Pretty nice stuff for an animal hospital."

She scrubbed a little harder.

"You are good, you know."

Anna peered at him from the corner of her eye.

"I mean," he said, "that you are a damned good veterinarian. Last week when you sewed up that rabbit, I was really impressed. I couldn't believe how you kept the little fella so calm. Your voice was soothing, gentle—hell, I think that I might even have let you take a needle to me after that."

Anna put down her brush and picked up a clean rag. "Thank you," she said, not knowing how else to comment.

He winked at her. "Just speaking the truth, your ladyship."

Anna self-consciously shoved at her hair again, lamenting the fact that she hadn't used more hairpins that morning. Never had she looked less a baroness.

Godfrey, singing under his breath, began wiping down the window frames, the meager sunlight bathing his face. Against the white of his shirt, his skin glowed a conspicuous brown. *The sun,* Anna realized. After spending so much time hatless, Godfrey had assumed a tan worthy of a farmer. Though considered common, the sun-warmed tones of his face made him look more real to Anna, more down-to-earth. It had been vexing during the early months of their marriage to acknowledge that her husband's complexion was softer and more lily-white than her own.

Together they worked side by side, Godfrey singing and humming. And dribbling water down his shirt.

"What . . . what is that you're singing?" Anna finally asked. "The tune is most unusual."

"Yeah, it's great, isn't it? It's by Eric Clapton, one of your boys."

"My boy—"

"That is to say, he's English," Godfrey quickly corrected

with a smile. "He writes some terrific stuff. Do you want to hear it?"

On her hands and knees, Anna glanced up at him. "Do you mean . . . sing to me?"

"Sure. I can't remember exactly how the song starts, but I know the refrain pretty well."

He cleared his throat and began to sing. To sing of a forever love that was light and laughter, his voice so hypnotically alluring—a low, rumbling sound that resonated within her.

Anna sat there, breathless and unmoving. Thoroughly mesmerized. His voice was doing all manner of interesting things to her stomach—warming, fluttering, tightening it.

She blinked slowly. Godfrey had stopped singing.

He dropped down beside her, so close that she sat back on her heels. "What did you think?" he asked.

She had trouble taking a breath. "V-very nice."

"Thanks," he murmured, but he wasn't looking into her eyes. He was looking lower. At her lips.

Heavens, he was going to kiss her. The realization hit her early enough that she could have turned away. Quite easily.

But she didn't.

She was curious. Never before had she wanted Godfrey to kiss her. Not once. But in that moment Anna wanted to know what it would be like. She *had* to know. She had a sneaking suspicion that she might possibly enjoy it.

He bent toward her inch by inch, leaving her plenty of time to back away. His eyes silently questioned her. She ignored the question.

With infinite gentleness, he settled his mouth atop hers. She sat so still—so very, very still. His lips were warm and pleasantly rough, drifting over hers in a slow, swirling motion.

He found her hands in her lap and threaded their soapy fingers together. It felt . . . agreeable.

He kissed the corner of her mouth, tickling its edges,

then the other corner. All the while their fingers slid against each other, in and out, in and out.

Anna did not move. She did not breathe. She simply absorbed the sensations, wondering where they came from and why she'd never experienced the like before.

Just when she thought her lungs would burst, Godfrey pulled his mouth from hers. She hauled in a ragged breath, and he smiled crookedly. Without a word, he picked up his rag again and went back to scrubbing the window.

As he sang quietly to himself, Anna imagined that she could feel his humming all the way down to her toes.

# *Chapter* 16

FIVE DAYS LATER Nick was thinking that maybe, just maybe, he was starting to make some headway. It wasn't much, but it was progress—kind of like that childhood game "red light, green light." As long as he took teeny-tiny baby steps, he kept moving forward, chipping away at Anna's defenses. But if he tried to cover too much ground with a giant leap, alarm bells went off and he was sent back to square one.

At least Anna had reached the point where she would allow him to pull out her chair for dinner; where they could sit together in the same room while he read the newspapers and she sewed. When he offered to help with her work in the menagerie, she hadn't precisely jumped at the offer but neither had she refused his assistance.

And though they weren't yet the picture of domestic bliss, Nick was hopeful. Hopeful for more reasons than one.

He wiped his stinging eyes with his shirtsleeve, then braced both palms on the handle end of the ax. Across the Channel the distant French coastline floated above the sea like a sailor's mirage. Nick squinted into the horizon, the

wind ruffling his hair. Though a cool front had blown in
this morning, sweat trickled down his spine, hot and sticky.

He rolled his head from left to right, trying to ease a kink
out of his neck. Evidently party-hearty Godfrey had been in
pretty sorry shape when Nick had inherited his body. Although he'd looked good, he hadn't any stamina. An afternoon of hewing fence posts had left him with aching
muscles right into his fingernails.

Nevertheless, Nick was glad for something productive to
do. After two weeks of inactivity, the last few days spent at
hard labor were a welcome change. James, who seemed to
do everything at Cliff House from taking care of the horses
to drawing Nick's baths, had eyeballed him kind of funny
when Nick had asked to help out with the chores. In fact, it
had taken quite a lot of convincing for the servant to take
him seriously. Starting him out easy, James had first set
him at the task of replacing loose shingles on the house.
Yesterday Nick had graduated to hard-core wood-chopping.

"My stars, just look at you. There must be enough posts
here to run a fence all the way to Folkstone."

Nick grinned and tipped his head to the side.

A splash of brilliant yellow against the gray sky, Beverly
ambled toward him like a winter-sprung daffodil.

"How's it going, Bev? Nice dress."

She spread her skirts wide like a young girl. "Do you like
it? John always favored this frock. He did rather fancy the
color."

"I've always been partial to yellow, myself," Nick said,
hoisting his ax over his shoulder. "Nice day, huh?"

"Glorious," she said. "Simply glorious."

Nick followed her gaze out to sea.

God, it was beautiful. But hardly the paradise he had
imagined it to be. Even in a place like this, a time like this,
bad stuff happened.

"So what have you been up to the last few days?" Nick
asked. "Haven't seen much of you around."

He had noticed that Anna's aunt was in the habit of vanishing into the attic for literally hours on end, then reappearing like a technicolor ghost.

"Goodness, you would not believe," she said with a dramatic sigh. "I have been busy cataloging my mementoes. It is an arduous task, but I feel that I must have everything in order."

Nick grabbed another chunk of wood and propped it up on the hewing stump. "Oh, so you're one of those, huh? A neatnik?"

"A neatnik? Heavens, the turns of phrase you use." She laughed softly. "No, I am scarcely a 'neatnik,' and therein, I fear, lies the nature of the problem. All these years I have been tossing my precious souvenirs willy-nilly into this or that trunk, and now I must try to make some sense of them before I go."

"Before you go?" Nick twisted around. "Where are you off to?"

Beverly merely smiled and turned her attention to a bird flying past.

A touch of disquiet settled over Nick. He couldn't imagine that as protective as Anna was with her aunt that she would allow Bev to travel anywhere without her. Was Anna thinking of going away?

"Does, uh, Anna know that you're planning a trip?"

Beverly wrinkled her nose. "No. And I would appreciate it if you would refrain from mentioning it to her. She is so frightfully good to me, the dear girl, but she cannot help but treat me as if I were a child. I'm not, you know."

Nick balanced the ax blade on the block of wood. "I know you're not," he answered her very seriously. "But I also know that Anna would be sick with worry if you took off without telling her."

"Oh, gracious, you needn't fret about that. I assure you I will not go without first saying my good-byes."

"You sure?"

"You have my word."

Well, he couldn't ask for more than that. While he might

not be convinced that Bev should be traipsing about on her own, that was Anna's decision to make—not his. As long as Bev promised to talk to Anna before she left . . .

*Hey.* He sent Beverly a long, thoughtful look. Should he ask her about the incident at the Kingsleys?

Whereas Nick had been biding his time, hoping that Anna would come clean with him, his patience—never considerable—had been starting to wear just a tiny bit thin. Every day that passed brought him that much closer. That much closer to the day of Godfrey's death.

Though he had told Anna that he would give her as long as she needed, the truth of it was that Nick was working on a deadline. Six weeks and counting.

Six weeks, or perhaps much less, for him to accomplish his purpose.

And as far as his mysterious "heaven-sent" mission was concerned— Well, it didn't much matter because, for Nick, this business with Anna had become personal. He had his own goals now; to earn Anna's trust . . . to right Godfrey's wrongs.

He would like to believe that mending Anna's broken spirit was part of his karmic assignment. But how was he to really know? When it got right down to it, he still didn't have a clue as to *why* he'd done the soul flip-flop with Godfrey. And at this point in the game, did it make a difference? All he could do was follow where his instincts—and his heart—were leading him.

Yes . . . his heart.

He cared about Anna. Maybe more than he should have. Nick was determined that he would not leave Anna suffering from the legacy of Godfrey's abuse. He would not leave her in pain, afraid.

So should he keep waiting in the hopes that Anna would confide in him, that she would learn to trust him? Or should he try to get the answers out of Bev?

*Baby steps,* he reminded himself.

Then Beverly let out a startled "oh."

"I'd almost forgotten the reason I came looking for you. The post arrived."

From a miniature purse swinging at her hip, she fished out two items and handed them to Nick.

The first was indeed a letter addressed to "The Rt. Hon. Lord Woodbaine of Cliff House, Aylesdown." But the second letter didn't look to Nick as if it had come via the mail—but, then again, what did he know about the 1810 postal service? The second letter was a thick piece of paper folded into an envelope with the initials "A.W." scrawled across the front.

"Thanks," he murmured.

"My pleasure," Beverly said. "But now I must return to my labors. I have yet to even glance at the trunk John and I brought back from India." With an airy wave of her fine-boned hand, she headed back to the house.

Frowning, Nick laid down his ax and studied the two letters. He tucked the note for Anna behind the first letter, then broke the wax seal on the one addressed to Godfrey. He shook out the paper, his eyebrows lifting. In his day penmanship such as this would have earned a sharp ruler on the knuckles from Sister Mary Theresa. It was a letter from the offices of Modell and Crawton.

*My Lord—*

  *It is with the greatest pleasure that we inform you that your uncle, Lord Barnes, has forwarded to our Offices the Requisite Papers so that we, as your solicitors, may commence preparation of the documents required to secure your inheritance. We have taken the liberty of notifying your creditors of your soon anticipated and much improved circumstances. Once the terms of the bequest are met, kindly contact our Offices at your earliest convenience in order that we may facilitate all legal proceedings.*

                                   *Faithfully yours—*
                                   *Nigel Crawton*

"Lawyers," Nick muttered. Whether 1810 or 1997, they never did speak plain English.

He read the letter again, boiling the message down to one key word: inheritance.

*So Godfrey's Uncle Barnes was planning to leave his nephew some moolah, hmm?* Apparently enough to keep the bill collectors from breaking down the door. Servants and fancy house aside, it appeared from the tone of this letter that funds were tight for the Woodbaines.

He scanned again the line about "terms of the bequest." What terms? The money came with strings attached?

Nick refolded the letter and tapped it against his thigh. Out of the blue, he had a strong and sudden hunch that this inheritance might have been the reason Godfrey had been racing back to Cliff House the night he was thrown from his horse.

But how could he find out? He sure as hell didn't want to contact Godfrey's uncle; anyone who shared blood with that wife-beating creep. . . . And the idea of leaving Anna to go see this Nigel fellow in London didn't much appeal to him, either. *Maybe—*

Maybe he could write Godfrey's solicitors and ask for an explanation or a clarification of Lord Barnes's terms.

Why not? What were they going to do, refuse to give him the information? Seemed as good an idea as any. Though Nick did wonder if the lawyers would notice if his handwriting failed to match Godfrey's. It struck him as funny that after years of completing daily police reports, he'd been at Cliff House almost three weeks without writing a single word. He didn't have the vaguest idea what his handwriting might look like penned in Godfrey's hand.

Nick glanced back to the letter and his eye caught on the note tucked beneath it. The secretive-looking note for "A.W." Clearly, it was intended for Anna. And clearly, he had no damned business opening it.

He broke open the seal. Out fluttered a piece of paper. Nick flipped the envelope over and back again. There was no message. He bent over and picked the paper up from the ground and saw that it was money. Paper money. Unlike any he'd seen in the London of his time, the bill was a five-pound note.

Who would send Anna money in an unmarked envel—

*Shit.*

Nick sent a harried glance to the house. What day was it?

"Thursday, damn it," he muttered.

Leaving the ax and fenceposts where they lay, he sprinted up the slight slope behind the stables. He burst into the front door, almost knocking over Mara.

"Lady Woodbaine?" he asked.

"You didn't pass her comin' in m'lord? She just this minute left to go into town."

Nick grimaced, turned around, and dashed back out the door. Godfrey's riding boots weren't meant for running, he decided, as he pounded the hundred yards or so across the grass to the stables.

Luck must have been with him or Anna would have mowed him over in the gig as she drove out of the stable doors.

"Nick," she gasped and pulled up hard on the reins. He jumped aside, the hot, grassy breath of the horse full in his face.

"Whoa," he murmured, flattening himself to the stable door. That had been a close call.

"Hey there, Anna. Where are you headed?"

He tried to sound casual, which wasn't at all easy when he was practically panting from his short sprint across the yard. Then and there, Nick vowed to whip Godfrey's sorry physique into shape.

Beneath her cloak, Anna was wearing one of her nicer dresses, the silvery-blue one that matched her eyes.

"I am driving into Aylesdown," she said cautiously.

"Oh, yeah?" Nick waved a hand in front of his dirt-streaked shirt. "Would you mind waiting five minutes so that I can clean up and join you? I haven't seen the town yet and I really would like to."

He kept the easygoing smile pinned to his face, determined not to react to the wariness that he had come to always expect from her.

"I, um . . . It is rather late and dusk falls so swiftly these days—"

"I promise I'll be ready in a flash," he said. "Back before you know it."

He thought to himself that Anna did a fair job of hiding her fitful sigh.

"Very well. I'll pull the gig to the front of the house and wait for you there."

Nick felt his shoulders relax. "Great. Thanks, I won't be long."

As he was loping back to the house, Nick suddenly stopped and twisted his head toward the stables.

"Well, what do you know?" he whispered softly.

Anna had called him "Nick."

# *Chapter* 17

ANNA WORRIED HER lower lip as her boot tapped impatiently at the gig's floorboard. The horse snorted, he, too, objecting to the delay.

What could be taking Nick so long?

*Nick?*

She covered her eyes with a gloved hand, the cotton silky and cool against her brow. So . . . he had won that small victory from her after all. His gentle teasing and constant reminders, day in and day out, had worn her down. She could not say when it had happened but, sometime in the last few days, she had begun to think of him as Nick.

In truth, it had not been so difficult. He was so very changed in every way that she had found it a natural consequence to think of him differently. To think of him as Nick.

The name did seem to suit his present temperament. A "Nick" could crawl under furniture in pursuit of a lost bunny, and a "Nick" could roll up his sleeves and wield an ax with strength and skill. Godfrey could not—would not—have done either of those; he would never have allowed himself to be mussed or soiled for any reason.

From what Anna could determine, her husband had not requested of anyone else that he be called Nick. Aunt Beverly referred to him always in the third person, a custom Anna thought rather unusual, and to James and Mara, of course, he was still Lord Woodbaine. Yet not the Lord Woodbaine they had served these past years. Anna had heard the whispered conversations, the servants' awed voices commenting on how affable and obliging the master had become. The entire household was in agreement that his lordship's disposition had taken a decided turn for the better.

And if the servants were falling under Nick's spell, Aunt Beverly was positively smitten. She and Nick had become bosom bows, playing cards together of the evenings, taking walks together in the mornings. His patience with her amazed Anna more than any other alteration in his character, for Nick would sit for hours listening to Aunt Beverly's often rambling, disjointed tales of youthful adventures and farflung travels.

At times Anna felt almost envious of her aunt's ease with him. It was as if Beverly had simply closed the door on the man who was Godfrey. And opened the door to Nick.

But for Anna, the matter was not so straightforward. Though she might eventually find it in herself to forgive her husband for what had gone before, not everything had been left in the past. Looking forward, Anna knew that her life would forever be scarred. Forever. And although more and more drawn to Nick, she did not believe it within her power to forgive Godfrey.

After but a few more minutes of waiting, Nick emerged from the house, his hair dripping wet as if he'd plunged his entire head into the washbasin. Idly, Anna wondered if any in town would recognize her husband. He looked like a country squire, though even a gentleman farmer would deign to wear a hat.

She gave a mental shrug, glad at least that he'd left off criticizing her appearance. Since the accident, she had heard only compliments from him, compliments she had almost begun to take to heart.

"I didn't keep you waiting too long now, did I?" he asked, accepting the reins from her as she scooted over on the seat.

"You shall catch your death of cold," she chided, "out in this chill air with your head uncovered."

Nick merely grinned as they set off down the road. "Did you ever think that might be my plan?" he asked. "After my tumble, I kinda liked lying around in bed all day while you nursed me back to health."

Anna refused to return his playful grin, though it was harder and harder to do of late. Nick, it seemed, was inordinately fond of making jests and teasing—yet another distinction between Nick and Godfrey.

"Anna," he asked as he slapped the reins over the horse's rump. "Do you know anything about an uncle of mine, a Lord Barnes?"

"Why?" she asked sharply. "Do you remember him?"

Alarm rippled through her, shimmying along her nerves in an instinctive warning. Dear heavens, was this not precisely what she had been fearing? That, of a sudden, his memory would return and, with it, the man she had married. The real Godfrey.

"No, not exactly," Nick answered. "I think I saw his name written down somewhere."

"Oh." She breathed more freely. "I am surprised that you would have seen his name. He is but distantly related, I believe."

"So, he and I aren't close?"

"Not to my knowledge. But I imagine that it is possible you could have contacted him while in London this past year."

"What about other family?"

"Yours?"

"Mm-hmm."

Again, trepidation washed through her. What was the reason for his sudden interest?

"I know only of Lord Barnes, and a cousin by the name of Baker who lives to the north. And your sister, of course."

"I have a sister?"

"Yes, she lives in Ireland."

"Really? What's she like?"

Anna laced her fingers together in her lap, selfishly relieved that his memory still suffered.

"I have never met her. She is a nun, nine years your senior. You have been estranged from her for a very long time, I believe."

"No kidding." Nick fell silent. "So, neither one of us has much family left, huh?"

"No." Anna's brows knitted.

Occasionally over the previous four years, she had pondered what she would do once she no longer had Aunt Beverly, her last of kin. She had always suspected that she would simply leave, sneak off in the middle of the night with her meager savings. Perhaps try to find employment in Dover or Canterbury.

But now . . .

She peeked at Nick behind her bonnet's brim. Now she was not so certain.

It seemed that not an hour went by where Anna did not have to forcibly remind herself that, regardless of the memory loss, and regardless of the new appellation, underneath it all this man was still Godfrey Woodbaine. Yet when she was with him, she had a difficult time remembering that. It was as if, ever since their discussion about the smuggling, he was on a mission to be as genial and as amusing as possible.

Yesterday, he had succeeded in even making her laugh. Accompanied by Aunt Beverly on the pianoforte, he had performed some bizarre little dance that he had called the "macarena." While Aunt Beverly laughed until tears ran down her cheeks, Nick had danced around the parlor, fluttering his hands and wiggling his posterior.

It had been silly, ludicrous, absurd. But Anna rather believed that had been his goal.

Never would Godfrey have poked fun at himself in such a fashion, no mater how well-intentioned the fun. Nick, on the other hand, enjoyed humor and made a point of finding some in each and every day.

At the moment, however, he appeared solemn, his features strained. She wondered what held his thoughts. He must have had a purpose in asking to join her in the trip to town; she wondered what could it be.

She gathered her nerve to inquire. "Is anything amiss?"

He blinked as if she had startled him from his reverie.

"Oh—what? No. No, I was just thinking." He smiled, but it was a distracted smile. "Actually, Anna . . ."

"Yes?"

"You pay all the bills, don't you?"

She had not been expecting that particular question. "Not all," she said. "I oversee Cliff House, but you have always managed the monies for the London town house."

Nick's eyes narrowed. Anna vaguely thought that she'd forgotten how very long his eyelashes were.

"And how do I pay for the town house?" he asked. "Where do I get the money to live on when I'm there?"

"There is a small income," she offered reluctantly.

Nick flung her a look of surprise. "From a job? Do I actually work?"

"Oh, no." She made an amused sound under her breath. "Indeed not."

"Then what do you mean by an income?"

Anna pretended great interest in the arrangement of her glove's seams. "Well. When we married, I came with a thousand a year from my great-uncle."

"What do you mean you 'came with'? Like a dowry?"

"Yes, like a dowry. The income is distributed by my

uncle's London man of affairs. It isn't a tremendous fortune, but—"

"A thousand pounds a year?" Nick interrupted. "That
doesn't sound like enough to live on."

Anna bristled. "Thank you very kindly, but most of us
could get along quite nicely on a thousand a year. And,
allow me to remind you that, at the time, you were glad
enough for that meager pittance."

Nick dropped his chin to his chest, wagging his head.
"Don't get your feathers ruffled. I was simply trying to cal-
culate how much it must cost to keep a house here on the
coast and one in the city. We can do that on a thousand
pounds a year?"

Anna studied her gloves again. "I . . . I would not know."

"I thought you said you paid the bills for Cliff House."

"I do."

"Then how much of the thousand goes to the Cliff House
expenses?" he persisted in the slow, patient voice one
might use with a child.

"None of it."

"None. But—" Then, with an aggravated groan, he
tossed back his head. "Damn it, I should have guessed,
huh? Diamond tie-pins, ivory walking canes, fancy clothes.
*Damn him,*" he muttered.

Anna arched a curious brow. She had remarked on Aunt
Beverly's habit of referring to Godfrey in the third person,
even when speaking directly to him. But to hear Nick-God-
frey so allude to himself . . .

"And I would suspect that the thousand pounds doesn't
even cover it, does it?" Nick asked.

"I would suspect not. Rent alone for the town house is
eight hundred a year."

"Perfect," Nick drawled. "Just perfect. While your husband is living the high life in London, you're struggling
just to put food on the table. That's the reason you got involved in the smuggling scam, isn't it?"

"I had to do something."

"Jesus, Anna, but it's breaking the law—don't you get it? What if you'd been caught?"

"It was a risk I had to take," Anna said. "And what else were we to do? In the beginning Aunt Beverly had a small sum tucked away. Those monies were enough for a short time, at least. After that, I sold what jewelry I owned that was of any value, yet even those funds did not last us forever."

Nick shifted the reins to one hand, resting his free hand upon his knee. "God, what a piece of work. What on earth did you ever see in . . . me, Anna?"

For the first time in years she gave him an honest response. "Very little."

"Yet you married me anyway?"

She shrugged and pulled her cloak tight as a gust of wind rocked the open gig. "What choice did I have?"

His fingers clenched on his knee. "There is always a choice," he argued. "Always an option."

"And what might those have been, pray tell?"

"I don't know," he said testily. "Couldn't you find a job or something?"

"Ah, yes." Anna folded her hands in her lap. "Let us suppose for a moment that, astonishingly enough, an uneducated girl of seventeen had been able to secure a position as a governess or a lady's companion. Though I believe it most unlikely that I would have been able to find such a position, let us imagine, shall we? What, then, would you have had me do with Aunt Beverly? Leave her alone at Cliff House? In her condition?"

"All right, all right. I'll concede the point that jobs for women aren't so easy to come by in these days. But damn it, Anna, you should have been out the door the moment I first laid a finger on you."

"I see. And allow you to place Aunt Beverly in one of those ghastly asylums?"

Nick jerked around to face her. *"What?"*

Annoyance was beginning to stiffen Anna's spine. "Naturally, you would not recall that, either, would you? The fact that you threatened to commit Auntie to a mental institution?"

"Jesus Christ, are you shitting me?"

"I beg your pardon?"

"Sorry." Nick combed his fingers through his hair. "I mean it, I'm sorry. I just can't believe it, you know? I just can't believe that your lovely little world of white cliffs and green fields could produce—" He waved off whatever he was going to say with an irritable sweep of his fingers.

"I guess," he said more to himself than to her, "that the mean, the bad, and the ugly aren't confined to any particular time period, are they?"

Anna didn't exactly understand, but she shook her head. "No."

"No," Nick echoed quietly.

Nothing more was said until they reached the outskirts of Aylesdown.

"This is it?" he asked.

"Yes. I told you it is a small village, unimportant."

The carriage wheels rattled over the aged gray stone of the medieval bridge, announcing their arrival as surely as the mail guard's horn. Anna thought to herself that Mr. Lewis, the butcher, must have been hard at work, for the scent of curing bacon floated on the wind.

A few heads turned as they drove into town, but none were faces Anna recognized.

Nick slowed the horse to a walk.

"I, uh, brought along a letter I need to mail," he said. "Which end of town will I find the post office?"

"You wish to send a letter?"

"Yeah." He deliberately avoided her gaze, looking past her to the row of shops. "I had a note from my attorneys in London. I'm getting back to them."

"Oh." She could not help but wonder what business he could be conducting with his solicitors *sans* memory.

"Very well, we can leave it off at the inn to be taken on the Dover mail coach."

"What about a stamp?"

"A stamp?"

"Postage. To pay for the letter?" Nick pulled the gig alongside the road at the end of town nearest the church.

"Do you expect that your solicitors will refuse the letter?"

"No-o," he answered slowly.

"Then, I don't understand. You have no need to worry about the postage, have you?"

A frown eased between his brows. "I suppose not."

After a swift, almost cautious glance around the street, Nick climbed from the gig. As he came around to assist her, Anna noticed how his coatflaps swayed from side to side as he walked.

Even his gait had altered since the accident, she realized. Godfrey had previously sauntered along in an indolent, straight-backed stroll. Now his stride was an ambling, rolling motion like the movement of the waves upon the shore.

He reached for her gloved hand. Their fingers touched. She lowered her eyes.

Spark. Awareness. Thrill. Anna did not know how to label the feeling his touch seemed to generate in her of late. Ever since he'd kissed her while they were cleaning the menagerie.

A brush of knee against knee in the carriage, the slight pressure of his hand at her elbow as he led her into dinner. It was a feeling that demanded more of the same—a hungry, urgent feeling. One she'd not experienced with him before. With any man.

Anna found the sensation disconcerting. Excruciatingly so. Where before his touch had repelled her . . . now, dear God, she feared that she had begun to crave it.

With a new familiarity—one she permitted—Nick tucked her hand into the warm crook of his arm. She kept

her face downcast. Did he sense it, as well? Was his pulse
suddenly rapid, his breath tight?

"Where to first?" he asked.

Anna cleared her throat, resisting the insane impulse to
flex her fingers in the tautness of his arm's muscle.

"The inn?" she suggested, checking that her reticule
rested at her hip. "It is early enough yet that your letter can
make the afternoon coach to Dover."

"The Black Oar?" he asked.

In unison their eyes raised to the painted wood sign
swinging in the wind ahead of them on the walk.

"Well?" he asked.

There was no reason to pretend that she did not understand his question.

"The customs officers must be in town," she answered.
"There will be no run across the Channel tonight."

"Good."

Together they began to walk down the cobbled walkway
fronting Aylesdown's business square.

"Sleepy little town," Nick commented as Anna dipped
her head to a neighbor across the way.

In the center of the village green—if a patch of grass the
size of a large shawl might be so dubbed—stood a cross
that was reported to have been from the town's first church,
one that predated even the fourteenth-century St.
Michael's. The people of Kent historically took great pride
in their churches and cathedrals, and Aylesdown's St.
Michael's featured some of the region's most intricate and
lovely stained-glass windows. So fine were they that local
residents claimed one had to travel all the way to Canterbury to find their equal.

Entering the Black Oar, Anna narrowed her eyes, adjusting her vision to the dark shadowed interior. In the front
room, seated before the fire, were three gentlemen whom
Anna presumed must have been the excise officers from
Dover. Their legs stretched out before them, the trio drank
their ale while periodically pounding the table to under-

score their loud laughter. They did not look to be hard on the trail of blockade runners.

A reputable alehouse and inn, the Black Oar was not a frequent haunt of Anna's. Rarely did she have business to conduct within its walls and never had she dined there or sampled the homemade brew. Therefore, it was with surprise that she heard the innkeeper's wife address her by name, as Mrs. Scranton emerged from the kitchen, wiping her hands upon her apron.

"Lady Woodbaine, now this is a pleasure. Are you in for a spot to eat?"

"No, not today, thank you." Anna sent a guilty glance behind her, as if suspecting that the mere mention of her name would alert the prevention men to her illegal deeds. "We have a letter for the afternoon mail coach."

"Ah, you've plenty of time then. Won't be leavin' for another hour. Are you sure I cannot tempt you with a chop and potatoes? You're wastin' away to nothin', lass."

Anna fidgeted with her reticule. "Not today, Mrs. Scranton. Only the letter."

Taking that as his cue, Nick withdrew from inside his coat a thick packet of paper. He held it out to Mrs. Scranton, who hesitated in accepting it, her tiny black eyes raking him up and down—and not with approval. Sniffing, she took the letter by its corner, holding it as if it were soiled or transmitted contagion.

Heat spilled into Anna's cheeks. *Why had she not realized—*

She took hold of Nick's arm and steered him around. "Thank you so much, Mrs. Scranton, and kindly give our regards to your husband, won't you?"

In a matter of seconds she had Nick out the door, the day's sunshine bright in their eyes. The aroma of curing bacon that had been so appetizing earlier now settled uncomfortably upon Anna's stomach.

"I take it," Nick said dryly, "that Mrs. Scranton isn't president of my fan club?"

Anna guided them back down the walk, embarrassment keeping the color high in her face. "I had forgotten that Mr. Heyer takes most of his meals at the alehouse."

"Ah." Nick's mouth flattened. "So the good doctor entertains the locals on Saturday nights with tales of domestic violence?"

"I-I do not know." Anna paused before the milliner's window under the pretense of admiring a white tulle-and-satin bonnet. In actuality, she chose to present her back to the street until the mortified flush faded from her complexion.

"I don't get it," Nick said. "If the whole goddamn town knew what was going on, didn't anyone try to help you?"

Anna's teeth ground together. "Please. Please don't swear so."

"All right," he said. "But what about your holier-than-thou Mr. Hancock? Did he know what was happening?"

She pretended to shift her gaze to a straw hat banded in green stripes.

"There was nothing that anyone could do," she said quietly.

Though she had often thought to herself that there *ought* to have been something, some action that could be taken.

"What about reporting it?"

Anna pursed her lips in annoyance. After years of keeping her secrets safely buried, she felt vaguely resentful of Nick's incessant efforts to exhume them.

"Report it to whom?"

"The authorities, the police?"

She did not answer him, her attention focusing on a hairline crack running almost invisibly through the milliner's window glass. Suddenly she pictured herself as the glass and her shameful secret as that seemingly insignificant threadlike fracture. The smallest blow to that vulnerable spot would shatter everything apart.

Anna shifted away from the window.

"You don't seem to understand that it would have accomplished nothing," she said. "Who would condemn a titled gentleman for disciplining his wife as he saw fit?"

"Are you telling me," Nick countered, still not yielding the issue, "that a man can beat up his wife and everyone turns a blind eye, yet another man might be hanged for smuggling silk hankies into the country?"

His voice was rough with angered disbelief. A disbelief that made Anna realize how unexpectedly the tables had turned in a reversal of their roles. Always before, she had been the young naive one, the unsophisticated rustic, gullible and immature. . . .

"It is the world we live in," she told him.

He backed away with a frown, as if he didn't know which way to turn to escape the reality of what she told him.

Unlikely as it seemed, Anna almost sympathized with him in that moment. She, too, had felt that same disillusionment four years ago. Four years earlier when she had been forced to accept that this *was* the world she lived in, its laws and its mores beyond her power to control.

She reached out to him in an instinctive gesture of solace. "I know that—"

"Oh, pardon me."

From the door of the mercantile, Mr. Hancock stumbled upon them. Literally. The vicar evidently had not been heeding his direction for, exiting the store, he bumped right into Nick.

All three of them stilled, the tension thick and undeniable. Anna held her breath. She had not shared a private word with the clergyman since that day she had visited him at the vicarage and become aware of his affection. She'd continued to attend church every Sunday, but had made a point not to linger after the service.

"Is . . . is all well with you both?" Mr. Hancock asked.

Anna nibbled at her lower lip, unable to take her eyes from Nick, praying that he would not make a scene.

*Please, don't say anything. Dear God, please.*

Surely she would die of mortification if he breathed a word to the vicar of what they'd been discussing. It would be so like him, though. Like the new him, that is. Direct, outspoken. Painfully blunt.

"Actually, Reverend, I'm glad we ran into you."

*No. Oh, no.* Anna's knees weakened.

Nick dug into his coat and pulled out a five-pound note, pressing it into the vicar's hand.

"Would you do me a favor and return this to your stepfather for me? Tell him that Anna is now officially out of the business, okay?"

"The business?"

In astonishment Anna realized that Nick must have intercepted her most recent payment from Lord Robeson.

"Yes." Nick smiled pleasantly. "And would you pass a message to your mother for me, also? Could you let her know that she'll need to find herself another boy toy? My gigolo days are over."

"Gig—" Mr. Hancock's blond brows stretched to his hairline.

Anna feared she might swoon. Or cry. Or laugh.

"Oh, and one last thing," Nick said as he moved to her side and wrapped his arm around her shoulders. "Just so there's no misunderstanding—"

And there, before, God, the vicar and all of Aylesdown, he kissed her.

And worse yet . . . she kissed him back.

# Chapter 18

WITH ONE FINAL gasp Nick slumped forward, resting his sweat-soaked hands on his sweat-soaked knees. Sweat soaked every other part of him as well. His legs were trembling like overcooked spaghetti, and his lungs were threatening to burst out of his ears.

*Damn.* Going for a run had seemed like a good idea. But after only ten minutes at a fairly brisk pace, he'd been breathing heavily. Fifteen minutes out and a side ache had begun to stab at his ribs. After twenty minutes Nick was mentally drafting his will.

He pushed himself upright and made himself start walking before his muscles began to cramp up. The chill air felt good on his overheated skin, the smell of the ocean reminding him of the runs he used to take along the Marina Green.

Running had always been a release valve for Nick. When the stress got to be too much, he'd go out for a few miles, usually along the Marina or sometimes in Golden Gate Park.

During the last few months—before he'd gone traveling through time—he had been running just about every day.

Not so much due to pressures from the job, but because he'd gone over seven agonizingly long months without sex. For Nick, seven months was just about his outside limit. While most runners raved about the exhilarating "rush" or the phenomenon of "second-wind euphoria," Nick ran to blow off sexual frustration.

And that was the reason he was running now. He had enough sexual frustration bottled up inside him to launch a rocket. With no relief in sight. The way Nick saw it he was caught between a rock and a hard place.

*No pun intended.*

On the one hand, he had made enormous progress in his efforts to draw Anna out of her shell. She didn't jump out of her skin when he came up behind her; she didn't flinch if he gestured or waved his arm in her direction. She smiled, she laughed. She seemed younger, prettier, more carefree. Once or twice she had actually attempted to flirt with him.

Though he knew that he was no expert on battered-wife syndrome, in Nick's opinion, Anna was starting to heal. To trust again. Bit by bit, the tension was easing from her.

And increasing in him.

That was the unsavory flip side; the intimacy developing between the two of them placed Nick in the worst possible Catch-22. The closer they became, the more he desired her and the more she trusted him. Yet the more Anna trusted him, the more Nick became convinced that he couldn't— shouldn't—make love to her.

After all, how could he, in good conscience, take her to bed, allowing her to believe that he was her husband? She trusted him. He would be lying to her. If not exactly in word, in deed.

He had considered trying to tell her the truth, but each time he played out in his mind how he might explain it to her, he felt like he was reenacting an *X-Files* episode.

*Anna, pass the bread and by the way, I'm really not your husband, Godfrey. I'm a vice cop from two hundred years into the future.*

Or . . . *Anna, sweetheart, before I throw you down on this bed and have my way with you, there's something you should know. I switched souls with your real husband, okay?*

Nope. Nick didn't see how he could tell her without her thinking that he'd gone off the deep end. And truthfully, when you got right down to it, the question of whether or not it was honorable to make love to Anna was only part of a much larger question: Would his sense of honor even permit him to return to the future? To abandon Anna?

Knowing now what he did about Godfrey, how could he live with himself if somehow their souls were to switch back tomorrow?

Especially . . . if he had already made love to her?

Nick could imagine no greater nightmare. After earning Anna's trust, they share the ultimate intimacy, then he disappears and leaves her to the real Godfrey.

He shuddered, either chilled by the thought or the drop in his body temperature.

"I can't do that to Anna," he murmured. "I can't."

Sure, Godfrey was destined to die. And die soon. But soon enough? If their souls did miraculously flip back tomorrow, Anna might be stuck with that monster for another four or five weeks. What might Godfrey do to her? What if he hit her again?

Nick's fingers curled into fists, his mouth going dry with fear. Damn it, he wouldn't allow it. He wouldn't allow Godfrey to reclaim his body. At least . . . At least, not before that body was dead.

*That's the answer,* Nick realized.

If only he knew how to make it happen.

Goose bumps puckered his cooling flesh, as another shiver vibrated through him, rattling his teeth. A slow jog back to the house would warm him up and keep him from getting stiff tonight. Or, at least, keep his *muscles* from getting stiff.

He had just broken into an easy jog when a horse and

rider appeared on the horizon as a distant blur of brown and red. Nick slowed to a walk again, placing his hands on his hips. They didn't get a lot of callers at Cliff House, so naturally he was curious as to who the visitor might be.

Mr. Kingsley had stopped by only yesterday to report on the twins' health, and the doctor was supposed to be in Folkstone until the day after tomorrow. The vicar never wore anything but black, and since the rider of the dappled brown horse was wearing a bright red coat and a feathered hat—

*Oh, jeez.*

Nick smirked and glanced down at himself. Hot-and-heavy Ursula was going to be in for a shock, that was for sure. He'd had to do some interesting improvisation in order to outfit himself in something approximating running attire, and though modest by 1997 standards, the drawers Nick was wearing classified as underwear in 1810. Poor old Ursula was either going to have a coronary or jump his bones on the spot.

Oh, well, there was nothing to be done about it. She was riding straight for him, and unless he could weave himself a grass skirt in the next five minutes . . .

As she rode up alongside him, Nick turned to greet her, crossing his arms over his chest in a stance just shy of belligerent. The light of day proved less forgiving than candlelight, he thought to himself. While still a fine-looking woman for her age, Lady Robeson had to be closer to fifty than forty, which made her a good fifteen to twenty years older than lover-boy Godfrey.

"My stars," she murmured in her husky Mae West voice. "Stephen had said you'd been behaving oddly, but I had never thought I might find you thusly." Her eyes skimmed over his bare legs, a blond brow lifting in appreciation. "Though I must confess, it is so very good to *see* you again."

Nick cocked his chin and looked up at her, determined not to offer any excuses. He hated to give excuses.

"I'm guessing that Boy Wonder gave you my message," Nick said, cutting right to the chase.

"Why, yes." She smiled silkily as she slid from the saddle with the ease of an experienced horsewoman, tucking her riding crop beneath her arm. Her heavy perfume was out of place, clashing with the briny scent of the sea and the crisp-smelling grasses.

"I did receive the message, though poor, darling Stephen was convinced that he must have misunderstood you."

"Yeah." Nick gave a self-conscious, one-shouldered shrug. "I do feel kinda bad about that. I hadn't meant to offend Mr. Hancock; I was simply trying to make a point."

"Point taken, darling. I am here, am I not?"

She emphasized the word *here* with a subtle arching of her back that drew into emphasis her generous curves.

"Well, I appreciate you riding all the way from Ravenshead just to say good-bye." His nod was curt, yet duly polite. "Thanks. It's been a real pleasure knowing you, Lady Robeson."

Her throaty laugh followed him as he set off walking in the direction of Cliff House, a good three miles yet up the coast. The tinkling jingle of the reins accompanied the muffled thumping of her horse's hooves as she and her mount kept pace with him.

"Oh, Godfrey, dear boy, I have not ridden all morning merely to make our farewells. I presume you wish for us to renegotiate our agreement?"

*Renegotiate?* Nick's step faltered for an instant, but he kept striding along, wishing he'd had enough sense to bring an extra shirt. At this rate, he was likely to freeze to death before he made it home.

"But, of course, allow me to guess," she said softly. "Hmm, I see that you've lost your taste for rings, so it must not be your jeweler. . . . Is it your tailor who plagues you, darling?"

Nick ignored her, though inwardly he was beginning to get a bad feeling about this conversation.

"Come, let us not play coy," she implored. "How much will it take for you to be returned to your coatmaker's good graces? And I to yours?"

Nick jerked to a stop, his blistered heel causing a faint grimace to flicker across his face. What he'd give for a decent pair of running shoes.

"Are—" He squinted into the hazy winter sun. "Are we talking about money here?"

Ursula reached out and trailed a finger down the center of his chest. Even through her leather glove, the tip of her nail felt razor-sharp against his skin.

"Money," she conceded with a reluctant smile. "And love."

"Love?"

Nick gave a breathless laugh and rubbed at his eyes with the heel of his hand. Lord, just when he thought Godfrey couldn't sink any lower in his estimation—

"So, uh, you help me out with my creditors in exchange for . . . ?"

Ursula's lips curled into a sensuous, thick-lipped pout. "Not in exchange, darling. I like to think it but a happy coincidence that I am in a position to lend you a few pounds every now and again."

Right. He could well imagine what kind of *positions* Ursula had been in.

Suddenly her hand relocated from his chest to hers, where she splayed her fingers over her bosom in a gesture of surprise.

"I say," she whispered, her pale blue eyes growing wide. "You do not remember, do you? Stephen had made mention of you suffering some sort of memory loss, but I had not given it any credence."

"Well, I suggest you give it all the credence you want," Nick replied. "I'd like to say that what we shared is only a distant memory but, to tell you the truth, marchioness"—he regretfully flipped his hands palm up—"it's even farther away than that."

"I don't believe it."

But her wavering, slightly intrigued smile told him that she did. She sidled closer, her perfume potent enough to asphyxiate. Nick choked back a cough.

"Are you sure," she asked, "that you have not simply found someone else in London?" Her arms curved around his neck like two sinuous snakes. "Someone younger? Wealthier?"

Nick gripped her wrists and dragged her arms back down to her sides. "Though there might be younger and wealthier women in London, I promise you I'm not interested in any of them. The only woman holding my interest, at present, is my wife."

"Your wife?" Ursula tittered. "Oh, dear, now you are toying with me, you unscrupulous wretch. Let me guess. Your tailor *and* your wine merchant?"

"Sorry, but no," he answered in a patient monotone. "There is no tailor. No wine merchant. No jeweler." Nick pressed a finger against his temple. "And no memory."

Her lashes fluttered irresolutely. "This isn't necessary, you know, this little sham. . . ."

Nick had had enough. Pneumonia did not figure into his immediate plans, and this discussion was starting to sound like a broken record.

"Look—"

"Let us see if you have forgotten this," Ursula challenged. And the next thing Nick knew her tongue was attempting to give him a tonsillectomy. And doing a damned fine job of it, too.

"Whoa," Nick gasped when he finally wrestled her away. Strong for a woman, she hadn't been easy to pry off.

"Look, Ursula," Nick said, breathing hard. They both were. "I'm flattered, I really am. But it's over. I'm sorry. I don't want to hurt you; you're a great-looking woman, and I'm sure there are men aplenty who'll be lining up to take my place. But you have got to understand that our relationship is over."

For the space of a second she took his measure, frowning with uncertainty. She was obviously trying to determine if he was just pulling her leg. She must have concluded that he was serious because she gave a small sigh and stepped away.

She beckoned her horse forward while calmly adjusting her hat.

Nick felt a grudging admiration for her. She took her loss like a champ. With class. He considered telling her that she could do far better than Godfrey, that she didn't have to pay for a man in her bed. But, ultimately, he decided to say nothing.

"Need a hand?" he offered as she placed one booted foot into the stirrup.

Her cool, collected smile was every inch a marchioness. "No, thank you."

With regal grace she pulled herself into the saddle, her skirts flowing into the horse's mane so that Nick could not distinguish the brown pelt from her chocolate-colored skirts. She gazed down at him from her perch, her chin high, her disappointment but a vague clouding of her eyes.

"Thank you," she repeated. "But I can manage very well on my own."

Nick saluted her. "I'm sure you can, my lady. I'm sure you can."

Foolish.

*Foolish, foolish girl,* Anna mocked herself.

She reined in her horse, cupping her hand over her eyes, scanning the miles that billowed before her like a bolt of green-and-brown flecked fabric rolled out for display. Winter's advent was leaching the color from the bright Kent landscape, fading the sky to a dismal gray, dulling the once-verdant meadows. Even the ocean had taken on an ashen cast.

Anna lowered her hand, her gaze anxious across the barren fields. Could Nick possibly have come this far?

According to a horrified Mara, who had seen Nick slip away from the house dressed only in his unmentionables, he had been gone approximately an hour. Anna had been at her bath, so the servant, employing her own confused sense of logic and duty, had opted not to disturb Anna at her toilette.

Not to disturb her when her husband roamed the coast clad only in his drawers and shirt.

Perhaps it was senseless to fret, but Anna fretted nonetheless. His inexplicable behavior might be connected to another seizure, she brooded, or he might have become confused and lost his way or fallen and struck his head again. The cliffs sheared away from the fields so precipitously that if Nick were disoriented following a paroxysm . . .

Worrying her lower lip, she hunched over her horse's neck, the animal's warmth comforting in the cool gray of the day. Should she turn back? she wondered, thinking it unlikely he could have covered this distance.

Then, in the field sloping below her, flashed a patch of scarlet. Anna leaned forward, her pulse quickening before frustration quickly sagged at her shoulders. The scarlet-coated figure, standing beside a fine-boned chestnut horse, was too heavy-set to be Nick.

*But . . . wait.* The figure separated, dividing into two persons, not one. An auburn-haired man, the lower half of his legs bare, and a woman, blond and statuesque, wearing a riding costume.

Her husband and Lady Robeson.

Emotions tumbled through her. Anger for her own gullibility, disillusionment for her newly sprung hopes, and resignation for the never-changing circumstances of her life.

*Blast him.* And blast her for being ten kinds of fool.

Had the kiss they'd shared in Aylesdown's square meant nothing to the scoundrel? The kiss she had fully participated in? The same kiss that had incessantly plagued her thoughts morning, noon, and night?

"Blast you, Nick," she repeated aloud, shocking herself with her language. "If it's Lady Robeson you want, then I wish you happy," she lied.

Prepared to head back home, Anna nudged her knee into her mount's side, at the same moment that she suddenly pulled the reins taut. A confused whinny from the horse questioned her mixed signals. She had begun to turn around when her mind had unexpectedly reconstructed the picture of the two of them as they had separated. Had Lady Robeson not been pushed from Nick's arms?

Hesitating, wondering if she might be victim of mere wishful thinking, Anna studied the tableau below. Nick's carriage implied a certain apology, yet did not beseech. Lady Robeson, more difficult to read, looked to Anna almost defeated, her head lowered, her eyes downcast, even as pride kept her back stiff.

Anna kneaded the bridge of her nose, baffled by the bizarre spectacle. On the surface, it appeared to have been a lovers' rendezvous, though why Nick would have gone so far as to meet Lady Robeson half-clothed in the open fields, Anna could not say. Yet, there was more beneath the surface—she was certain.

Lady Robeson climbed into the saddle, unaided. Nick saluted her with a two-fingered wave from his brow, the small courtesy revealing all that Anna had been looking for. It had been a salute of farewell, of permanent farewell.

Her mouth fell open, and she started as horse hooves rumbled across the valley. Fortuitously, Lady Robeson rode straight inland toward the road to Ravenshead, so she could not see Anna atop the slight rise. The humiliation had she been discovered spying upon their tryst would have been unbearable. Even if the scene she had witnessed had proved to be a parting.

Her gaze found Nick again, standing alone amid the drying grasses and the incoming fog. Slowly, he wiped the back of his hand across his mouth before he turned toward home and set off running.

Anna debated whether or not to offer him a ride.

*No,* she decided, still sufficiently unsettled to believe a cold no more than he deserved for gadding about in his unmentionables.

Though when he returned home, she would be waiting for him. Waiting for an explanation.

# *Chapter* 19

"P<small>SST</small>."

Nick jerked awake as the pointy end of a parasol whacked against his shin.

"Hey—"

Anna awarded him a mock glare and leaned over, her shawl slipping from her shoulders. The light from the stained-glass window behind her flickered across her hair in bands of rich, golden bronze.

"You were snoring," she accused in a whisper.

"Oops. Sorry." Nick sat up straighter, recalling why fifteen years had passed since he'd last attended any kind of religious service. Hancock was killing him.

The vicar, who had already been droning away for two excruciating hours, obviously was not familiar with the old axiom that less is more. He'd been rattling on and on and on . . . It was the Energizer Bunny with a Bible.

However, in an ironic twist, Nick had to confess that he'd been moved to prayer by the vicar's sermon: *Oh, God, please let him be done soon.*

A glance to Anna found her sitting serenely, hands

folded, expression alert, as if she were hanging on the vicar's every word. Since the subject of today's sermon was gluttony, Nick failed to see what the ascetic Anna could relate to in Mr. Hancock's lessons on overindulgence. The woman ate like a bird, dressed like a nun, and had to be bullied into sharing a glass of sherry with him before dinner. If Nick hadn't known better, he'd have thought that Anna was gunning for canonization.

*Hell, she deserves to be a saint after sitting through this ordeal every Sunday.*

To keep from dozing off again, Nick entertained himself from the privacy of their second-story box by watching the parishioners below. Even the most stalwart began to fidget as the clergyman launched into his third hour of discourse. Most of the youngsters had fallen asleep either on parents' laps or stretched out along the pews. The Kingsley girls, Kate and Joan, sat at their father's side, both neat and clean and wearing their Sunday best. Mrs. Kingsley, Nick had learned, had been confined to bedrest by Mr. Heyer.

Nick searched among the pews for the doctor, but failed to spot Heyer's distinguished, silver-topped head. He hadn't spoken to the man since the night of the Robesons' dinner party, though he'd been hoping for an opportunity. Already sick and tired of apologizing for Godfrey's sins, Nick would have welcomed a chance to talk with the doctor, who seemed like an honest man. The kind of man he had always respected.

Nick bent over and whispered in Anna's ear. "Are Hancock's sermons usually this much fun?"

Anna's lips pursed. "Do not say that I didn't warn you," she returned in a hushed voice. "Frankly, I do not know why you were so insistent on accompanying me. You have never attended services before."

Nick's features creased with chagrin. His reasons for wanting to join Anna this morning probably weren't worth divulging. Not unless he was looking for a marital rumble.

His main reason for tagging along today had been to observe one more time Anna's interactions with Mr. Hancock. He was pretty much convinced that he'd been wrong to ever believe Anna had been messing around with the vicar, but he wanted to be sure. He wanted to be sure because he had decided to go for it. To go for Anna.

And why the—damn, Anna had asked him to cut back on the swearing—why the *heck* not? He cared for her deeply, he wanted her badly, and as Shakespeare had said, "a rose by any other name." Did it really matter what label he wore when the *inside* him wanted to be with her?

At any rate, Nick's worries had been put to rest. Prior to the service, the vicar had greeted them on the church steps, wearing his heart on his clerical sleeve. It was obvious to Nick that Anna clearly did not return Hancock's sentiments, even if she were vaguely flattered. And Nick vaguely annoyed.

Nick's second reason for attending services was more convoluted. Despite being, as he called it, "piously impaired," Nick had come to the decision to place his dilemma into the hands of a higher authority. For after evaluating the soul-switching problem from every angle, turning it upside down and inside out, working at it backward and forward and sideways . . . he was nowhere. As surely as he knew that he *had* to return to 1997, he knew with equal certainty that he couldn't.

It was impossible, a lose-lose proposition. Either way, someone lost. Usually Anna.

So Nick had opted to take a shot on church. Not that he and God were on the best of terms—definitely not after this soul-swapping prank. But when you'd been raised in the church, and when you'd seen first-hand the comfort religion could provide in the dark hours, you understood the power of faith. It was always there. A safety net.

And if ever a man were teetering alone on the high-wire, it was Nicholas Michael daCosta.

Anna shifted in her seat, stretching her neck as if it ached.

"Are you all right?"

She smiled softly, no longer distrustful of his solicitiousness. "Yes, only tired."

"Trouble sleeping?"

She avoided his gaze as she answered. "A little."

Nick knew about not getting enough sleep. He had been awake late into the night, doing push-ups, playing solitaire, learning how to darn his own socks. Anything to keep him from walking the few yards down to Anna's room.

"I think you're blushing," Nick teased. "Next, I'll believe that you've had trouble sleeping for the same reason that I have."

He gave her his best Groucho Marx leer.

"Oh, my." Anna's cheeks flamed even brighter, and her shawl suddenly required an inordinate amount of arranging around her shoulders.

Nick did a double-take. That blush would have been admissible as a confession in most states.

*Was she up nights because—*

*Was she thinking the same kind of thoughts that—*

"Hallelujah, praise the Lord," Nick murmured.

"Shh." Anna looked flustered. And frightened. Most likely, she was already regretting revealing so much.

Nick cautioned himself to slow down. An admission of poor sleeping habits wasn't precisely an invitation into her bed.

Yet, that quiet "oh, my" lingered in his thoughts all the way home.

Anna had never felt so delightfully out of control. Prone to unexpected giggles and blushes and all manner of girlish foolishness, she was as much unlike herself as her husband was unlike himself.

At all hours of the day she found herself thinking of Nick, always looking for him from the corner of her eye, wondering what task he was at or where he might be. A thrill would catch her breath ever so slightly when he entered the room, heat rushing into her face and stomach. A casual touch upon her shoulder, or a meeting of their fingers as he helped her with her cape, was enough to make her pulse race, her eyelashes flutter of their own accord.

She felt silly and young and . . . happy.

Godfrey had never made her feel this way. This commotion of mind and feeling that, oddly enough, was pleasing. Thrilling even. And that seemed to demand fulfillment.

Though not altogether naive as to where these feelings led, Anna had a difficult time reconciling this scintillating awareness with the act that Godfrey had perpetrated on her. The pain and humiliation she had endured lying beneath Godfrey seemed to have no connection to the stirrings deep within her, deep within her private places.

Perhaps, she mused, these feelings made the act more tolerable. Many years ago Aunt Beverly had told her that a woman could take pleasure from it as well as a man. But after being with Godfrey, Anna had assumed that she was not one of those women.

Nick caused her to wonder. To spend far too much time wondering.

Beside her on the seat, blissfully unaware of her wayward thoughts, Nick whistled and turned the gig toward Cliff House. In high spirits, he did not appear glum following Mr. Hancock's unusually tedious sermon. Perhaps, she thought in amusement, he was refreshed from his nap.

Smiling, Anna laid her hand in her lap, her fingers unconsciously cradling her middle. When she realized what she was doing, her smile dimmed, uncertainty flickering through her like a candle in the breeze.

*And what of this?* she asked herself.

She had sworn that she would never forgive Godfrey for stealing her dreams. She had worn it in the days that death hovered at her door and she had willed it to take her. The last barrier between them, Anna's loss had stood as the final stronghold, the rampart she refused to bring down.

But somehow, in the last few days, that rampart had

come down without her knowledge. Godfrey had not been forgiven; yet Nick had. Always she would mourn the loss. Always. For the rest of her days. But for the first time since she was a child, Anna sensed that happiness was hers for the taking. That she could simply reach out and pluck joy from the tree of life and know happiness with Nick.

She would forever be shadowed with regret, she knew. But better to live with the shadows than never to enjoy the light.

"Home sweet home," Nick said, waving to James as they pulled up in front of the house.

On his hands and knees digging trenches and piling stones, James jumped up and loped toward them, brushing the dirt from his hands.

"I'll take the gig in for ye, yer lordship," the servant called, reaching up to take the reins.

"Thanks, James," Nick said. "But it's Sunday, you know. You should be taking the day off."

"Oh, I'm just fussing about, m'lord. Don't want the rain to be washing into the house." He glanced up to the darkening sky. "Looks to me like the first big storm of the season is on its way."

Nick clapped him on the shoulder. "I'll change and give you a hand."

James nodded affably, as if he'd come to expect no less from his titled employer.

Nick helped Anna down from the seat, and together they walked into the house.

"It's getting darned cold to be using the gig," Nick commented. "But you tell me it's not kosher for me to drive the carriage?" He took her cape and bonnet from her and hung them on the hall hooks.

"No," Anna answered, with a scandalized laugh. "It's not at all the thing for you to serve as your own driver."

"But I don't see the difference between driving the whiskey and driving a coach. And I don't know why James should have to sit out in the cold while you and I cuddle up toasty warm inside the carriage."

Anna ignored the reference to cuddling up.

"If you persist in these egalitarian views, you are going to need to change your political affiliation," she teased, as they headed down the hall toward the warmth of the parlor.

"Well, politics isn't— *Shit*."

Anna drew back. Nick had been trying very hard to curtail his cursing.

"Whatever—"

But she did not complete her question, for Nick was already charging through the parlor door. Anna followed, terror piercing her heart as her gaze fell to Aunt Beverly stretched out on the floor in a crumpled pile of fuchsia and green.

"Oh, my," Anna breathed. "Oh, my."

Nick squatted over Beverly, pressing his ear to her bosom.

"Heartbeat, but it's thready. She's breathing, thank God." Lifting his head, he ordered, "Send James for Dr. Heyer. *Now*."

The fearful urgency he injected into "now" sent Anna flying down the hall and out the front door.

"James," she called in a near-shriek.

"Yes, m'lady." The man appeared from around the corner of the house as if returning from the stables.

"Take Lord Woodbaine's horse and race for Mr. Heyer. It's . . . it's Aunt Beverly."

No further words were needed. James pivoted and loped back to the stables as fast as his stumpy legs would carry him.

Anna dashed back inside to discover Nick halfway up the staircase carrying a limp Aunt Beverly in his arms.

"Wh-what shall I do?" Anna asked. *What shall I do if Auntie dies?*

"Fetch Mara—"

"She leaves at noon on Sunday."

Nick's features tightened. "Then come on. I'll need you to start a fire in Bev's room."

Up the stairs Anna trailed him, weak-kneed with relief that Nick was here to help. That she did not have to face this alone. Like the day at the Kingsleys' home, his extraordinary self-confidence comforted her when she felt her own composure slipping beneath the strain.

At a glance Anna saw that Aunt Beverly had been rearranging the furniture. Along the far wall, Uncle John's desk and chair squeezed up against the bed. The curtains were open, revealing masses of slate-gray clouds crowding the sky, turning day into night.

Nick lay Aunt Beverly down while Anna fumbled with the phosphorous box, her hands shaking. Instead of a fireplace, a small faience stove was used to heat the room. Anna dumped in the coal as kittens scrambled out from all corners of the room, mewling plaintively as if they sensed that their patroness was unwell.

When Anna completed her task, she turned to find Nick sitting on the side of the bed, massaging Aunt Beverly's hands, while talking to her in the same way he might have had she been conscious.

"Not to diss Mr. Hancock," Nick was saying in his bantering way, "but I can understand why you skip out on those services every Sunday, Bev. The vicar's heart might be in the right place, but Billy Graham he isn't."

Anna tiptoed closer. "How is she?"

Nick forced a smile. Anna could see that it was forced; she knew him well enough now.

"She's hanging in there."

"Is . . . is there not anything that we can do?" Anna's voice hitched, her imagination envisioning the worst.

"Nothing that I know of. The best we can do is to keep her quiet until the doctor comes."

"What do you think it is?"

"I'm guessing either stroke or myocardial infarction."

"Really?" Anna swayed and dropped into the chair in

front of Uncle John's desk. "That does sound rather serious."

Confirmation he did not give, asking instead, "How old is she?"

"Aunt Beverly will be vexed with me for telling you"—Anna essayed a watery grin—"but she is seventy-two."

"Has she had trouble with her heart?"

"No. At least, none that I am aware of."

Her dizziness passed, Anna rose, clutching to the bedpost as she squeezed through the narrow space between the desk and bed. She sat down across from Nick, taking one of her aunt's weightless hands in hers.

Nick flattened his ear to Aunt Beverly's chest again. "She's weak and irregular."

Anna gazed with a pained tenderness upon her aunt's chalk-white face. "She has always been thought of as irregular, I fear."

"Yeah." Nick smiled crookedly. "She's a heck of a gal. One in a million."

"Yes, she is," Anna murmured, feathering her fingers across her aunt's temple.

"She didn't say anything to you?" Nick asked. "About not feeling well?"

"No. Did she to you?"

"Mmm, not exactly. She mentioned something about going away."

"She did?"

*Going away?* How could Aunt Beverly go away, the woman who had been mother and friend and companion to her? The single person who had been a loving constant in her everchanging, unpredictable life?

Anna stroked Beverly's hand, noticing how its bones were as brittle as seashells, its skin as transparent as water. *So fragile, so frail,* Anna thought. Yet she also remembered that hand, younger and stronger, holding hers throughout their many years together.

She remembered Aunt Beverly holding her hand at her

parents' funeral, then through the months of nightmares that ensued. She remembered her holding her hand when Uncle John told her about the engagement, then again when she'd been so terrified the morning of her wedding. And then, of course, she remembered Aunt Beverly's hand in hers last year when Mr. Heyer had saved her life while shattering her dreams.

Such strength in these fragile fingers. Such strength.

Anna smothered a sob as tears began to tumble down her cheeks one after the other like reflections of the raindrops speckling the window panes.

Nick pushed off the bed. "Anna, I'm going to go downstairs and make us some tea. It's probably going to be a long night, and I'm sure the doctor and James will appreciate a hot drink when they come in from the rain."

She nodded, unable to speak.

He paused at the door, opening it wide. "Shout if there is any change."

His hurried footsteps echoed down the long hallway as thunder rumbled through the sky.

Anna sniffled and wiped her face with her sleeve, not relinquishing her aunt's hand.

"You cannot do this, Auntie," she whispered. "You cannot. I know that you miss Uncle John, but I must be very selfish and insist that you remain with me a little while longer. Are you listening, Aunt Beverly? Can you hear me?"

Her aunt groaned, her gray head twisting on the pillow. "Anna?"

"Yes, Auntie, yes. I am right here."

Anna's heart sang.

Beverly wrinkled her nose, her hazel eyes squinting open. "Have I misplaced my spectacles?"

"Oh, they must have fallen. Shall I fetch them?" she offered eagerly.

Beverly clenched her fingers. "No, child. It does not matter."

"Not matter?" Anna's momentary elation burst. "Y-you will need your spectacles. Y-you—"

"My darling girl. My time has come."

"No, no." Anna wagged her head in spasmic jerks. "You are recovering, you are getting well. You must not talk like that."

"Shh, child. I beg of you, please don't fret so. I am not afraid. There is nothing to fear, Anna. I am only moving onward as I am meant to."

"But I don't want you to move on," she protested. "I want you here. With me."

"But you do not need me any longer, darling."

Anna threaded her fingers through her aunt's, clasping tightly as if her grip alone could hold her to this world.

"Of course I need you. Of course I do."

Beverly's faint smile lit up her face. "No, darling, you don't. He is going to take care of everything. He will make it all right again."

Anna scowled, confused. "Are you speaking of Ni—er, Godfrey?"

"We have spoken of this before, Anna, but you must learn to trust him." She closed her eyes, as if marshalling her strength to speak. "After what you have been through, I know it is the most difficult lesson left to you, child, but you must trust again."

"I . . . I am trying," Anna confessed. "I am trying to trust him, Auntie."

"Yes, your spirit is strong, resilient. It will stand you in good stead, my dear."

Panic raced through Anna's veins as her aunt's voice weakened. "But, Auntie, surely you do not have to leave us. Not yet."

Another hint of a smile. "You will see, Anna, that when your time comes, there is no fighting it. Fight though we will, we cannot triumph over time or fate."

# *Chapter* 20

WE CANNOT TRIUMPH *over time or fate.*

Nick stood in the doorway, the tea tray balanced in his hands, Beverly's words resounding through him with the indisputable ring of truth.

Is that what he had been doing all these weeks? Spinning his wheels to no purpose, fighting a destiny that could not be altered? Either his or Anna's?

Anna looked up from the bed and saw him, her eyes misty and stricken, her pale lips quivering.

And in that moment Nick realized that his need to protect her was greater than anything else in his life. Greater than his need to fight time or destiny. Greater than his need to return home to his family, his job, his friends.

In that moment Nick made a tremendous realization. He would not be leaving Anna. He would not be returning to his own time. He loved her. Her loved her like he had never loved another woman. Like he had not known himself capable of loving.

As if Mother Nature wished to spotlight the magnitude of his soul-shattering realization, thunder boomed overhead, sounding like a cannon had been shot from the roof. Outside the window lightning split the sky in jagged bolts of electric white.

"She's awake," Anna whispered in the lull following the thunderous blast.

Nick nodded and forced himself to move. He walked across to the desk and cleared a space for the tea tray, then set it down, amazed that his hands were not shaking.

Schooling his expression to one of cheerful calm, he came around to stand at the opposite side of the bed. Bev did not look as well as he had hoped. Though she was awake, a gray hue beneath her skin made her appear bloodless, almost cadaver-like.

"Hey there, good-lookin'," he said, testing her forehead with his palm. It was cool. "You've got to be more careful where you take your beauty naps, Bev. The parlor floor isn't the most comfortable spot."

Her wan smile required an exertion. "Beauty naps," she scoffed raspily. "As if I need any."

"Yeah," Nick conceded. "No point in gilding the lily, huh, sweetheart?"

Anna looked to relax, their jokes apparently reassuring her. "I fear, Auntie, that such outrageous flummery will soon turn our heads. Yesterday, he professed that my eyes were more lovely than all the seven seas. Have you ever heard such nonsense?"

Across the counterpane Nick's smiling eyes met Anna's. He *had* said that. Though, at the time, Anna had brushed aside the silly flattery, he was glad that she'd remembered it.

"I need to speak with you," Bev said, stretching her arm out to Nick.

"Sure." He took her hand and perched himself on the edge of the bed.

"Anna, dear." Beverly rolled her head to the left. "Might we have a moment?"

"Oh—" Anna's eyes flickered with surprise. "Yes, of course."

Nick saw that she was hurt by her aunt's request, yet couldn't think what he could say to comfort her.

Anna stood and smoothed out her skirts. "I'll just go downstairs and light a lamp in the front hallway for James and the doctor. It has grown very dark with the storm."

After bending over to plant a kiss on her aunt's cheek, she left the room quickly, her footsteps fading down the corridor.

"I know."

Beverly's hushed whisper jerked Nick around, for he'd been staring at the door, watching Anna leave.

"You know?" he repeated. He felt like a kid caught passing "I-like-you, do-you-like-me?" notes in class. "Jeez, is it that obvious? I only figured it out myself a minute ago."

Beverly's thin gray brows arched together. "You did?"

"Yeah." His gaze lingered on the door again. "I'd always been attracted to her, but, I mean, this is the real thing. *Love* . . ." He bent his head and laughed self-consciously. "What can I tell you, Bev? It just feels right."

The crinkly lines of her face softened. "Yes, it is right. It might take Anna longer to see it, but have faith. She will."

"You think so?" Nick clasped both hands around Beverly's small fist. "After everything that she's been through, all that she's had to endure—"

"But that wasn't you."

"What—"

She smiled sleepily. "I have known all along that you were not Godfrey."

A bowling ball may as well have been dropped on Nick's head.

"H-how?"

"Your aura," she answered in a very serious, very quiet manner. "The instant I saw you lying in that bed, I knew that you could not be Godfrey. Each spirit gives off an aura, you see, its own light. Your light differs enormously from Godfrey's."

"Uh . . ."

What was he supposed to say to that? Time to break out the crystals, incense, and Yanni tapes?

"You think that I'm losing my wits, don't you?"

"Lord, no, Bev. It's not that. You've got more wits than the rest of us combined. It's only— Well, you know, it's weird."

"As weird as taking over another man's body?"

He expelled a long *whoosh*ing breath. "I suppose not, when you put it that way. Jeez, who am I to say what's weird or what's normal anymore? It seems that everything I've ever believed in has been blasted apart since I took over this body."

"Has it?" she asked. "Or had you merely forgotten what it was you truly believed and have only again been reminded of it?"

Nick thought that over for a minute. He had rediscovered a lot of himself since he'd come through time to Godfrey's body. He'd regained pride in being a cop, remembering why he'd first decided to serve. He'd finally found love, when he hadn't believed he'd ever experience it in his own time. And simmering on the back burners of his psyche were a few other issues he was still laboring to come to terms with.

"You're one smart cookie, you know that, Bev?"

"A macaroon?" she teased, though her voice wobbled.

He bent forward, hoping against hope that she might give him a clue to this crazy life-death-soul-swapping-time-traveling puzzle he'd fallen into.

"How much do you understand of this?" he asked. "Do you understand how it happened, the switch? The hows or the whys or . . . any of it?"

"I wish that I did understand. I wish that I could provide you with all the answers you need before I go."

Nick's heart skipped. "Do you have to leave?"

Her grin was a pale shadow of her normally radiant smile. "You know as well as I do that you go when called."

"Yeah. I guess I do. Have you any idea where you're headed, Bev?"

A spark of humor lit her eyes, creating the illusion that the spark of life was rekindled in her as well. But Nick knew better.

"Perhaps," she said in a faint whisper. "Perhaps I am headed whence you came."

A knot formed in Nick's throat. She was fading. Fading fast.

He spun around, thinking that he ought to call for Anna, but when he turned, she was already materializing on the threshold, her face a study of contained grief. He signaled her forward.

"So," Beverly rasped. "Before I say good-bye, I would like to know— Is your name 'Nick,' as I've heard Anna call you?"

"Yeah," he answered. At last he understood why Beverly had never called him Godfrey.

Anna came to stand beside him, and he relinquished his seat on the bed to her. She touched his sleeve as he stepped aside, the brush of her fingers conveying her question. Nick paused, studied his boots for a heartbeat, then answered her with a grim tightening of his mouth.

She made no sound, but he heard her anguish. He heard it inside him as surely as if she had cried out.

"Good-bye, Nick," Beverly said.

"Bye, Bev, darling. It's been an honor." To Anna, he murmured, "I'll be outside in the hall if you need me."

In the cold, shadowy hallway Nick pressed his back up against the wall and slid into a boneless crouch, burying his head in his hands. It was hitting him now. Hitting him smack-dab between the eyes. He had lost his only true friend in this place.

Just as he had lost his only true friend at home.

*Bev. Chris.* His pain doubled, was now twice what it had

been. Grieving over the loss of Beverly hammered home the realization that he had never had a chance to properly mourn Chris. He hadn't been able to, he'd been too busy chasing leads halfway around the world. Heck, he didn't even know if his partner had lived or died. And under the circumstances, he would probably never know.

But, at least, he could grieve. He could grieve jointly for the loss of two good friends.

Like Chris, Bev had accepted Nick for who he was. She had been the only one in all this craziness who had accepted him right from the start. The only person who hadn't cringed or glowered or winced when he'd entered a room. He'd never had to win Bev over because she had known all along that he wasn't a wife-beating sociopath. Because— Nick smiled—she'd seen it in his aura.

While they had all believed Aunt Bev to be a little fruit-cakey, the truth of the matter was that she had seen what no one else had been able to. Perhaps she had only seemed like a space cadet because she had been in touch with so much more than the rest of them. She had more to take in. For all they knew, she really could have been talking to dead Uncle John and holding seances up in the attic.

He had to hand it to her—Bev was really together on the spiritual front. She was not afraid of dying. She had no reason to. She'd looked death in the eye with dignity, and Nick respected that. Especially since he knew that very soon he might have to do the same.

Downstairs the front door slammed. Nick pushed himself to his feet.

"Lady Woodbaine?" a man's voice called.

At the top of the staircase, Nick met Mr. Heyer coming up, a black satchel in his hand, water trickling from him in a steady stream.

"I knocked," Mr. Heyer said, "but I didn't think anyone could hear me over the storm."

The man radiated hostility.

"We're just glad you're here," Nick said. "Though I'm not sure that anything can be done."

"Leave that for me to judge, shall we? Where is she?"

"In her room." Nick indicated the closed door behind him. "Can I get you anything? A blanket or a towel? There is some tea, but I don't know if it's still hot."

Suspicion dripped from the doctor's thin smile. "A linen would be appreciated."

Nick went in search of clean towels while Mr. Heyer proceeded to Beverly's room. From so many hours spent exploring the house for clues, Nick remembered that towels and the like were kept in the upstairs closet on the other side of the house. After piling his arms full, he hurried back to the other wing. He rounded the hall corner, then skidded to a stop.

Mr. Heyer, satchel in hand, was just closing the door to Beverly's room.

With choppy, wooden steps, Nick walked toward him. The doctor glanced up as he neared.

"My condolences, Lord Woodbaine."

*Damn.* Nick snapped his head to the side, dropping his gaze to the parquet floor. "Anna?"

"She asked for some time alone with her aunt."

Nick nodded. "I appreciate you coming out, Mr. Heyer. I'm sorry it . . . it was too late."

"I am sorry, too. I always liked Lady Radcliffe."

A drop splashed on the floor between their feet, reminding Nick that the doctor was soggy to the skin.

"Let's go downstairs and get you warmed up," Nick offered. "I'll make us some more tea."

The doctor followed Nick down the stairs to the parlor. In a matter of minutes Nick had a fire going in the hearth and a hot pot of tea steaming on the parlor's sofa table. Mr. Heyer's coat was hanging over a chair to dry.

Nick retrieved the brandy decanter from the sideboard and splashed a generous amount into his teacup. "Mr. Heyer?" he offered, lifting the decanter in invitation.

The professorial frown reappeared. "Don't mind if I do," he said. Nick poured him a shot and the two men faced off, Nick on the sofa, the doctor in Anna's favorite chair nearest the fire.

"How is your health these days, Lord Woodbaine?"

The question's guarded delivery made Nick sit up a little straighter, as he sensed that Mr. Heyer was on a fishing expedition.

"Right as rain," he answered.

Mr. Heyer tapped his fingertips thoughtfully against his cup. "The vicar had mentioned to me that you had experienced some memory loss after the accident. I was surprised to hear of it since you hadn't called me in again."

Nick gave the doctor a calculated smile. "To tell you the truth, Mr. Heyer, I decided that I was better off without my memory. Once I learned what a schmuck I had been, I figured that the man I was prior to the accident wasn't worth remembering."

"You don't say." The doctor's eyes gleamed behind the owlish spectacles. "Nonetheless, it must have been a difficult adjustment. How has Lady Woodbaine fared?"

*So, that's the direction the wind is blowing.* Nick drained his cup and set it aside. "To be honest with you, Mr. Heyer, she's fared a helluva lot better than she has in the past. And I promise you, you won't ever be summoned to this house again to tend bruises or bumps she took from my hand."

Mr. Heyer helped himself to another shot of brandy, omitting the tea this time.

"I am glad to hear you say that, Lord Woodbaine. Though you'll pardon me if I remain skeptical."

Nick shrugged, as one of Bev's kittens, Lucky, jumped into his lap. "Not at all. It's taken weeks and weeks to convince even the people living in this house that I am a changed man. I wouldn't expect you to be persuaded any easier."

"And Lady Woodbaine? Call me presumptuous, but I am

surprised that she could be swayed under any circumstances to view you in a different light."

*A different light,* Nick thought. Exactly how Beverly had described that aura thing.

"Particularly," the doctor continued, "considering how Lady Woodbaine almost died last Christmas at your hand."

Nick's fingers curled in the kitten's fur. "I, uh . . . I don't remember that incident, Mr. Heyer. Want to refresh my memory?"

The doctor's glower could have frozen a blowtorch at ten paces. "I don't relish the retelling of it, Lord Woodbaine—"

*Oh, yeah, tell it to the folks at the Black Oar.*

"But if you, in all honesty, do not recall the events—"

"I don't," Nick said.

"Very well, then." Mr. Heyer placed his cup on the table, then laced his fingers together, his arms steepled at the elbows. "Lady Woodbaine was in a delicate condition—"

"What do you mean by 'delicate'?"

The doctor pursed his lips. "She was expecting. Expecting a baby. By my estimation, she was perhaps four months along."

*The baby clothes.* Nick drummed his fingers along the curved top of the sofa, dreading what he was about to hear.

"Not to belabor the tale, but, evidently, there was some manner of quarrel between you and Lady Woodbaine. I understand that you slapped her, then pushed her. Pushed her so that she fell down the staircase. James was sent for me. When I arrived—"

The doctor paused and lifted his interlocked hands to conceal the lower half of his face.

"She lost the baby and nearly lost her life. The situation was such that I had to do what I could to save her, you understand. But . . . she will never be able to bear children again."

Nick had seen it coming; he had. Yet it still felt like he'd been broadsided by a Mack truck. His fingers quit their drumming and instead clutched the sofa back squeezing until his knuckles cracked. Squeezing as if they gripped Godfrey's sorry neck.

"Are you sure?" he managed to ask.

"Absolutely."

"Does Anna know that she's . . . barren?"

"I had to tell her—it would have been wrong of me not to—though I confess she did not take it at all well. In fact, in retrospect, I can see now that I ought to have waited to inform her, since I believe that the news impeded her recovery. If not for the responsibility she felt for her aunt, I wager that Lady Woodbaine would have died last December. That she would have willed herself to death."

"I see," Nick said. "And how did *I* take the news?"

The doctor's features hardened. "You left for London, even as your wife's life still hung in the balance."

*Of course.*

As a cop, over the years Nick had been exposed to the cruelest, the most sadistic lowlifes ever to roam God's green earth. Time and time again he'd seen the worst of humankind and blamed it on "the times." The times they lived in. Drug addiction, broken homes, the problems of the inner city—they were to blame for the world's ills, he'd told himself.

*Well, welcome to an 1810 reality check, Nick daCosta.*

Even paradise was tainted.

Nick crossed a leg over a knee, making an internal count to ten. He had to calm down and focus—not get carried away by fantasies of tearing Godfrey apart limb by limb.

"I thank you for being straight with me, Mr. Heyer. And, though it comes too late, you also have my deepest, sincerest thanks for saving Anna's life."

The doctor condescended to giving him a curt nod, as he retrieved his coat from the fireside chair.

"Let me ask you something, Mr. Heyer," Nick said, rising from the sofa. "When you treated me following the riding accident, did I appear to you to be in good health? Aside from the injuries, I mean?"

Mr. Heyer shrugged both arms into his coat sleeves. "From what I could tell, you seemed to be in perfect health, Lord Woodbaine. Your wife was concerned that you had been lying out in the cold for an indeterminate length of time, so she asked that I examine you thoroughly. I found nothing untoward. No heart irregularities, no infection. Your lungs were clear."

The doctor picked up his black bag and looked ready to head for the door.

"One last thing?" Nick said.

The doctor hesitated, his annoyance only barely hidden.

"Considering all that has happened to Anna, all that I've done," Nick said, "you must have been surprised that she decided to rescue me that night."

Mr. Heyer signaled his impatience by switching his bag to his other hand. "As I said to you at Ravenshead, had I been in her shoes, I would have left you there to rot. But was I surprised? No, not at all. She's an exceptional young woman, your wife. Exceptional. She deserves far better than you."

Nick's lips compressed into a tight line as he silently cursed Godfrey to hell and back.

"You know what, Mr. Heyer? I couldn't agree with you more."

# *Chapter* 21

"IF YOU LIKE, I could call at Cliff House tomorrow. Although I am scheduled to visit the dame school in Postcliffe in the morning, I could come by, let us say, early afternoon? A partner in prayer can be so comforting, and I would be happy to condole with you, Lady Woodbaine."

*Happy to condole with her?* The vicar's choice of words was unfortunate indeed.

Through the black lace of her bonnet, Anna peered up at the well-meaning clergyman who looked today like a large crow in his black overcoat.

"Thank you kindly, Mr. Hancock, but while your offer is appreciated, I do not believe that I am ready to condole with company quite so soon."

"Yes, naturally, your private grief must be attended to. Of course," he muttered awkwardly. "Should have thought of that."

Anna craned her neck and peered around the tall clergyman, searching for Nick among the handful of mourners. As reclusive as the family had always been, Anna had not expected that many would appear for her aunt's service. Of the score or so who had, perhaps half had been people whom Anna had met through her animal hospital, families whose pets and livestock she had treated. She was grateful that they had come.

The men had carried the casket out to the church grave-yard well over a half hour ago. Nick had reappeared at her side, then vanished again. Where had he gone?

A light mist had been falling the entire afternoon, a respite from the incessant downpour of the previous two days. The rain had turned St. Michael's lawn into a muddy morass in which Anna's boots were sunk nearly ankle-deep.

Cold, wet, exhausted, and emotionally drained, she wanted only to go home.

"Here he comes," she whispered to herself.

Striding toward her with his rollicking gait, Nick did not appear slowed by the thick muck sucking at his Hessians. He walked with purpose as if eager to return to her. Even in this inclement weather, he had refused to wear a hat, so that his wet auburn hair shone as sleek as a seal's pelt.

"Sorry to have been gone so long," he said, cradling her elbow in the protective way she had come to expect. And to enjoy. "I ran into Mr. Kingsley, who extends his deepest sympathies."

"How kind," Anna said.

"I thanked him for us."

"Yes," Anna said. "That was good of you."

Unconsciously, she leaned into him. For so long Anna's family had comprised but two people, Uncle John and Aunt Beverly. Then, she'd been left with only Aunt Beverly. Now she had no one but Nick.

"Thanks again, Reverend, for everything." Nick reached out and shook the clergyman's hand. "The service was . . . nice."

Under her veil, Anna's lips curved in a bittersweet smile. If not exactly poignant, at least the vicar's eulogy had been mercifully brief.

Again the heat of Nick's hand warmed her arm. "Anna, I told James we were ready to go home. Are we?"

"Yes. I am very tired. Thank you again, Mr. Hancock."

"My pleasure," the vicar said, a shade too enthusiastically. "Please call on me if I can be of any assistance to you in your suffering."

Anna murmured something appropriate beneath her breath and allowed Nick to guide her to the waiting carriage. He sat beside her on the banquette, and she rested her head against his shoulder. With his other hand, he tucked the carriage blanket around her legs.

"Are you warm enough?"

"Yes. Thank you."

The next thing she knew her eyes flew open with a start when the carriage rattled over a rut in the road. The abrupt awakening found Anna with her cheek snuggled against Nick's shoulder, her hand splayed across his chest. Against her fingers pulsed the comforting and steady rhythm of his heart.

She tipped her head back.

His eyes caressed her and she was close enough to note the reddish tips of his dark eyelashes.

She lowered her face into his shirtfront. "I guess the emotion of the day must have caught up with me. Are we almost home?"

"We just turned onto the road to Cliff House."

At the back of her mind Anna reflected that she ought to remove herself from his embrace, yet she could not find a reason to do so. She needed his strength right now. She needed his comfort. Had Aunt Beverly's last words to her not been a plea for her to trust in him?

The coach stopped, rocking slightly as James jumped from his perch. He opened the carriage door and helped Anna to the ground. Her boots and the hem of her skirt were heavy with dried mud.

From the front windows of Cliff House light spilled into the advancing dusk, while above the chimneystack curled charcoal-gray spirals of smoke. Mara, returning earlier from the church service, had obviously set to work making the house as welcoming as possible.

"My, what is that delicious smell?" Anna asked as they stepped into the front hall.

"I'm not sure," Nick answered, shaking the drizzle from her cloak. "But I did ask Mara to cook up something special tonight. I told her to put together a meal that would tempt even your finicky appetite."

"Oh, Nick." Anna spun around, not wishing to devalue his thoughtfulness. "How considerate of you—"

"But?" he prodded.

Her smile was apologetic. "But with the additional expense of mourning, we simply cannot afford such luxuries."

"You mean since I've taken you out of the smuggling business?" He motioned her to sit down on the front hall's bench, then dropped to one knee to help her remove her muddied boots.

"It didn't bring in an enormous sum of money," she admitted, "but it did help pay the butcher."

He worked the lacings on her right boot. "Well, I don't think we should have to worry about the occasional lamb chop anymore. I wrote my solicitors again. I told them not to renew the lease on the London house."

"You what?"

Nick glanced up. "Was that a bad idea?"

"No, not at all. Only, I, um—" Flustered, Anna tucked a strand of hair behind her ear, her fingers trembling. "I hadn't known that you were considering remaining at Cliff House. Permanently, that is."

"Would you rather I didn't?" His hands wrapped around her foot, kneading her arch through her wet stocking.

"If you want," he said, "I could write them again and say that there's been a change of plans. I can do that if that's what you want, Anna."

In the lustrous light of the oil lamps, his eyes shone as twin pools of palest green. He awaited her answer and

Anna knew in her heart he would abide by it. She could say "yes, leave" and he would be gone on the morrow.

She dropped her gaze, and confessed in a whisper, "No. I do not want you to return to London."

"Good." He smiled as if she hadn't just made an exquisitely momentous admission. "So we should have enough moolah around here to eat better, don't you think?"

Anna's second boot hit the floor.

"I would think so," she answered. After living so long on five pounds here, five pounds there, a thousand pounds a year would seem like a fortune.

Her other foot received the same lavish attention as the first, as Nick worked the tension from her toes and arch, warming her foot in his hands.

She groaned inwardly when he stopped.

"Why don't you go upstairs and have a rest before dinner?" he suggested, standing up and casually brushing at the knees of his trousers. "It's been a heck of a day, and I don't want you falling asleep in your soup tonight."

Even after the short nap in the carriage, Anna did still feel very tired.

"Perhaps I will," she agreed. She moved toward the staircase, then paused and turned back to Nick.

"Thank you," she said, her gratitude sincere and heartfelt. "Thank you for everything."

He gave her a wink and shooed her upstairs.

In her room Anna changed out of her soiled dress and wet stockings and lay down in her chemise and petticoat. Once settled in her bed, however, she could not sleep. Her mind was too active, ranging back over the events of the last five weeks.

Her life had changed so much in such a short span of time.

Had it only been last week that she and Nick had shocked Mr. Hancock by sharing that kiss in the center of Aylesdown's square? So much had happened, it felt to Anna as if years had passed since that kiss. Or perhaps it only felt like years because she had spent hours upon hours reliving it.

Rolling over on to her side, Anna plumped her pillow with a restless jab, her emotions turbulent. She hurt for the loss of her aunt. She felt raw and needy and aching. Aching for her husband's embrace. Was it unseemly? What would Aunt Beverly say?

In all likelihood Aunt Beverly would counsel her to cease her dithering and get on with it. Her aunt had made no secret of the fact that she believed Anna should accept Nick as her husband. Completely. In every sense.

But for Aunt Beverly, the marriage act had been an agreeable experience, an intimacy which she had spoken of freely and openly. Anna could not say the same of her own marital encounters.

Though obligated to Lady Robeson, when at Cliff House, Godfrey would still come to her at least once a week. Anna had often questioned why he had bothered, for he had not seemed to take great pleasure in it. And, most assuredly, she had taken none.

But that had been Godfrey—not Nick. Nick's kiss, she had to admit, *had* been pleasurable for her. She had begun to enjoy his touch, the comfort she took from his nearness. Amazingly, she looked upon him now without even seeing Godfrey; in five weeks, he had become wholly distinct from the man he had been.

With a fitful sigh, Anna flipped onto her back and stared at the ceiling. A lace-wispy cobweb waved to her from the corner. She shut her eyes; they popped back open. It was no use. Too much filled her thoughts. Too much filled her heart.

She rose from the bed and dressed herself in an ink-black bombazine gown, once she had worn five years earlier following the death of Great-Uncle John. In the cheval glass Anna scrutinized her reflection.

A bit outdated and a fraction too loose, the dress would have to suffice until she finished sewing her new mourning wardrobe. The addition of a lace fichu softened the gown's drab color, and after pinching her cheeks to a rosy color, Anna felt reasonably satisfied with her appearance.

At the top of the staircase she sent a final, forlorn glance to Aunt Beverly's room. *If only—*

The door stood ajar.

*That's odd,* Anna thought, certain that she'd sealed off the chamber earlier that morning. She went to shut the door, her black kid slippers silent over the wood floor. She faltered on the threshold of her aunt's room.

Sitting among the shadows with his back three-quarters to her, Nick slumped forward, his hands clasped between his knees. Head bent low, hair falling over his brow, he sat perched on the edge of Uncle John's old chair. His pose was one of abject despair.

Shame shot through Anna in a guilty spurt. Immersed in her own anguish these past two days, she had failed to think of Nick, to consider that he might need to mourn, to contend with his loss. While she had done little more than weep and pray these forty-eight hours, Nick had seen to the business of ordering the casket, scheduling the funeral service, and seeing to her needs. He'd not yet had the time or opportunity to grieve. Nor had Anna, in her self-indulgent absorption, considered that he might need to.

Noiselessly she entered the room. The curtains were drawn, no candles or lamps lit. Against the shadows, Nick's snowy-white shirt gleamed, stretching taut across his back. Anna noticed how the shirt's fabric hugged muscles newly defined from his recent labors. She came to stand behind him, placing her hands atop his shoulders. His muscles tensed, then relaxed in recognition.

"I am sorry," she whispered.

He shook his head.

The room was icy, to the point where Anna could see her breath. Beneath her hands, Nick felt cold, deathly so. With tentative strokes, Anna smoothed her fingers back and forth across the tops of his shoulders, instinctively wishing to comfort, to console.

He let her soothe him. Neither spoke. They simply took solace from each other, the mere act of being together setting them on the road to healing.

After a few minutes Nick tilted his head back, as if seeking, demanding more of her touch. Anna's knuckles brushed against the hair at his nape. So silky, as soft as the kittens' fur. She wove a hand through the thick auburn mass, and he pivoted slightly to gaze up at her. A pinkness rimmed his eyes, revealing what Anna would not have believed possible two months ago.

Moved with compassion—and something else—she cradled her fingers against the side of his face, the merest hint of evening stubble tickling her palm. He turned his face into her hand. His lips were like a warm murmur against her skin.

Anna's entire body began to pulse. Her heartbeat throbbed in every limb, in every nerve, in every pore.

Nick pressed his mouth into her hand, the contact now sure and purposeful. Anna closed her eyes, her other hand still threaded through the hair at his nape. Slowly he kissed his way up a finger, the tip of his tongue gliding along its length.

Anna began to shake, her legs quivering beneath her. When she opened her eyes, Nick's gaze impaled her. Ripped right through her, its naked demand undeniable.

"Anna?" he whispered hoarsely.

Her breath emerged as frosty little pants puffing in the air.

*This is it.* She hadn't thought the question would be thrust upon her so soon. Was she ready? Would she ever be ready?

She averted her eyes. "Yes."

He growled a soft sound as he stood, his hand clasping hers tightly. He led her out the door, Anna's attention focused on the hall's diamond-patterned parquet floor. At the back of her mind, she wondered if he would take her to his room or to hers. He opted for hers.

The view from her window framed an indigo sky smudged with streaks of violet and slashes of crimson. A sky that hovered between night and day, that wed the wonder of light to the mystery of darkness.

At the center of the room, Anna stood, her fists curled, pinning her sights to the farthest point on the horizon. The door shut behind her with a portentous click.

"Are you sure?"

Barely audible, the words shivered through her. How could she explain that she would never be sure? Never be sure until she tried? For her, it was a riddle that would not be solved unless she saw it all the way through to its end. It might very well be the same numbing ordeal she'd endured under Godfrey. Or maybe . . . Maybe it would be different. As Nick was different.

In answer she whirled around, clutching to him, burying her face in his shoulder. His arms encircled her, just holding her. Holding her safely, surely. After a minute or two, his hand cupped her chin and he lifted her face to meet his gaze.

"Anna, are you sure you want me to make love to you?"

*Yes,* she thought. *Yes, if it truly is making love.*

"It's been a while for you, hasn't it?" he asked.

She nodded.

Nick's brows inched together. "Has it ever been good for you?"

Flames stole into her cheeks. "No."

"It will be this time," he promised.

Gently he pulled her along with him to the bed. He pushed apart the bedhangings and started to sit, but Anna nudged him aside to turn down the counterpane. She then went ahead and lay down, hoping she did not look as stiff as she felt. Nick crawled up after her, stretching out beside her, propping himself up on an elbow.

"Shoes first?" he asked.

"Very well."

Before she could sit up, Nick was at her feet, sliding her slippers from her. A muted *thud-thud* told her the shoes had been tossed to the carpet. She lifted up and peeked down the bed to see him kneeling, his legs apart. He cradled her foot in the vee of his legs.

Her face afire, she sank back against the pillows, feeling as naive as any virgin. Then Nick began that wonderful kneading of her toes and arch and ankle again, that wonderful rubbing that drew the tension from her body as if by magic. His thumbpad circled the sensitive flesh curving at her arch, his fingers squeezing the tendons at her ankle.

He probed and rubbed and stroked her feet, and Anna lost track of time, floating ever nearer to a place of utter contentment. The anxiety that had gripped her only minutes earlier melted away into nothingness. She could not remember the last time she had felt so pampered, so cared for. So indulged.

All the while, her heel pressed against him, pressing against the hard part of him inside his trousers.

Warm and relaxed, she felt Nick glide up and over her body, not touching her, but hovering above her. She lifted her heavy lids. He smiled and bent over to kiss one eyebrow, then the other. He feathered kisses from her temple to the corner of her mouth.

"You are so beautiful, Anna," he murmured against her jaw. "So beautiful. To think how far I had to come to find you."

Anna smiled, not understanding, though she liked hearing him call her "beautiful." She raised her arms and hooked them around his shoulders, pulling him closer. His mouth captured hers and she sighed. This was what she had been seeking—those same feelings, that subtle stirring deep inside her.

He kissed her, his tongue rimming her lips, then rimming her teeth and tongue. It was exciting, surprisingly so. Her contented languor gave way to a quickening, a faint unex-

plained urgency. Tentatively she entwined her tongue with
his. She felt his smile against her lips.

"That's the way, sweetheart. Don't be afraid to jump
right in," his husky voice teased.

"I don't know how," she confessed.

He trapped her earlobe between his teeth. "Just follow
my lead. And if there's anything you especially like, you let
me know, all right?"

So far, Anna was liking everything very well indeed.

The lace fichu disappeared, leaving her neck vulnerable
to tiny biting nibbles, deliciously indescribable, that stole
her breath.

"I-I . . ."

She was going to comment that she very much enjoyed
that particular activity when Nick's palm cupped her breast
and she forgot what she was about to say. He kneaded her
gently until she began to twist beneath him in an instinctive
movement. His hands shaped and molded her, his thumbs
flicking over the sensitive tips. She moaned.

"Yes, love, yes," he whispered. "Just help me get this
dress off, will you?"

Together their fingers fumbled with the buttons, Nick re-
warding her with kisses after each button had been undone.
As he pushed the gown from her shoulders down to her
waist, Anna was secretly glad that she'd abandoned her
stays these last months, for it would have taken forever to
remove them.

"God, you're so perfect," he whispered as he tugged at
her chemise, pulling it up and over her head. "So perfect."

Anna could not bear to look at herself. She was now bare
from the waist up, exposed and vulnerable. When Nick's
hot breath fanned across her nipple, she gasped and tried to
push back.

"Easy, love. Easy."

Soothingly he lay her down again only for her back to
arch of its own volition when his tongue flicked over the tip
of her breast.

"Oh-h," she gasped, shocked at the force of the sensation.

"Again?"

She could scarcely breathe, but she managed a "Yes."

His tongue lapped her once more.

"Oh," she cried out, daring to open her eyes.

Contrasted against the white of her bosom, his hair shone a rich, lustrous copper, and the sight of his head at her breast sent a thrill shooting into her stomach.

He lifted his head and his eyes glowed like a cat's in the expanding darkness.

"Like that, do you?"

He suckled her in earnest, his lips and teeth drawing at her until she wanted either to laugh or to cry. Never did she want him to stop. Never. A tautness was building inside her and with each pull of his mouth, she felt herself draw tighter. Closer.

His hand snaked up her calf and she was powerless to prevent it. His fingers grazed over her knee, then became tangled in her petticoat. Sitting back on his heels, he began peeling her stockings from her legs.

Dazed and panting, Anna realized that he planned to divest her of every bit of her clothing. Petticoat and gown were stripped from her hips until she lay amid the bed linens as naked as the day she was born.

She made a furtive grab for the sheet, but Nick proved swifter than she. His callused palms stroked from her knees along the sides of her legs up to her waist.

"Beautiful," he murmured before his tongue dipped into her navel and she shuddered, biting into her lip.

"I . . . I don't know how much more of this I can take," she gasped.

Nick's rumbling chuckle promised more. Much more.

He yanked his linen shirt off in two brusque movements, then threw off his trousers and drawers. Grateful that darkness continued to blanket the room, Anna could only make

out his silhouette in the shadows. It was nonetheless impos-
ing.

His skin was so hot Anna moaned when Nick blanketed
her with his body.

"Anna," he whispered.

"Yes?"

"Kiss me."

She obliged him, keenly aware of the crisp mat of curls
sliding over her sensitive breasts, the rigid shaft burning
into her thigh. . . . The hand spreading her legs open.

His fingers touched her, pinpointing the center of her, the
point from which all her body's pulsing originated. She
sighed into Nick's mouth as his thumb pressed against her,
circling and circling.

*Is this how it is supposed to be?* Anna wondered fever-
ishly. This pleasure bordering pain, this hunger that seemed
incapable of being quenched?

He kissed her with deep thrusts of his tongue, mimicking
the motion of his finger inside her. His thumb continued
circling, driving her ever higher to a madness, a madness
that had her hips writhing.

"That's right," he urged at her ear. "Don't give up on it,
sweetheart. It's yours for the taking."

*What?* Anna wanted to ask. *What?* She was reaching for
something, but what was it?

She pulsed, she throbbed. She felt so tense, she feared
she might snap in two.

"Nick," she pleaded.

"Easy, sweetheart," he whispered. "It's coming."

His thumb circled her relentlessly, the pressure building
and building. Anna thrashed her head back and forth
against the pillows.

"Nick, please," she begged, almost sobbing.

"Here we go, love. Hold on."

Suddenly a warm wetness settled between her legs, the
tip of a tongue scraping across the core of her. She came
apart. Nick gripped her hips firmly, holding her still as he

brought her to a place she had never imagined. A place where your body betrayed you, sending your soul on a dizzying ride through ecstasy.

Sensation was still rippling through her when Nick sheathed himself inside her. She bucked against him. He withdrew, then slipped into her again, his fiery length sliding along her throbbing flesh.

"No," she whimpered. "I can't. Not again."

He chuckled into her neck. "You'll be surprised what you can do, my love."

His hands cupped her buttocks, tilting her up as he moved again, in and out.

Anna clutched at him, certain that she could not survive another trip into such pleasure. He rocked against her, setting a rhythm that demanded she join him on the ride. The pace increased, frenzied and wild. And unlike before, this time it came upon her slowly, working through her abdomen up into her breasts, emerging as a strangled cry from her throat.

"Nick!"

She exploded, her journey complete.

"Anna," he groaned. His fingers dug into her buttocks and he jerked, his hips grinding against her.

And there at the pinnacle of her pleasure, Anna suddenly realized that she had flown high enough to see the truth.

*This man was not her husband.*

# Chapter 22

Nⁱᶜᵏ'S HEART THUNDERED as if he had just run the four-minute mile. He grinned into the side of Anna's sweat-dampened neck. If he'd run it in four minutes, judging from the sound of Anna's labored breathing, she must have shattered the world record.

Either way, they both came out winners, he thought with satisfaction.

He kissed the curve of her jaw.

"My love," he murmured, "that was unbeliev—"

"Who are you?"

The three staccato words punched through the darkness, hitting him right in the gut.

Nick went stock still. Beneath him, Anna lay as stiff as the figurative board.

"Who are you?" she repeated. Emotions too numerous to name layered her voice.

Nick rolled onto his side, allowing his splayed fingers to linger on the smooth roundness of her stomach. She did not push away his hand.

"What," he asked carefully, "do you want to know?"

He felt her abdomen rise and fall as a tremulous breath shuddered through her.

"I want to know how this could be possible. How you could look exactly like Godfrey Woodbaine and yet not be my husband. Are you his twin?"

"No."

"Who . . . are you then?" she asked tremulously, her voice pitched an octave higher.

"My name is Nick daCosta."

The shadows were too deep for him to make out her expression, but he could feel the shock work its way down her body.

"Anna, is it okay if I light a candle? I'd like to be able to see you if we're going to talk about this."

She took several seconds to answer. "If you like."

Nick climbed from the bed, batting away the hangings. Goose bumps gathered on his arms and legs as he fumbled across to the fireplace. The dying coals cast enough light for him to see by and he stoked the fire, then lit a three-pronged candelabra he took from the mantel.

Returning to Anna's side of the bed, he found her sitting up against the pillows, the sheet pulled high around her neck, her eyes enormous and wary. The flickering candlelight revealed gold threads in the dark blonde hair tumbling about her shoulders.

Nick felt a little embarrassed as he approached her wearing only his birthday suit. Or Godfrey's birthday suit.

He set the candlestand on a round side table and crawled back into bed. Anna scuttled aside. Nick couldn't be sure whether she was trying to make room for him or simply trying to distance herself from him. She clutched the sheet up to her chin, and the two lay silently in the candlelight for several minutes.

Nick clenched his jaw. This wasn't going to be easy. He reached out and pried Anna's right hand loose from the sheet. She let him weave his fingers through hers.

"Anna . . . are you afraid of me?"

A knot shifted along the long column of her throat. "No," she whispered. "Not really."

"Good." Nick breathed a little easier. "Because what I'm going to tell you is going to make you think that I'm a lunatic. You do know that I'm not a lunatic, don't you?"

He gave her an imploring smile.

The tension in her gaze relaxed. Just a smidgeon.

"Okay." Nick tipped back his head and wondered where in the world he ought to start. "Do you remember when you found me after the riding accident? When I first said I had lost my memory?"

She nodded.

"Yeah. Well, this sounds incredible, I know, but the truth of the matter is that I never lost my memory . . . because I was never Godfrey. You see, I was driving and I had a serious car accident—"

"Car accident?"

*Oh, right.*

"A car is like a carriage without horses."

Her brows drew together.

"At any rate, you're just going to have to trust me on this one, but when I woke up after the car accident, I realized that something amazing had happened. Something unbelievable. When I awoke I was no longer in my body. I was in Godfrey's."

Anna recoiled, her head pulling back on her shoulders like a startled turtle. "I-I don't understand."

"Believe me, neither did I. And I still don't completely. But for some reason, when Godfrey had his riding accident and I had my car accident, we somehow switched bodies."

She stared at him for a good long minute, first skepticism, then alarm passing over her features. "So," she asked, evidently piecing together the puzzle, "Godfrey has *your* body?"

Her eyes darted to the door as if she expected to see her real husband come bursting upon them any second.

"No," he assured her. "I mean, yes. But he's not likely to

show up here. At least, I don't think so." Nick squeezed his eyes shut and reopened them. "Damn, this is hard to explain."

"How?" Anna asked. "How did it happen?"

"I don't know."

"How then do you know that Godfrey is in your body? Have you seen him?"

Nick scratched at his chin. "Uh, you know those seizures I have?"

"Yes . . ."

"This is going to sound totally wacko—bear with me—but during those seizures, it's like Godfrey and I— Well, it's like our minds mix together. It's tough to describe, but it's sorta as if both our spirits are in both bodies. At the same time."

Anna's pupils dilated until her eyes shone almost black. "Where is he? Where is Godfrey?"

*Oh, Jeez. Here goes.*

"He's in the future, Anna. Almost two hundred years into the future." Nick winced, waiting for the fallout.

*And a one, and a two—*

Anna pulled her hand from his. "You expect me to believe that?"

"Anna, I'm sorry. It's incredible, it's insane, but it's the truth. I wish I could have told you from the beginning, but I knew that you'd never fall for such a cock-and-bull story."

"Yet . . . I am supposed to fall for it now?"

Nick gusted a sigh. "All right, let's look at this from a different angle: Am I Godfrey?"

Anna frowned and tucked her hair behind her ear. "No, I don't think that you are."

"So you accept that I am Nick daCosta in your husband's body?"

"I guess that I must. Yes."

"Okay. So if you've bought in that far—if you believe that souls can switch bodies—is it so much harder to accept that my soul came from 1997?"

"1997?"

Anna's breathless laughter might have held a hint of hysteria. But, at least, she no longer had the sheet clamped around her like a shield of armor.

"1997," she repeated, shaking her head in wonder. "You are telling me that you come from the future?"

Nick nodded.

"I—" Anna pressed the tips of her fingers against her eyelids. "I-I don't know what to say."

Slowly she lowered her hands. "What is it like then? The future?"

He smiled. "It's wa-a-y different. You wouldn't even recognize it as the same planet. We have cars, like I told you about, and airplanes, machines that fly in the air. We have electricity, which is power, like coal in a way. And radio and television—too complicated to describe. And *toilets*. Man, I never appreciated toilets like I do now, let me tell you.

"In 1997, there are many, many more people in the world. Especially where I come from, San Francisco."

"The colonies?"

Nick's smile broadened. "Yeah."

Anna traced her lower lip with her finger, her expression thoughtful. "I had thought there was a foreign element in your speech."

"Foreign?" Nick laughed. "You want to talk foreign? You should hear how this voice sounds to my ears."

She raised her gaze to his, her eyes like silver in the muted light. "And who is Nick daCosta? Who are you in the future?"

Nick felt his throat swell with emotion. She believed him, by God. She believed him.

"Nick daCosta is a man who loves you, Anna. A man who had to travel into the past to find the only woman ever meant for him. He's a police officer, a movie addict, and a pretty decent guy who sometimes has a tendency to be too stubborn and hardheaded."

"A police officer? You were in the army?"

Nick noticed that she didn't say that she loved him in return. It hurt him a bit, but he understood that it might be asking too much of her at this point. She'd had a mountain of stuff to deal with today. He had to be patient.

"Not exactly," he explained. "It's like a . . . a constable. My job was to make sure that people obeyed the law."

"Oh. That's why you disliked Lord Robeson's smuggling so very much."

"The main reason, yeah."

Anna's lips parted. "Were you married? Did you have a family?"

"I was married when I was younger, but we divorced. Lisa's been out of my life for a long time now. I have a mom and three sisters."

"My." Anna shook her head. "And what did you look like?"

Nick screwed up his face. "Well, I didn't look much like this, I'll tell you that. I was all-right looking, but not what you'd call gorgeous or anything. Dark brown hair, dark brown eyes. Shorter, but in better shape physically."

"I think that sounds very handsome indeed," Anna murmured as she touched his cheek with her finger.

Nick dropped his gaze, goofily pleased that she thought so. "Thanks, but I'm sure Godfrey doesn't agree. I don't think he would have under any circumstances."

"What do you mean?"

"Well, the last I saw, the body he inherited from me wasn't looking so good. That car accident really messed me up. Broke my back, shattered my jaw. I was burned pretty badly over my shoulders and arms, too."

"I don't understand."

"You see," Nick explained, "the whole time that I've been here, falling in love with you, Godfrey has been in the year 1997 fighting to stay alive. He's been stuck in a hospital in London, tied to a traction device, receiving skin grafts and undergoing operations. Loads of fun."

"You know all this from the seizures?"

"Mm-hmm."

Anna pondered for a moment, anxiety filtering into her eyes. "Nick . . . if you do not know how your bodies initially exchanged, then how do you know that they might not switch back?"

Nick's toes curled. He ought to have known that Anna would eventually arrive at the same question he'd been battling these last few weeks. It was only logical, after all.

But how could he tell her the truth? How could he tell her that during the last seizure, he had sensed Godfrey's efforts to reclaim his body? That he had no idea if or when the switch might take place?

God, she'd be terrified. Terrified out of her mind. Yet if he were to share with her what he knew about Godfrey's imminent demise, it's not like she'd find that very comforting, either.

So, Nick made a decision. He would have to lie to her. White lies.

"Now, why would I be sent here if I wasn't meant to stay?" he asked with a grin. "Obviously the fates intended for us to be together, Anna. Godfrey was a mistake, so God fixed it."

"Do you truly believe this has all been divinely directed?"

"Yeah, Anna, I do think so. Before I came here, I'd lost touch with all that stuff, but—" He shrugged. "If finding you two centuries in the past isn't a miracle, I don't know what is."

Anna said nothing for a few seconds, obviously lost in thought. "Aunt Beverly knew about you, didn't she? That is the reason she didn't fear you, the reason she liked you as well as she did."

"Yeah, she knew. Though I never told her. In fact, she didn't let on to me that she knew until . . . the end. I don't know how, but she could see that I wasn't Godfrey."

"So what do we do from here?"

Nick studied the white moons of Anna's fingernails, a small sadness creeping over him. He was going to have a hard time withholding so many secrets from her.

"I don't know, Anna. What do you say we just enjoy what we've been given?" He lifted her knuckles to his lips and murmured, "Let's just live each day we have to its fullest."

# *Chapter* 23

Nick crept out of bed the following morning, careful not to disturb the mass of tangled limbs and bedding sleeping beside him. Though sunlight flooded the room—it had to be nearing noon, Nick guessed—Anna was out cold. Like a light.

Taking into account the emotional fallout of the funeral and then last night's shocker and add to all that three rounds of lovemaking . . . He figured that she had plenty of reason to be zonked. Besides a nice, long rest would do her good. That and a hearty meal.

*Poor Mara,* Nick thought as he slipped into his pants. After asking the servant to put together a special meal, he and Anna never did make it downstairs to dinner last night. They'd been too busy.

Nick walked back to his bedroom to put on some clean clothes, and it was like walking into a meat locker. Without a fire going during the night, the room's temperature had dropped to below freezing. A thin layer of ice had crusted over the water in his washstand, resulting in Nick taking the fastest sponge bath known to man.

He hissed and cursed as he cleaned himself up, dreaming of the days of central heating and hot running water. Man, would he ever get used to living like this? Or was it, he asked himself, a moot point? Today would be what . . . the second of December? So unless Godfrey's destiny had somehow been altered, this body would be dead within a month.

Nick had less than thirty days left to spend with Anna. He was going to have to live a lifetime of loving in that short time.

The thought almost sent him running back to Anna's bedroom to wake her up. But he didn't. He couldn't let on to her how important every minute was from here on out. He couldn't let Anna see that he was scared. Scared of losing her.

Nick finished dressing and headed downstairs to apologize to Mara. The little cook-slash-maid accepted his apologies, grinning as if she knew exactly what had kept the two of them occupied abovestairs. Nick tried to play it cool, but he could sense a certain swagger to his step that announced loud and clear he was a man in love who'd had himself a helluva night.

He grabbed a quick breakfast, then decided to make one more visit to the rocks where Godfrey had cracked open his head. He might only be grasping at straws, but he had the suspicion that there was something he'd forgotten. Something important. A lingering sense that a vital piece of the puzzle was yet missing.

Of course, that might be nothing more than wishful thinking, he told himself. He never had been able to give up even when the odds were stacked sky-high against him. Go gracefully into the night? Never Nick daCosta. He went kicking and screaming and swearing like a sailor . . . or like Shirley Sokolov, he amended with a faint smile.

What he needed to find was a loophole. A loophole, an escape hatch, a secret path out of his dilemma. Because as it stood right now, Nick was simply waiting to die. Waiting for Godfrey's destiny to catch up with him.

Even if he knew how to trigger the soul-switch, he couldn't "activate" it. He couldn't abandon Anna. It might be one thing to leave her safe and secure in her Regency England world, but to leave her in the hands of Godfrey . . . No goddamn way.

As Nick saw it, a best-case scenario would result in Godfrey's soul dying when Godfrey's body died, thereby sending Nick back to his own time and to his own body. In the worst-case scenario, Nick would die with Godfrey's body, leaving psychopath Woodbaine to live as Nick in 1997. Neither option sat very well with him since neither option meant a future with Anna.

There had to be an answer. And he had to find it.

The ground was soggy, making *squish-squish* sounds under his boots. Sunny and windy and cold, far colder than any San Francisco day, it felt like December. Like Christmas hovered just around the corner with its promises of roast turkey and mistletoe and Mom's special-recipe eggnog.

Nick frowned, wondering what Christmas would mean for his family this year. Would Godfrey be out of the hospital? If so, would he take over Nick's identity—actually travel home to Chicago for the holidays? Nick hated even to think of it. Hated to think of his mother and sisters sitting down to Christmas dinner with Godfrey, the wife-beating degenerate.

*An answer,* Nick told himself. He couldn't give up.

After spending nearly an hour exploring the site of the accident, studying the same damned boring rocks over and over, Nick gave up. On the rocks—not on his crusade.

Heading home on the trail, he again pored over every nuance, every angle of his situation. *Loophole. Escape hatch. Trapdoor.* There had to be a way that he could be with Anna, ensure her safety, while also keeping Godfrey out of his family's life. But how?

Absorbed in thought Nick walked along, kicking fitfully at stones on the path. Abruptly his eye caught on a gray lump of something concealed a few yards away among the grasses and weeds. Curiosity steered him toward it—

*Jesus!*

Vertigo slammed into him, weakening his knees. He fell to the ground on all fours, breathing hard. Focused on the object in the grass, he hadn't realized how close he had come to walking right off the cliff. Less than two feet in front of him, the earth cut away at a sharp ninety degrees to plunge straight down into the ocean.

Gingerly he retrieved the item that had caught his interest and backed away on his hands and knees. It was only a cap. A common cap of the variety he'd seen Mr. Kingsley wear. Thinking it might belong to James, Nick went ahead and stuffed it into his coat pocket. He stood up slowly, sending another watchful glance to the cliff's edge.

Man, it was deceptive. The upward slope produced a sort of optical illusion whereby you couldn't see the foaming breakers crashing below on the rocks. If a guy wasn't paying attention, it would be way too easy to just stroll off the edge into oblivion.

*Hey . . .*

Might he just have saved Godfrey's life? Maybe it had been something as simple as that. Maybe Godfrey had been walking along here and had slipped in the mud on the bluff's rim?

Man, why hadn't he considered the possibility before? The mere fact that he had altered the course of Godfrey's life might mean that he had already altered the course of Godfrey's death. After all, it was reasonable. Who knew? He could have unwittingly changed Godfrey's destiny any number of times in the last few weeks, in any number of ways. Perhaps Godfrey's fate had already been altered. Perhaps he wasn't going to die after all.

*Whoa.*

Nick stopped in midstride, Beverly's deathbed words

ringing through his head: *"We cannot triumph over time or fate."*

Had the message been directed to him? Had she been trying to tell him something?

Cocksure, never-say-die daCosta would have a helluva time accepting that. Nick didn't know if he could. How could he reconcile himself to the fact that he couldn't win? That he couldn't outsmart the fates?

He was still debating the question when he strolled into the parlor at home and found Anna sitting in her favorite chair, her Bible open in her lap. She glanced up as he entered and Nick's heart did a backflip in his chest. Her bashful smile and bright blush made her look softer, younger, happier. Beautiful.

*Whatever happens,* Nick vowed, *I swear on all I hold holy that I will do what is best for Anna.*

"Mornin', sweetheart," he drawled, walking across the room to her.

"G-good morning."

Considering her upturned face an invitation, Nick leaned over and bestowed on her a rousing, soul-stirring, groin-tightening kiss. She initially answered him, before pulling away with a low, embarrassed murmur.

"Really," she mumbled, "Mara might come in. . . ."

Grinning from ear to ear, Nick dropped to a crouch beside her chair.

"So did you wake up wondering if last night had been a dream?"

"Gracious, I—"

Anna flushed a perfect scarlet, unable to decide what to do with her hands. They fluttered over the Bible, then brushed across her hair, then slid along the chair's arms. Nick wanted nothing more than to take her upstairs and show her how to put those hands to good use.

Red-cheeked, she glanced to the open doorway. "It was lovely," she whispered.

Nick chuckled. "Yes, it was . . . lovely. But actually I

was referring to our conversation. About me coming from the year 1997 and all that other mind-tripping stuff."

"Oh." In the light of early afternoon, her eyes shone a deep, deep blue that reminded Nick of a sapphire pin his Nona used to wear.

"I must admit," Anna said, "that I continue to wonder how such a thing is possible."

He indicated the Bible. "Were you looking for answers in there?"

"Yes. I was."

Her calm, unwavering faith amazed him. Especially since, up until now, Anna's lot in life had pretty much stunk to high heaven.

"Find anything useful?" he asked.

She tipped her head to the side, her dark blond curls sliding to one shoulder. He noticed that she wasn't wearing one of those hideous little white caps that reminded him of Granny from *The Beverly Hillbillies*.

"Exodus 20:14 had been giving me cause for concern," she said soberly.

Nick frowned. His scripture was rusty, but even he knew Exodus 20 listed the Ten Commandments. *Craven images, coveting . . .*

"Thou shall not commit adultery."

"Oh." Then he caught her drift. *"O-h-h.* Christ, Anna, you don't think that you've sinned because—I mean, jeez, I'm as good as your husband. That is, I'm a thousand times better than that worthless pile of sh—" He caught himself. "Okay then, technically speaking, if I'm not your husband, who the heck is?"

A mischievous smile dimpled her mouth.

And Nick realized that he'd been had. "My God, you're putting one over on me, aren't you, you little tease?"

Anna pressed her lips together. To keep from laughing at him, he guessed.

"All right, Jezebel, come here."

Nick pulled her to her feet, cupping her buttocks and

grinding his hips against hers. Her eyes danced with laughter and he couldn't resist. He kissed her long and deep, tasting strawberry jam on her tongue, holding her to him as if he would never let her go. As if their days together were not already numbered.

"My," she breathed when he finally let her up for air.

"My," he agreed, waggling his eyebrows.

She gave him a look from under her lashes, one part coy, one part reprimand.

Nick laughed and pulled her down with him onto the sofa so that she was sitting upon his lap.

"So," he said, "aside from doubting whether or not you're a loose woman, was there anything else you wanted to discuss? About our conversation last night?"

Anna thumbed her lower lip. Nick found the gesture wildly distracting.

"I imagine, like you, I'm curious as to how the exchange took place," she said. "It does seem incredible, doesn't it? I should never have believed it possible if I weren't actually living it."

"Yeah, me, neither. You couldn't have known what you were getting into when you saved my life that night, could you, darling?"

"About that night." Anna's forehead wrinkled. "There is something I've often wondered about. . . ."

"Let 'er rip," Nick invited.

"When you were unconscious, you called out for someone. Someone named Chris."

Nick's gut spasmed. *It still hurt.*

"I did, huh? Well, remember how I told you that I was a police officer? Well, cops often work in pairs and my partner, Chris, and I were really good friends. We were close."

Anna snuggled in his arms. "I'd like to see this future of yours, Nick. It sounds so interesting."

"It is interesting, but you know what? I used to think it was worlds apart from this time and this place. But, it's not. People have always been pretty much the same through history. There are the good ones, the rotten ones." He slid his palm up to cup her breast. "And, let's not forget, the sexy ones."

Anna sputtered and pushed herself from his lap. "You are incorrigible," she laughingly chided as she adjusted the front of her dress.

Nick gave her a lascivious wink. "Don't you mean 'insatiable'?"

Blushing, Anna stepped over to the sideboard where she picked up a folded paper.

"While you were out, you incorrigible, insatiable man, a letter came. From Godfrey's London solicitors." She handed it to him. "Don't you think it's curious? Yesterday I would have handed this to you without a qualm. Today . . . I wonder if I should."

He took the letter, turning it over in his hands. "Thanks."

For some reason, Nick found himself hesitant to open it in front of her.

Anna must have sensed his reluctance, for she watched him a moment then announced with false briskness, "You know, I think I'll have a look at Osiris. James says that he's been off his feed the last day or so. He claims that the horse is grieving for Beverly and it's nothing to fret over, but I think I'll check on him nonetheless."

She started for the door.

"Would you like to take a walk later?" Nick asked.

Her smile was magical. "I would like that very much."

The sound of the front door closing caused Nick to blink, then laugh at himself. He'd been in a daze, like some lovestruck kid. *You got it bad, daCosta. Real bad.*

He flopped down on the sofa and opened the letter, groaning as he saw the lines and lines of illegible handwriting filling the page. Damn, he'd have a fullblown headache before he was done reading this chicken scratch. He attacked the first line.

" 'Delighted to hear from you—' " Nick sighed. "Yeah, yeah, let's cut to the chase, shall we?"

He read on. As he already knew, Godfrey's uncle, Lord Barnes, had agreed to revise his will leaving all of his dough to Godfrey, his closest living male relation.

"Right," Nick said. "Only he's living in the twentieth century."

Then the letter went on to detail in a half-dozen sentences Lord Barnes's incomparable generosity and the depth of his regard for his nephew. . . .

"Blah, blah, blah. Yeah, okay, here we get to the heart of it. 'The sole provision—' "

He must have been confused by the legalese. Nick backed up and reread the last paragraph. That's what it said all right.

According to the offices of Modell and Crawton, Godfrey could only inherit after he produced an heir. No heir, no money.

"This can't be right. There must be some kind of mistake."

Mr. Heyer had plainly stated that Anna could not bear children after her miscarriage. So how in the hell did Godfrey expect to meet the stipulations of his uncle's bequest?

Pain spiked through Nick's temple, and he realized that he had his jaw clenched like a vise. He told himself to relax, but then his legs began to shake. And his arms. The letter drifted from his fingers.

*Damn!*

The next moment he was flat on his back on the floor.

Godfrey could tell that he was close this time. Very close. He recognized the acanthus-leaf medallion at the center of the parlor's ceiling; felt the plushness of the room's Oriental carpet beneath his back. *His* back. Not the borrowed broken one he'd been saddled with this past month or longer. His back.

Yes, he was close. Tantalizingly close. This time all his senses were involved. He could smell the fire's smoky fragrance, and the hint of saltwater in the air. Hunger gnawed gently at his stomach—his stomach, not Nick's.

For weeks and weeks now, Godfrey had been waiting for this opportunity, desperately hoping to precipitate one of the episodes that brought the two of them together in this incomprehensible manner. But without being able to identify the catalyst to the seizures, or to distinguish a pattern to their frequency, Godfrey had been forced to wait. To wait until the window of opportunity opened to him yet once again.

*So you fancy yourself in love with her, do you?*

Godfrey's derision skated through Nick's consciousness as easily as it had through his own. This time there seemed to be fewer barriers between them, the mingling of thought and emotion almost without any boundaries or limits.

*Bedded her yet, colonial? Have you been between my devout wife's skirts yet? Taken your pleasure in her, plowed her till she wept?*

Godfrey searched Nick's mind for the answer, but could not find it. Apparently there remained a few barriers after all.

Every vile oath, every vulgar epithet emanated from Nick's thoughts, his enmity powerful and focused. Yet not so powerful that Godfrey could not shunt it aside, dismiss it with ease. Of course, Nick loathed him. As he loathed the coarse American. Loathed him for masterminding this harrowing trip into the world's future.

He was convinced that Nick held the key to this exchange, that he alone was responsible for Godfrey's plight. Responsible for the torture he had suffered at the hands of the white coats.

But Nick was not thinking of the future, Godfrey saw. His thoughts were elsewhere.

*Ah, you've learned of the inheritance, I see. What a pity. I had hoped that you would not.*

*How?* The question flowed from one mind to the next.

*How did you plan to cough up an heir for your uncle after what you did to Anna?*

No conscious answer was necessary. Nick had only to enter Godfrey's thoughts to locate the response.

The milksop American was stunned.

*You heartless butcher! I swear I'll kill you.*

Indifferent to the other man's rage, Godfrey concentrated on the parlor's familiar landmarks. Or what he could see of them while lying flat on his back on the floor.

*Murder your own wife? Did you really think you could get away with it? Like you got away with beating her?*

*She is of no further use to me.*

*Because of you. Because you almost killed her.*

*An accident.* Godfrey gave a mental shrug. *Naturally, I was not pleased that she lost the child.*

*Then when you learned she was barren—*

Bored, Godfrey did not choose to focus on the plans he'd made for his wife, but Nick reached into Godfrey's psyche and found what he was looking for.

*There is a young woman in London you plan to marry. . . . My God, that's the reason you were riding back to Cliff House in the dead of night. To murder Anna!*

The American was distracted. Godfrey decided to make his move, to seize his chance. His chance to reclaim his body. For, if he did not attempt it now, who knew when next he might have another opportunity? When next they might again come together like this?

*No!* Nick's will blocked him. *There is no way in hell I'm letting you anywhere near Anna again.*

*Stop me,* Godfrey challenged.

Godfrey held the upper hand. With nothing else to think of these past weeks, he'd fixed his energies on but one goal: returning to his body. By strength of will, he drove them back, drove their souls back into the whiteness. Into the void between time and space.

Nick fought him, but Godfrey was not going to relent.

He battled on. Their spirits careened through the white emptiness and it was like the first time their souls had switched—only in reverse. Godfrey could see the vague outline of the rocks where he had fallen, hear the retreating hoofbeats of his fleeing horse. At the same time, he saw through Nick's eyes the strange metal carriage bursting into flames, a grave marker crushed into rubble. And beside the fiery debris stood another grave marker. It read: Anna Woodbaine 1788–1810.

*No-o-o-o!*

# *Chapter* 24

"GEORGE, YOU SILLY thing. What are you doing out here in the cold?"

Anna scooped the big, orange cat off the frost-covered porch and carried him back into the house.

"Were you looking for Auntie, George? Osiris misses her, too. He's not eating." She scratched the cat's round stomach. "But that's not a problem for you, is it, my furry friend?"

The cat purred and Anna smiled, looking up the staircase toward her aunt's chambers. It was funny, but, though she missed her very much, Anna didn't feel as if Beverly were truly gone. So much of her remained. Like the scent of her lavender water haunting the rooms. Like her beloved kittens frolicking from one end of the house to the next. In many ways Anna felt that Aunt Beverly was still with them. That the essence of her had not yet left Cliff House.

Anna put George down and hung up her cape in the foyer. Wherever Auntie was, she had to be pleased. Pleased to see that Nick and Anna had finally overcome their secrets—most of them, at least—and found happiness.

Anna shook the foggy dampness from her hair. But how, she wondered for the hundredth time, had Aunt Beverly recognized that Nick was not Godfrey? It would forever remain a mystery. Perhaps as great a mystery as how Nick came to be in Godfrey's body.

George meowed plaintively from down the hall.

"Me-o-oww," he whined again, his call loud enough to echo through the lower part of the house.

"Goodness," Anna muttered. "Such a fuss you're making, George."

She followed his cry into the parlor.

Terror seized her by the throat.

"Nick!"

She rushed over to where he lay as stiff as a corpse between the sofa and the sofa table. She had to kneel at his head for she didn't dare move him or try to wedge herself in between the furniture on either side. After what he had told her last night, Anna didn't think she ought to touch him. In reality, she was afraid to. Afraid that somehow she might come into contact with Godfrey.

Staring down at his rigid yet trembling body, Anna knew a frustration so acute it was unbearable. Dear Lord, if only she knew how to help him; if only she understood more of what Nick was experiencing. She suspected that these episodes could hardly be pleasant for him if he were somehow engaged with Godfrey's spirit. What caused these seizures? And more important, how might they put an end to them?

Anna bit at her knuckles as a dreadful thought came to her, further whetting her fears. *Could these attacks be . . . life-threatening?*

She scanned the length of him, looking for signs of injury. Her frantic gaze landed on a piece of paper lying beside the table's lion-claw foot. The letter from Godfrey's solicitors. She hesitated, aware that Nick had been reluctant to share its contents with her. It was not right to read his correspondence without his permission. But, an inner voice argued, might something in the letter have triggered his seizure? Some unhappy tidings, perhaps?

Her fingers quivering, Anna reached out and picked up the letter. With one eye on Nick and the other on the parchment, she scanned the lines. When she was done, she feared that she might become sick to her stomach.

She hadn't told Nick. He didn't know the painful secret she'd kept close to her heart. He didn't know that she would never be able to give him a child.

"Oh, dear God."

She ought to have told him yesterday, but she hadn't been ready. Last night she had gone as far as she could, exposed herself as much as she was able. Though their lovemaking had been exquisite, it had taken a leap of faith for Anna to open herself even that much, to make herself vulnerable again. Vulnerable to a man.

For the same reason, she had held back from telling Nick that she loved him. Again, she knew that she should have told him—she knew that he was hoping to hear the words from her. But after four years as Godfrey's wife, it was not so easy to throw off all of her defenses. Last night she had not revealed her love for Nick because she was afraid. Afraid of leaving herself open to hurt.

Anna glanced again at the letter, realizing that this could hurt her. Hurt her in more ways than one. In truth, it already had done damage by giving rise to insidious suspicions: *Had Nick known about the inheritance?* The wording of the solicitor's letter suggested that he had. That the letter he had posted from Aylesdown had been a request for clarification of Lord Barnes's terms.

Is that the reason Nick had taken her to bed last night? Had he hoped to get her with child so that he might inherit the fortune?

Anna squeezed her eyes shut, her head beginning to throb with tension. She couldn't allow herself to think along those lines. She couldn't.

Yet, even if Nick's intentions had been honest and honorable—even if he did love her—might he not resent her once he learned the truth? How would he feel when he realized that he would never be able to inherit Lord Barnes's riches because she could never fulfill her part?

Anna pressed her palms into her temples until her wrists ached. She was driving herself mad with this endless circle of suspicions and doubts. Completely mad.

Nick loved her. He did. Why could she not accept that and let go of her fears once and for all?

*Trust,* her aunt had counseled her.

"Oh, Auntie," she breathed. "I am trying to trust him. I truly am."

"No-o-o-o!"

Nick's roar set Anna back on her heels, as his body suddenly came to life. His arms flailed about, one cracking against the side of the sofa table with bruising impact. His chest heaved up and down like a bellows, his gasps soughing through the room, loud and harsh.

Anna held her breath.

She bent forward, looking upside down into his face.

"Anna?"

Were those tears glistening in his eyes?

"Oh, jeez, Anna." He reached up and pulled her down to him, cradling his cheek against hers. His beard's stubble grated against her skin, but she did not pull away. Instincts alone conveyed to her the depth of his need. The need simply to be held.

"Are you all right?"

Slowly Nick released her.

"Yeah," he answered, though his voice sounded painfully gruff.

They both sat up on the carpet, Anna unsettled by Nick's pallor.

"What happened?"

He leaned against the sofa, and drew one knee up close to his body. He stared down at the floor as he said, "Another seizure."

"Do you know what caused it?"

His head jerked from side to side. "I never do."

"Was"—she could scarcely force out his name—"Godfrey there?"

Nick lifted his head, his eyes wet and glowing. Glowing with a love that made Anna ask herself how she ever could have doubted him. How she ever could have believed this man to be Godfrey.

"Yeah," Nick rasped. "He was there."

"Did . . . did you learn anything?"

"I— No, not really." He rubbed his hand across his face.

"Not really?" she pressed.

"Well." Nick shrugged. "He sure is one angry S.O.B. But that's pretty much it."

Anna swallowed. "Do you think that you're always going to have these seizures, Nick? Might we stop them?"

"Don't worry about it, Anna. Please? They don't really bother me. They're just like unanticipated naps."

He grinned in that charming, lopsided way that was wholly his. Godfrey had never smiled like that.

Anna was prepared to dispute his definition of a nap when a large blur of orange leaped between them and vaulted into Nick's lap with a sonorous purr.

"Ooph," Nick said, puffing out his breath. "George, old fella, you got to start thinking about a diet. You could have emasculated me, you big furball."

Anna started to smile—

Before Nick's words reminded her of the letter.

*Trust,* she told herself.

"Nick."

"Mm-hmm?"

"I am ashamed to tell you—I know that I shouldn't have—but when I walked into the parlor and found you on the floor and then I saw the solicitors' letter laying beside you . . ."

He glanced up from stroking George's ears. "You read the letter?"

Anna nodded.

"So I guess you didn't know about the inheritance?"

"No."

"What do you think about it?"

*Oh, no.* In that moment Anna felt she would have paid any price, sold her very soul, not to have to reveal her secret. Her loss.

She bowed her head, twining her fingers together. "Nick," she whispered. "I can't."

He tilted toward her. "Can't what?"

"I-I can't help you with . . . that." She gestured feebly to the letter.

"Wha—? Oh, Anna." His arms closed around her and drew her against his chest with infinite tenderness. "Anna, sweetheart, I know," he murmured. "Mr. Heyer told me."

Relief and shock warred within her. A lump rose in her throat.

"You don't feel . . . cheated.?"

"Cheated?" Nick squeezed her so tight her ribs ached. "Are you kidding me? Against all odds, I found *you*, Anna. Found you when logic would have said I never, ever could. For God's sake, I don't feel cheated at all. I feel like I've been blessed."

Tears stung at her eyes and she gathered a fistful of his shirt into her fingers as if she would never let him go.

"If anyone has the right to feel cheated, it's you, Anna." His voice gentled, sounding almost like George's comforting purr. "You really wanted a baby, didn't you?"

Anna buried her face into his front, the heartache as fresh as it had been a year ago.

"So much," she confessed.

"Lord, I wish I could give you a baby, Anna." He caressed her hair. "I wish I had the power to make it all right for you again."

She closed her eyes and let the tears come. And amazingly, her loss seemed a little less painful than it had a moment earlier.

"You do make it better, Nick. Just by being here with me, you make it better."

Nick was dying inside. For Anna's sake, he put a good face on it, but the next hour proved to be pure, unmitigated torture.

After Anna dried her tears, she suggested they take that walk they had talked about. Nick, though coming apart at the emotional seams, could deny her nothing. Hand in hand, they strolled along the cliffside trail, the day more beautiful than any Nick had ever seen. The irony of it all hit him square between the eyes.

As they walked, Anna asked about the future, about his life in particular, his family and friends. Nick teased and joked and smiled, putting on an Oscar-caliber performance. Yet all the while he could think only of how the clues had finally clicked together. Clicked together with the sound of a death knell.

Of course, it all made sense now. The pieces of the puzzle had combined to form a pretty clear picture of how it must have played out. The first go-around, that is.

After Anna's miscarriage, Godfrey had left for London, not knowing if his wife would live or die, but knowing that she could not bear children. In London he had either run into or sought out his distant relative, Lord Barnes. As his debts piled higher and higher—probably too high for Lady Robeson to take care of—Godfrey had cozied up to Barnes, wheedling himself into his uncle's good graces. When Barnes had started making noises about an heir, Godfrey had put together a plan. He'd lined up some sweet little London miss to drag to the altar the minute he'd rid himself of Anna. Murder had been his goal that night he'd raced back to Cliff House—Anna's murder.

But something must have gone wrong. Godfrey and Anna had both died. Probably during the murder attempt, Nick guessed, but he couldn't be certain. The truth of the matter he would never know.

Nor, God willing, would Anna.

With the sun glinting off her gold-brown hair, Anna walked at his side, completely unaware of the chaos running rampant through his soul. She had no idea of the bullet Nick had dodged that afternoon. No idea of how close Nick had come to losing his battle with Godfrey. A few seconds more and Godfrey would have overpowered him, would have forced the exchange of bodies. Only the shocking vision of Anna's headstone had spurred Nick on, had given him the strength to claw his way back to 1810.

But when might Godfrey try again? During their "mind-meld," as Nick mentally labeled it, he had learned that Godfrey was scheduled to be released from the London hospital any day now. What was Woodbaine's plan? From what Nick could tell, Godfrey was neither curious nor eager to explore the world of 1997. He wanted back. Back to his handsome face and back to his uncle's wealth. Godfrey was not going to give up until he had reclaimed his body. And Nick feared that he could not hold him off forever.

Nick gazed across the windswept fields and white-peaked waves, remembering when all of this had been no more than a dream. Well, he'd had his dream . . . and more. Now, it was time to wake up.

"Anna, I was thinking I'd make a quick trip into town before it got dark. Do you mind?"

She tilted her face up to him, and Nick put every detail to memory. The curve of her jaw, the arch of her eyebrow.

"No, of course, I don't mind. You will be home in time for dinner though?"

"Absolutely, positively," he promised, relieved that she didn't need to ask his reasons for going. That she, at last, had begun to trust him.

He left Anna on the porch with a sizzling kiss, one that left them both breathless and giddy. And wanting more.

Twenty minutes later Nick was pulling up in front of Aylesdown's tidy vicarage. He couldn't rightly say what had brought him, but, then again, he didn't know where else to turn. He was facing a major crisis point in his life. In his life, Anna's and Godfrey's.

He banged on the door with the side of his fist. Hancock answered his knock, recoiling slightly when he recognized his visitor.

"Lord Woodbaine. What a . . . pleasant surprise."

"Sorry to drop in uninvited, Reverend, but if you've got a minute—"

The vicar's blond brows formed one large yellow caterpillar across his forehead. "Is all well at Cliff House?"

Nick gave him a listless grin. "Just peachy. In fact, why don't you stop by and see Anna soon? It'll put your mind at ease."

"Yes, I will." He then seemed to recall why Nick was standing there. "Please. Come in."

"May I offer you a libation?" the vicar asked as they settled themselves in the parlor.

"No. Thanks." Nick glanced around at the blue-and-gold decor, thinking the room was a *Cal* fan's fantasy. It only lacked a golden bear and a football poster or two. "Actually, Reverend, I'm here for a little spiritual advice."

If the vicar hadn't already been sitting, he would have dropped to the floor like a lead sinker.

"S-spiritual advice? Why, that's wonderful."

*Uh-huh,* Nick thought wryly. "I'd like to talk to you about the soul. Get your interpretation."

Hancock blinked about six times in a row. "Yes, well. Ahem. Let us see what our scripture says." The clergyman reached for his Bible sitting on the side table. He spent a few seconds thumbing back and forth through its pages. "Now, what was it you specifically wished to discuss, my lord?"

Nick leaned forward in his chair, lacing his fingers together. "Well, I'd like to hear what you have to say about souls and spirits. About their immortality."

The vicar perked up. "Ah,yes. The word of God clearly tells us that He shall preserve our souls. Psalms 121."

"Uh-huh." Nick tapped his foot in a fanning motion. "But does He preserve it the same wherever it goes? What I'm trying to pin down is whether my spirit is mine no matter where it ends up. . . . For example, would you say that the soul is separate from the body?"

"Hmm. 'The Invocation' does state that we offer 'our selves, our souls and bodies' to the Lord. One could argue that each of those entities is distinct and separate from the other."

"Yeah, I suppose one could." Nick twiddled his thumbs, first forward then backward. "Tell me, do you think there is a logic to all this? A reason things happen when they do, why they do?"

Hancock nodded earnestly. " 'To every thing there is a season, and a time to every purpose under the heaven,' " he quoted.

"Yeah," Nick muttered. "The Byrds. I know that one."

"I beg your pardon?"

Nick shrugged, uncertain as to whether he'd found the answers he was searching for. Granted, the vicar did seem to be giving it his best shot. He probably viewed this as an opportunity of a lifetime—the chance to save Godfrey Woodbaine's unsalvageable soul.

"Can I ask you something?" Nick said.

"Please. I am at your complete disposal."

"Why didn't you help Anna when you knew that I was abusing her?"

The Bible landed on the floor with a *thud*. The vicar blanched.

"Oh, hey, I don't mean to come down on you," Nick explained. "I'm just curious. It's obvious that your calling is important to you, that you're sincere in your mission. I'm just wondering why you didn't do anything to help her?"

Mr. Hancock went from a pasty white to a bright tomato-red, his ears so crimson they looked as if they might spontaneously combust. Suddenly Nick was reminded of just how young the clergyman was. He probably hadn't even seen twenty-five yet. And Nick wasn't really being fair to him, was he? He could hardly expect Hancock to have all the answers when, at thirty-two, Nick was still figuring them out himself.

Like tolerance. The Nick who'd dropped into Dover six weeks ago wouldn't have been able to appreciate Hancock's youth, to cut the guy a break. That Nick had only seen the world as black and white, people as either good or bad. Today Nick was able to appreciate the middle ground, to understand that life also came in shades of gray.

"Look, I'm sorry," Nick said. "I wasn't trying to put you down—"

"I didn't know how to help her."

The whispered confession appeared to catch them both off guard. The clergyman looked stricken, as if the admission had cost him emotionally. Nick felt ashamed of himself, wishing that he'd not put the young vicar on the spot.

"Hey, who am I, of all people, to judge *you*?" Nick argued. "You've always been there for Anna and I am grateful for that. In fact, I'd like to ask a favor of you if I can."

"Yes, of course." Mr. Hancock's voice wobbled.

"If something were to . . . happen to me, would you give me your word that you'll take care of Anna?"

The vicar's eyes clouded with concern. "Are you—"

"No. No questions," Nick interrupted. "I just want you to promise me you'll take care of her. No matter what."

Hancock picked up his Bible and spread his palm across its leather cover. "You have my solemn word, Lord Woodbaine."

"Thanks." Nick sighed. "Thanks a lot. You know, since Bev died, Anna doesn't have any other family. I just need to know that someone will be looking out for her if, uh, something were to happen."

"Is there . . . is there anything more you wished to share?"

"No, I—" Nick winced as a stabbing pain lanced through his temple. "I—" Another pain. His legs went stiff.

*Oh, God, not again.*

The next minute Nick was in the throes of his second seizure that day.

# *Chapter* 25

"NICK, MARA ASKED if you enjoyed your dinner?" Anna repeated.

"Wha—?" Nick snapped out of his glassy-eyed reverie and sent a surprised look to the servant standing at his elbow—as if he hadn't noticed her there. "Oh. It was delicious, Mara. Great eats."

The maid dimpled and curtsied. "Thank you, m'lord." She cleared the plates and retreated to the kitchen.

"Nick, is anything troubling you? You've been rather distracted since returning from town."

"Have I?" He leaned across the table and made a show of slowly licking his lips. "I guess I must be eager to get upstairs."

Anna lowered her gaze, surprised to recognize that she, too, was eager. Last night had introduced her to a whole new world of intoxicating sensations. Sensations she looked forward to exploring again this evening.

She smoothed her skirts. "Well. Perhaps it isn't too early to retire. . . ."

Nick didn't need any more encouragement. In the flash

of an eye he had her by the hand and they were tripping their way upstairs.

"I shudder to contemplate what Mara must think of us." Anna giggled as Nick pushed open the door to her bedroom.

"Odds are she's thinking that we're lucky to be so desperately in love," Nick countered with a smile.

But as soon as he spoke, the statement seemed to hang in the air between them like an invisible curtain. Anna still had not said that she loved him. And judging by Nick's expression, he was poignantly aware of her omission.

"Nick, I—"

He didn't let her finish. His mouth swooped down upon hers, taking the truth from her lips if she couldn't give him the words. She opened to him, reveling in his sweet moistness, redolent of grapey-tart claret. He bent her back over his arm and she slipped her hands into his hair.

"Oh, Anna."

"Nick," she sighed into his mouth.

His tongue possessed her, ravished her whole while they yet stood before the fireplace, fully clothed. She clung to him, elated. Alive.

His hands gently squeezed her breasts through her dress, and it was both ecstasy and torment. She needed his flesh against her flesh, needed his warmth. She fumbled at the buttons of her dress, shoving aside her chemise, opening the way to him, silently imploring him to touch her.

He did. He touched her. He loved her. He worshipped her breasts with his fingers and his mouth until she was making soft sounds deep in her throat, her head thrown back, her knees weakening beneath her.

"Nick."

She must have started to fall, for he half carried her over to the bed. She pulled him down on top of her, a now familiar heat throbbing between her thighs, demanding relief.

"Oh, don't stop," she begged in a whisper. "Please don't stop kissing me."

He answered her with a throaty growl, his tongue leading her in a rhythm that left her swollen and tight and wanting. An urgency overtook them both. Anna tore at his buttons and tugged at his trousers. He shoved up her skirts, his fingers parting her delicate folds. She gasped to feel her dampness wet his hand.

"Nick," she pleaded. She'd had her taste of heaven, and she could not wait another second to experience it again. She needed the completion. She needed it now.

He came into her with a thrust that nearly lifted her off the bed. She cried out, twisting her hips, trying to bring him still closer, still deeper inside her. He took her as she yearned to be taken, with the same fervency, the same desperation that clawed inside her.

Their lovemaking was raw and frenzied and ever so sweet. Anna reached her climax with a swiftness that was unexpected. It ripped through her, up through her abdomen and into her throat. Nick caught her scream with his mouth and she bucked beneath him like a wild creature, the magnitude of her release pushing her to the edge of a faint. Nick groaned and pumped one last time into her. Exhausted, they both collapsed back onto the mattress.

Anna was just drifting off to sleep when she murmured against Nick's shoulder, "I love you, too."

She awoke in the middle of the night. Nick was tenderly stripping her clothes from her. This time, he made love to her with a maddening slowness, a gentleness that brought tears to her eyes. She climaxed twice before he took his release. Then he pulled her back against his stomach, and cradled her against his body.

"Never forget that I love you, Anna," he whispered against her hair. "My love for you is timeless, endless. Forever."

She snuggled against him, too exhausted, too happy to speak.

She was not certain what awoke her next—a noise, the faint stirrings of dawn, or the absence of Nick's warmth by her side. She burrowed into the pillows, feeling her muscles pull taut.

"Mmm," she groaned. To think that all these years, she had not known such pleasure existed.

She flipped onto her side, opening one eye to peek around the shadowed room. "Nick?"

The silence sent a sudden uneasiness wafting through her.

"Nick?" she called again in a louder voice, pushing herself up against the pillows.

No answer.

On impulse, she shoved aside the tangled coverlet and walked to the window. The cold plucked goose bumps from her flesh. She yanked aside the curtains, almost tearing the aged fabric from the rods.

There he was, his figure outlined against the mauve-tinged gray of daybreak. Fog rolled across the Channel in thick white waves lurking just off-shore.

Frowning, Anna pushed her hair back, blinking sleep from her eyes. Where was he going with such a purposeful stride? Apprehension rippled through her, though she had no apparent reason to feel anxious. Why should she? Nick was taking an early-morning stroll. That was scarcely cause for alarm. They both walked the trails almost daily, Nick often choosing to run along the path for exercise.

*Nonetheless* . . .

Anna whirled away from the window and ran to the wardrobe. She grabbed an old chemise and the first gown she happened to touch. Dragging on the chemise, she muttered irritably beneath her breath as her fingers fumbled with the gown's buttons.

What was wrong with her? Her stomach churned. Her unreasonable anxiety mounted. She did not even bother struggling into stockings, merely shoving her bare feet into her finest pair of leather half-boots. Her hair swung past her shoulders, but she left it loose.

She hurried down the stairs. The house was still. Mara

must not yet have risen. Snatching her cape from the foyer hook, Anna quietly pulled the front door closed. The fog had brought in a piercing breeze that stung her eyes and nose and lips with its December cold. She swung her cloak across her shoulders and pulled the hood around her face.

She headed down the trail. Her sense of urgency increased. Where was Nick? And why was it so important that she find him?

Along the ranging coastline, the fog had begun to creep over the cliffs, spilling onto the fields like white tulle. Anna picked up her skirts and broke into a trot. The penetrating wind chilled the length of her bare legs, as her boots slapped against her ankles. How, she wondered, had Nick outdistanced her so quickly?

With one hand holding up her skirts, the other keeping her wind-tossed hair from her face, Anna jogged along the trail. Her pulse pounded.

At last she spotted Nick off the trail a few hundred yards ahead of her. She slowed to a walk, gasping for breath. Her relief, however, was short-lived.

"What is he doing?"

He faced the eastern horizon where the sun rose like a giant yellow sphere above the ocean and the advancing fog. Anna narrowed her eyes. Wasn't he standing dangerously close to the edge of the cliff?

With his back to her he could not see her approaching from the distance. She would have called out to him, but she knew her voice would be lost in the moaning wind.

Anna judged that she was perhaps two hundred yards away when Nick suddenly went stiff, his arms stretching out at his sides. His silhouette shook like a leaf.

"No," she whispered. "No."

She hauled her skirts practically up to her waist and sprinted for him.

Nick was resigned. He knew what he had to do.

Twice yesterday, Godfrey had come within mere seconds

of repossessing his body. The second incident, at the vicar's house, had been even more blood-chilling than the earlier episode at Cliff House. Nick wasn't sure what had saved him that second time, but he suspected it had been when the vicar had taken hold of his hand. Miraculously the clergyman's touch had helped pull Nick back from the brink. Back from the future.

He'd woken in a cold sweat on Hancock's parlor floor, the young reverend clasping his hand. Nick—not wanting to open that particular can of worms—hadn't shared the real meaning of the seizures. He'd dismissed the attack as no big deal, and the vicar had bought Nick's explanation that the seizures were but aftereffects of his head injury.

But the episode at the vicarage had sealed Nick's decision. It was the final straw.

As it was, Nick had taken a huge risk stealing one more night with Anna. What if he'd suffered another seizure during the night? What if Godfrey had suddenly rematerialized in Anna's arms?

Nick shook his head. He'd been damned lucky, that's for sure. At least, he and Anna had been able to share one last night together. One last perfect night.

But Nick knew he could only push his luck so far.

If he were to delay, to let Godfrey reclaim his body, it would be like signing Anna's death warrant. Godfrey would kill her. And only Nick could prevent it.

He was going to have to kill Godfrey first. Or, that is, kill . . . Godfrey's body.

Nick gazed down at the rocks below, at the punishing surf battering the snow-white cliffs.

Anna, please God, would think it an accident. She would be devastated, his death following right on the heels of Beverly's. But better she believe that he had slipped from the bluffs than know that he'd taken his own life.

It was a gamble, no question. Already fate was working against him, since history had shown that Anna was destined to die in less than three weeks. But this was Nick's

only chance to save her. To save her before Godfrey returned.

The wind whipped at his hair and Nick let it lash into his
eyes. He clutched the gold pocket watch in his fingers and
said a silent prayer. Someone's soul would die in the next
minute. It might be his. Or it might be Godfrey's. But either
way, Anna should live.

Nick took a deep breath. Then he felt it. The stinging
through his temples, the stiffening of his limbs.

*Damn. Not now.*

Gritting his teeth, Nick fought desperately to lurch forward, but Godfrey entered into him and refused to let him
move. He had read Nick's motives.

*Only a few steps . . .*

*Do you honestly believe I will allow you to do this?*

Nick shut out the other man's thoughts, concentrating
only on the sound of the thundering breakers. If he could
manage to stay on his feet—

*Fool! Your plan will not work.*

*It must.*

Nick fought with everything he had, every bit of himself.
But like a puppet on a string, he was powerless to com-
mand his movements. But if he couldn't . . . neither could
Godfrey.

They vied for control, Nick laboring to dive forward,
Godfrey struggling to pull him back. Two men trapped in a
single body, engaged in a bizarre stalemate of corporeal
possession.

In their place of heightened awareness, Nick noticed how
the air smelled saltier, the wind bit with greater chill. It was
as if they were warriors forever suspended in time.

Then Nick's legs started to buckle.

*No, damn it. No.*

"Nick!"

Anna's frantic cry somehow penetrated his consciousness. Godfrey, taking advantage of Nick's momentary mental lapse, succeeded in turning him back a step.

Nick made out a blurry image of Anna racing toward him, her dark blond hair flying behind her like a banner.

*Go back!*

But, of course, he could not put voice to the words.

Her hands clutched at both his arms. "Nick, can you hear me?" she shouted. "You're too close to the edge."

Godfrey seized the moment and attacked with a burst of will, driving Nick perilously close to oblivion, to the white void that lay between their worlds. Nick knew that Anna was screaming, tugging at him with all her strength, yet he could neither hear nor feel her. He had to maintain his complete focus on keeping Godfrey away.

Nick felt Godfrey jerk his body to the side, then suddenly whirl him around in the other direction. He floundered, Anna clinging to him. His footing slipped. The earth began to give way.

*Anna!* his mind cried out in warning. But she would not release him.

Weightlessness.

An echoing cry.

They spun in the void. Three souls. Two bodies.

The rocks rose up to meet them with deadly force.

A flash of pain.

It was over.

Across the fields a lone horseman bowed his blond head, shocked numb by the tragedy he had witnessed. He had come too late. Dear God, always too late.

He clasped his Bible to his chest and prayed. Prayed for the souls of Lord and Lady Woodbaine.

# *Chapter* 26

NICK FELT HIMSELF pulling away, pulling away from the earthly confines of flesh and bone. He drifted up into the air, sailing ever higher until he could gaze down upon the jagged white rocks below.

Two broken bodies washed back and forth on the tide, tossed along by the unfeeling surf. One was the body of a man, floating facedown, his arms outspread. The other was a woman, her blond hair streaming like seaweed across the surface of the blue-green water.

*Anna.*

Pain knifed through Nick as keen as if he still inhabited a body. He reached out to her, desperate to hold her in his arms one last time. But his spirit continued to rise up and away.

*Oh God.* He had to go back. He couldn't leave Anna. He couldn't abandon her this way.

Panic blinded him. Or was it panic?

Suddenly his world went black, darkness spinning around him with lightning speed.

*No,* his soul cried, *I have to go back for Anna. I won't leave you, my love. I will never leave you.*

But his spirit whirled out of control, tumbling through the afterlife, through the infinite white space that lay between time. His mournful cry echoed across the centuries: *Anna-a-a-!*

"Mr. daCosta?"

A woman's soft voice broke into his consciousness.

"Is he asleep?" a man asked.

"He wasn't a moment ago," the woman answered. "I just stepped out for a minute to see that his discharge papers were in order—"

Nick opened his eyes. A middle-aged nurse was bending over him, her Christmas-tree-shaped earrings dangling on either side of her long face. She straightened up as their gazes met.

"How are you doing, Mr. daCosta?" she asked in an English accent reminiscent of Paul McCartney's. "I thought you might have fallen asleep there."

Nick glanced to the man standing at her side, a short bald guy whom, according to his nametag, went by the name of Dr. J. P. Baker. Dr. Baker was wearing the harried expression of a very busy man.

Nick tried to open his mouth to speak and couldn't. His jaw was wired shut.

*What's going on here? What's happened to me?*

The doctor pulled up one of those rolling stools doctors always use and took a seat next to his bed.

"All right, Mr. daCosta, we're going to let those vocal cords of yours finally get some exercise." He produced a pair of tiny wire-cutters, or some instrument that looked pretty similar. "Easy now."

The doctor made a few snips, and in a matter of seconds Nick was free of the metalwork. He experimented with moving his jaw up and down.

"Do you have any discomfort?" the doctor asked.

"I-I don't think so," Nick said. Though his voice sounded strange to him. Unfamiliar.

The doctor scribbled a note on a clipboard. "I want you to pay attention to what you eat for a few weeks, all right? Try not to open your mouth wide for foods such as rolls, apples, sandwiches—that kind of thing. After not being used for such a long period, your facial ligaments could be vulnerable to strain."

Nick rubbed his hand across the side of his face. *That's right.* His jaw *had* been broken. He'd been in a car accident. It was all slowly starting to come back to him.

"What about my back?" he asked. "The ruptured disk?"

Dr. Baker looked up from his clipboard with a frown. "Didn't you and Dr. Leslie have a postoperative consultation last week?"

"I, uh—"

Nick glanced at the nurse who was surreptitiously picking something from her teeth.

"Could you go over it with me one more time?" he asked.

Baker flipped impatiently through the chart. "Well, there's not much to discuss at this point. As Dr. Leslie said, the operation was a complete success; she doesn't foresee any problems whatsoever. There was no nerve damage, no bone fragmentation. It's probably best if you refrain from contact sports just to be safe, but otherwise, your spine is as good as new."

"Wow," Nick said quietly. "That's great."

"Now about the seizures—"

Nick jerked as if stung.

"The CAT scans and MRI came back negative. The neurological report and blood tests were clear. There are no signs of subdural hematoma, brain lesions, or injury. No indication of epilepsy in the EEG. I don't know, Mr. daCosta. I understand that you've been pushing hard to be released, but I am concerned about discharging you when we haven't been able to identify the cause of the seizures."

Nick felt as if the bottom fell out of his stomach as the memories suddenly tumbled forth. *The seizures. Cliff House. Godfrey . . . Anna.*

"H-how long have I been in the hospital?"

The doctor peered down his nose at him. "You were admitted October twenty-seventh. That makes just about six weeks, doesn't it?"

Nick raised his hands and stared at them. They were his hands. His fingers. There was the scar on his pinkie he'd got carving pumpkins a few years back.

Had he only imagined it? Had it all been nothing more than a dream—an extremely vivid dream played out in his subconscious while he drifted in and out of the coma?

"But, Anna," Nick mumbled under his breath. Anna *had* been real. And the pain he felt knowing that he had lost her was certainly real. Too real, in fact. Too painful.

He looked up to find the doctor studying him through narrowed eyes.

"No," Nick said. "Six weeks is long enough. I'm ready to get out of here. I, uh, I don't think you have to worry about me having any more seizures, Dr. Baker. I think I'm done with those."

The doctor twiddled the pen in his fingers. "Well, I'm not so sure about that, Mr. daCosta, but we're not going to hold you against your will. I would like you to see your own doctor when you get home. Schedule a follow-up physical in three or four weeks. And don't forget to leave Mrs. Huddleston the name and address of your physician, so we can send a copy of your record."

"Fine. Whatever you say."

The doctor signed his name to a half-dozen papers, then handed the clipboard to the nurse. "Mrs. Huddleston will help you get your things together for discharge. Best of luck to you, Mr. daCosta. You're an amazingly fortunate man to be leaving here in one piece."

Nick nodded, though he sure as hell didn't feel lucky. And he sure didn't feel as if he were in one piece, either.

Would he ever be whole again? Not when his heart had been ripped from his chest. Pictures of Anna flashed through his mind's eye—her slender silhouette as she walked the seaside trails, her gentle hands as she soothed a frightened animal. How could she be gone? Gone forever from his life?

The doctor extended his hand and Nick shook it, though he kept his gaze averted. The backs of his eyes were starting to burn, his throat filling, as the full realization of her death set in.

"Thanks very much," Nick croaked.

"Take care."

The doctor left, and as the door closed behind him, a tissue was abruptly thrust into Nick's hand. He looked up in surprise to find Mrs. Huddleston wrinkling her nose sympathetically.

"I'm sure it's an emotional experience for you to finally get to leave hospital. I know it's been hard on you these last few weeks."

"Yeah," Nick breathed, struggling to regain his composure. "It has."

"Well, I have some clothes for you right here and after you get yourself—"

"Clothes? Is my family here?"

Her Christmas earrings swung, sparkling under the lights, as she turned to him. "You don't remember?"

"Nuh-uh."

"Your mother was here for well over a week. Stayed in your room even. Lovely woman, Theresa. Just lovely. But she had to leave when your sister developed complications late in her pregnancy."

"Sophia?" Lord, he had completely forgotten the baby was due so soon.

Mrs. Huddleston paused in her sorting of the clipboard's papers. "Yes, I do believe it was Sophia. But not to worry," she added with a smile. "Your mother has been calling in every day and your sister delivered a healthy baby girl only yesterday."

"Wow, no kidding." Nick huffed a low laugh. "That makes niece number seven. Do you know what they named her?"

"I don't remember, I'm sorry. Oh, and that Mrs. Sokolov has been calling regularly, asking after you. We really aren't allowed to give out information to anyone other than family, but I did let her know you were probably going to be released today."

Nick dropped his head into one hand and massaged his aching temples. This was too much to absorb all at once. Shirley, the investigation, his job. Man, he had a life to get back to—responsibilities, obligations. How, in God's name, was he going to survive it without Anna? How was he going to wake up every day for the rest of his life, knowing that the only woman he'd ever loved had died almost two centuries ago?

The worst of it was that he wouldn't even be able to talk about Anna to anyone, to share his precious memories. Who was going to believe him? Who was going to believe that he, Nick daCosta, had lived six weeks in another man's body in the year 1810?

Shirley would have him parked in the shrink's office faster than you could say "Looney Tunes." And his mom would probably haul in Father Flynn to perform an exorcism.

No, only Chris would have accepted the truth.

Nick watched the nurse putter around the room, gathering together the flowers, plants, and cards he'd been sent.

"So have any arrangements been made for me to get home?"

"Your mother took care of most of the details, replacing your passport and the like."

"Did she leave an airline ticket?"

Mrs. Huddleston glanced up from placing the plants in a box. "To Chicago? Not that I know of. Mrs. Sokolov seemed to think you'd be flying back to San Francisco to say good-bye to your"—she lowered her voice respectfully—"your friend."

"Chris?" Nick sat up. "Chris is still alive?"

"Oh, well, I can't be sure," the nurse said. "Mrs. Sokolov had said they expected any day now that—"

"Where's the phone?" Nick demanded. The hospital pillow fell to the floor as his bare feet hit the chilly linoleum. "I've got to get on a plane."

Fourteen hours later Nick landed at San Francisco International Airport. He felt like hell. Nothing like an interminable plane ride to give a man plenty of time to grieve. His thoughts had been consumed with Anna from the moment the jet had lifted off from Heathrow's runway.

He'd had himself a couple of drinks on the plane, which hadn't helped any. Not by a long shot. They'd only loosened him up enough to where he could more easily feel the pain of his loss.

As he waited in line to deboard the plane, Nick thought again of how fate had outsmarted him. Beverly had been right all along, hadn't she? He'd not won. He'd not beaten the odds. Godfrey and Anna had still met their destinies, probably in the exact same way they had been meant to. But that realization was of little comfort to Nick right now. Not now when his heart was bleeding like a raw, open wound.

So what was he going to do, but rub salt into that wound. Heap tragedy upon tragedy. Shirley was picking him up straight from the airport so that they could race over to San Francisco General in order for Nick to make his good-byes to Chris.

*Jesus, what a day.*

Nick shouldered the duffel bag his mom had brought for him and walked up the little tunnel into the gate's receiving area. Shirley was waiting for him at the front of the crowd, her sharp gray eyes searching for him among the debarking passengers.

"Nick," she called.

He walked right up to her and hugged her so tight, she practically disappeared into his chest. He knew he was shocking the stuffing out of police captain Sokolov, but he was just so damned glad to see her.

They separated and she cleared her throat awkwardly, pretending to fuss with her hair. As if a tornado could have disturbed the helmetlike do that Shirley'd been wearing for the past twenty years.

"Hell, Nick, you didn't have to maul me," she grumbled, but she grumbled with affection.

"Chris?"

Shirley gave a curt nod. "Still hanging in there. The hospital got the court's approval to pull life support three days ago. Since then, it's been straight downhill." Her mouth pulled taut. "We should get going."

Driving north into the city, Nick stared out the window of Shirley's '79 Olds, telling himself that this was his home. Candlestick Park, Sutro Tower, the Pyramid. All familiar landmarks, yet distantly so. As if years had passed since Nick had last seen them. In actuality, years *had* passed. One-hundred and eighty-seven years, to be exact.

"So did you have a good talk with your mom?" Shirley asked.

"Yeah, I talked with her twice. Sophia and the baby are doing fine. They're all expecting me home for Christmas."

"Well, you take as much time as you need, you hear me? Two weeks, four weeks, whatever. After what you've been through, there's no reason for you to rush back to work until you're damned good and ready," she said fiercely.

Nick smiled at her hawk-nosed profile. "Thanks, Shirl. And thanks again for taking care of Internal."

"What?" Shirley shrugged. "What did I do? You were the one who told me to bring in Lenny. He sang like a freakin' parakeet, and the investigation was cleared. Just like that. It wasn't like I had anything to do with it."

"Yeah, well, thanks all the same. It's nice to have my badge and good name restored."

It was nice, even if he wasn't at all certain that he was going to be returning to the department. He had a lot of emotional baggage to sort through before he was ready to make a decision about where to go with the rest of his life.

Being a cop did have its advantages though, he remembered as Shirley parked the Olds in a red zone right in front of the hospital. Neither spoke as they got out of the car and headed inside.

As they rode up in the elevator to ICU, Nick rubbed his sweaty palms down the legs of his pants. Though he no longer blamed himself for Chris being shot—after all, he'd learned the hard way how difficult it was to alter a man's destiny—he still hadn't emotionally prepared himself to say good-bye.

Chris had always been there for him. Always. In life and in death. And Nick wanted to be there for Chris. To be there for his friend in those final, crucial moments as Chris left for that vast white beyond.

The elevator doors opened with a chime. Disinfectant fumes curdled the air.

"This way," Shirley said.

They walked down the hall and turned the corner to utter chaos. At least a half-dozen people were running back and forth between the nurses station and the red internal emergency phones and . . . a hospital room.

"Damn," Nick heard Shirley mutter.

"What?" Nick demanded. "What?"

They couldn't be too late. *No.* They couldn't be. To have come so far—

Nick sprinted down the hall and grabbed hold of a male nurse scurrying by.

"What's going on here?" Nick jerked his chin in the direction of all the activity.

"Oh, Lord, a patient—" The nurse caught himself. "I'm sorry, sir, are you a member of the family?"

Nick shook the man's arm. None too gently.

"Is it Chris?" Nick growled. "Christina Lewis?"

The nurse sent a furtive glance around the bustling hall, then bent forward to whisper, "They're calling it an honest-to-God miracle. She was dead. Had been pronounced dead for at least ten, twelve minutes. Then—wham—she just opened her eyes."

"Chris is . . . alive?"

The man confirmed it with a confidential nod. "The doctors say she's in perfect health. At least five of them have been in to examine her and not a one can explain it. The only thing that's got them worried is she keeps calling herself by another name. She thinks her name is Anna."

Nick pinned his gaze to the hospital room door and began walking.

"Hey, you," a voice called. "You can't go in there—"

"Who is that guy—"

Nick shoved past the faceless, protesting bodies and pushed into the room.

Two doctors stood talking at the foot of the chrome-and-white bed. They completely ignored him. A woman—Chris?—was sitting up in the bed, watching the two men with a puzzled frown. She turned toward the door as it opened.

Their gazes locked.

Nick couldn't breathe.

What was it Beverly had said about an aura? About people having their own aura, their own light? By God, he could see it. He could see her light, her glow. And this aura didn't belong to Chris.

The woman's lips moved, but made no sound.

Nick lurched a step closer.

"Anna?"

Her eyes widened.

"Nick. Is it you?"

He half stumbled, half staggered to the side of the bed. They clutched at each other's hands.

"Dear God, Anna, is it— Could it be?"

Or did he only wish it were so? It was Chris's body, Chris's voice—

"Chris?" he asked hoarsely.

"Oh, Nick, I saw her," she whispered. "I saw her in this place—this place of light. She said that she wanted this for us so that we could be together. She said to tell you not to worry. That her time had simply come."

Nick pressed his lips together, dropping his forehead to their joined hands.

"Thank you," he murmured, his chest aching with the beauty of what Chris had given them.

She had given them the gift of herself.

# *Epilogue*

"HOW ARE YOU feeling, honey? Do you want some more crackers? A Tums? Do you need to me pull over for a little while? There's another bottle of water in the backseat if you're thirsty."

Between questions, Nick jerked his anxious gaze back and forth from her to the road then back again.

Anna patted her husband's arm. "It was only a little morning sickness. And it's already passed. Really, Nick, I feel wonderful."

His fingers visibly clenched on the steering wheel. "I knew it. We should have waited to make the trip until after the baby came."

*Oh, boy,* Anna thought. *Here we go again.*

"Nick, I doubt we'll be doing much traveling with a newborn. And I really wanted to do this."

He relaxed, sending her a sheepish look. "Yeah," he agreed. "Me, too."

Anna reached over and gently brushed her knuckles across his cheek.

"Did I ever tell you that I think you're the handsomest man in the world?"

"Uh-huh. And remind me to have your eyes checked when we get home."

Anna's smile softened. She could tell him a thousand times a day, but Nick would never believe that she found him more attractive now than when he'd been inhabiting Godfrey's body. She suspected that he still felt partly self-conscious about the burn marks on his back and arms. Skin grafts and time had done a lot to repair the scars, but they still bothered Nick. More than he would confess to.

Of course, Anna could well empathize. It had been far easier to her to accustom herself to seeing Nick in a different body than seeing herself in a new one. She was tall now, curvier, with dark brown hair and blue eyes. Even after four months, Anna would find herself flinching as she passed by a mirror, asking herself who that woman might be.

Not that she had complaints, mind you. Not at all. Every single day Anna got down on her knees and gave thanks. Thanks for the gift she had been given. A chance to live again. A chance to love again. A chance to be a mother.

"We must be close," Nick said, shooting a glance to the map spread across the dashboard. "It should be coming up on our right."

Anna craned forward. "Do you really think the house might still be standing?"

"I don't know why not. You English love your old, drafty houses, don't you?"

"I'm a colonial now, remember? An 'Uh-meer-ican.' "

Nick squinted through the windshield. "Anna, I think I see it."

Her pulse fluttered as a squarish shape appeared on the horizon. "Oh, my goodness, Nick, I can't believe it."

In a matter of minutes they were pulling onto the paved road that led to Cliff House. Anna thought the stone-and-wood facade looked almost unchanged.

"Hey," Nick said, parking near the front, in roughly the same location James used to wait with the whiskey. "It seems to be some kind of museum or historical site."

"Oh, but, Nick, it's closed," Anna said. "What a disappointment."

"Well, we can still have a look around, can't we?"

Nick laid his arm across her shoulders, and they walked toward the shadowed porch.

"The stables are gone," Anna commented wistfully. "And the roses Aunt Beverly planted outside the dining room windows."

"But here's something new," Nick said. "A plaque."

They both came to stand before the front door.

Anna read aloud. " 'Hancock House. Built in 1762, the house was a private residence until 1811, when the Reverend Stephen Hancock of Aylesdown established here one of England's first shelters for battered women. The house remained a women's shelter until Reverend Hancock's death in 1858.' "

"Well, what do you know?" Nick said in a quiet voice.

Anna ran her fingers across the cold brass, tears slipping onto her cheeks.

"Oh, Nick. Do you think it was because—"

"Yeah. I do."

She turned her face into the roughness of Nick's wool jacket. "He was a good man," she whispered.

"He was, Anna. He really was."

Though they couldn't go inside the house, Nick and Anna spent a few hours exploring the grounds, peeking into windows and reminiscing. The cliffside trails had long since been overgrown, no smugglers or lonely young women to beat down the grassy paths.

For Anna, it was a closure, a final farewell to the ghosts of her past. She now could look toward the future. And only to the future.

"It's getting late, hon. We should think about finding somewhere to put up for the night."

Anna nodded. She had feared that once she arrived, it would be difficult to leave. But, in her heart, she was ready to leave Dover behind.

They were headed back to the car when a wiry, gray cat leaped into their path.

"Look, Nick, where do you think this little guy came from?" Anna bent down to pick the cat up, but he bounded away and meowed at her. "Oh, he wanted to play. Do you think he might just be Nefertiti's great-great-grandkitten?"

Nick grinned. "It's possible. Nefertiti sure kept herself busy."

The cat meowed again, switching its long tail.

Anna crouched down. "Is this your home? It used to be mine, too."

The cat dug its nose into the thick grass, its tail whipping from side to side.

"Hey." Anna scooted forward. "What's that you've got there?"

Something glinted in the late afternoon sunlight, something half-buried in the earth. She reached out—

"Jeez, Anna, don't do that. It's probably a mouse carcass." Nick hunkered down beside her. "Here, let me."

Using the car key, Nick dug the mud-encrusted object out of the ground. He stood up with his prize, brushing away the loose surface dirt as Anna peered over his shoulder.

"Huh," he said. "It looks like a locket. A portrait—"

They went utterly still.

"My father's watch," Anna breathed.

Nick pried his thumb around the clasp, and the watch sprang open. The time read sixteen minutes after twelve. Nick laughed softly and turned his face up to the sky.

"Thanks, Bev," he said.

And as they both glanced back to the watch, the seconds hand began to move. Time had finally been set right.